WELCOME TO THE BULL RUN

As the shrouds of a dream fell away, Terra stirred and looked up. A large flap of mottled skin was hanging just above her nose.

"Welcome-hello-howdy. I am Clahkto." The skin flap rose, and arching in the middle, exposed a pair of flat nostrils underneath. Below them, a lipless slit gaped open and displayed an uneven row of grayish teeth.

Terra stared transfixed at the grisly sight.

"Smiling-grinning I am doing, in your native custom," intoned the voice. "Hi there-greetings-how are you now? Welcome-hello-howdy to Satellite Hospital Outpost."

Novels by Sharon Webb

THE
ADVENTURES
OF
TERRA
TARKINGTON

Sharon Webb

BANTAM BOOKS
TORONTO · NEW YORK · LONDON · SYDNEY · AUCKLAND

For George Scithers
who was there at the birthing
of Terra Tarkington . . .

The following portions of *The Adventures of Terra Tarkington* appeared in *Isaac Asimov's Science Fiction Magazine* in somewhat different form:

"Hitch On the Bull Run" IASFM, 1979
"Itch On the Bull Run" IASFM, 1979
"Switch On the Bull Run" IASFM, 1980
"Twitch On the Bull Run" IASFM, 1981
"Bitch On the Bull Run" IASFM, 1981

THE ADVENTURES OF TERRA TARKINGTON

A Bantam Book / March 1985

ISBN 0-553-24862-6

Published simultaneously in the United States and Canada

Bantam Books are published by Bantam Books, Inc. Its trademark,
consisting of the words "Bantam Books" and the portrayal of a
rooster, is Registered in U.S. Patent and Trademark Office and in
other countries. Marca Registrada. Bantam Books, Inc., 666 Fifth
Avenue, New York, New York 10103.

PRINTED IN THE UNITED STATES OF AMERICA

O   0 9 8 7 6 5 4 3 2 1

Preface

The moon smiles down on the Interstellar Nurses Corps 29th Space Personnel Operations Training complex. Inside the vast and shadowy SleepTeach building of the 29th S.P.O.T. the students are hard at work, snoring gently as their single-file line of motorized cots trundles slowly through the long hallways.

Ahead, the wide doors of LESSER KNOWN ALIEN BEINGS, DISEASES OF whooshes open and the cot bearing the somnolent form of Ivy Hall, R.N. clicks into the room followed almost at once by Curtis Clef, R.N.

As Ivy Hall's cot wheels cross the threshold, LESSER KNOWN ALIEN BEINGS, DISEASES OF springs to life and its walls begin to softly whisper lessons to the sleeping caravan of nurses.

Now approaching the threshold is the cot of Terra Tarkington, R.N. The sleeping girl mutters and tosses for she had red beans for supper and her rest is disturbed.

Slowly, as if programmed, Terra's cot turns left ninety degrees. Clattering gently, it aims itself toward a door marked BROOM CLOSET. The door opens with a sighing hiss that breathes out a scent of dank mops and disinfectant. In a moment, the cot and Terra are gone.

LESSER KNOWN ALIEN BEINGS, DISEASES OF whispers its lessons to Chung "Hark" Harkwell, R.N., and to the gap that should have been Terra Tarkington (but was instead a grievous gap in her education) and then to Bevis Riviera, R.N., whose narrow nostrils hum with the passage of refrigerated air over sundry and dessicated nasal secretions.

Time and the nocturnal caravan pass.

The lessons concluding, LESSER KNOWN ALIEN BE-INGS, DISEASES OF whispers the seven danger signs of Pleiadean Stifled Stoma Syndrome to Chung "Hark" Harkwell, R.N., and to the gap where Terra Tarkington, R.N. ought to be, and to Bevis Riviera, R.N., whose nostrils quiver in a modulated sinusoidal buzz.

Then the great room falls silent and the procession clacks on into the hallway leading straight ahead to ALTERED ALIEN STATES, TREATMENT MODALITIES OF.

To the left, a blue light flares as a door marked ULTRA-SONIC DEHUMIDIFIER—NO ADMITTANCE opens silently and the cot bearing Terra Tarkington, R.N. clicks toward the caravan. With a smooth swiveling motion, the cot reinserts itself into the gap between Chung "Hark" Harkwell, R.N. and Bevis Riviera, R.N.

Outside, above the Interstellar Nurses Corps 29th Space Personnel Operations Training complex the moon smiles down benevolently. But what does the moon know?

INTERSTELLAR NURSES CORPS

Space Personnel Operations Training
is proud to present

GRADUATION EXERCISES OF THE 29TH S.P.O.T.

Processional............ "To Mars, Then the Stars"
Welcome .... Hobertann Holloway, Administra-
tor, Interstellar Nurses Corps
Salutary .... Bevis Riviera, R.N., Salutatorian
Song .... "To Alien Lands I Go, I Go,
To Alien Lands I Go" by the
29th S.P.O.T. Class
Honor Student Address . Humphrey Smet, R.N., Honor
Student
Other Student Address.. Terra Tarkington, R.N., Other
Student
Song .... "All Beings Great and Small" by the
29th S.P.O.T. Class

Valedictory. . . . . Corvis Kong, R.N., Valedictorian
Presentation of I.N.C. pins . Clyde Debien, Asst. Administrator,
  Interstellar Nurses Corps
Lighting of the Lasers . . A 29th S.P.O.T. Tradition
Recessional . . . . "To Boldly Go"

Reception immediately following in Parasitic Diseases of
Aliens Room.

Chapter 1

Dear Diary,

It seems odd to be able to stay up after dark. I keep expecting somebody to come in and make me swallow a sleeping pill so I won't be late to class.

I can't believe graduation is tomorrow. Tonight I have to boil the midnight oil to get my Other Student Address finished. You know how flabbergasted I was to be chosen, but did you know that the Other Student represents the exact arithmetrical mean of the class. To think that I am a significant statistic!

Well, it has to be an omen.

When one chooses to devote one's professional life to healing aliens, one must pause to reflect. And on reflection, it seems to me that there has got to be a sublime reason why our class was chosen to go off to Cygnus. Imagine it: the Swan—and us right in the neck. It's so poetic I can hardly stand it.

Just two more weeks and then I, Terra Tarkington, full-fledged member of the Interstellar Nurses Corps, take the Big Lurch out to the Swan Run.

I'll tell you what, it's a little scary. But I am ready to extend the torch of medical knowledge to alien unfortunates. I am ready to say to them, "Give me your tired, your poor, your huddled messes. . . ."

4

The lights dimmed. Gladiola Tarkington caught her breath as the Processional began. "Here they come, Bertram," she whispered and reached down to pat the slim cloisonné cylinder she always wore at her waist. But it wasn't there. Her eyes widened in shock for a moment before she remembered where she had left it.

"What?" said the red-eyed lady seated next to her.

Craning her neck for a better look, Gladiola clutched at the woman's arm. "Isn't it beautiful?"

The red-eyed woman sniffed and her nose lengthened in sorrow. "My boy—going off God knows where."

"Well, at least they're all going off together," said Gladiola with a bright smile.

"Halfway around the galaxy. For years— What if they don't come back?" She rolled her red eyes and added darkly, "What if they go native?"

Gladiola's bright smile wavered. "I never thought of that." Then optimism reasserted itself as the band of students in brand new Interstellar Nurses Corps dress uniforms passed single file by her aisle seat. "There she is. There's my Terra."

Humming softly with the music, Gladiola settled back in her seat to hear a welcoming address punctuated by sniffs from the red-eyed woman.

When Bevis Riviera rose to give the Salutary, the woman's eyes grew redder and she clutched at her program.

Bevis, expressive nostrils flaring, waxed eloquent. At least Gladiola assumed he was waxing eloquent. It was awfully hard to make out what he was saying over the red-eyed woman's sniffs.

At the close of Humphrey Smet's Honor Student speech, Gladiola leaned forward intently. The Other Student address was next. She nudged her neighbor, and with a whisper that carried through the auditorium said, "That's my daughter."

Though the red-eyed woman's lower lip was pinioned by her teeth, she tried to smile.

As she stood, Terra nibbled at a fingernail and glanced down at her notes. Her eyes were very wide in the dim light of the hall, and to Gladiola it seemed that they were misted. It was hard to really tell through the mist in her own eyes.

Terra laid her notes in a little row on the podium and looked out into the audience. "My subject is 'Women In Space' or 'Can She Be a Nurse and a Woman Too?'" She flourished the first of her notecards before the audience. This was followed by a dramatic pause as a little gust of wind from the air-conditioning duct swept the card out of her hand and sailed it toward her feet.

Terra retrieved the card and fixed her gaze on the audience. "What is a woman?"

The audience gazed back with interested, if somewhat puzzled, expressions.

"The ancient writer, Kipling, defined her as 'oregano, bone, and a hank of hair.' But women have come a long way since then. At the turn of this century, women of courage stormed the portals of the world's nursing schools and demanded to take their rightful place next to the men.

"Some of you may find this hard to believe, but history reveals that once most nurses were women. And this was so, up until the computer riots of the late twentieth century and the great Job Decimation.

"We women owe a great debt to those brave pioneers who restaked our claim to the territory of nursing. They would be proud to know that we carry that noble banner to the stars.

"Next week our class is leaving this earth for the depths of the galaxy and—" Blinking, Terra caught her lower lip between her teeth. She brushed her notes away into a little pile. Staring down at them, she said, "I don't want to give the rest of this speech." Then she looked up. "Instead, I want to tell you what I feel."

She glanced toward the rows of nurses in their bright new dress uniforms and then her gaze fell on her mother. "While I was sitting here, it came to me that we're really going away. I mean, we've all known that for a long time. But we knew it as a fact, not an emotion. And now it seems to me that we have to think about our feelings, too."

She gave a quick smile to her mother that faded into a wistful little look and said, "Sitting here, I suddenly thought about everything that we were going to leave behind, things we've known since we were children, things we love like ice cream and trees and puppies—and the people who mean something to us. And I want to say right here, I love you, Mom. And I love this earth." Suddenly she had to clear her throat. It was a moment before she could say, "Maybe I didn't know how much till just now.

"So, anyway, I think it's important that when this class is off in space we remember to treat each other like brothers and sisters and love each other, because we're all we're going to

6

have." Terra gazed around the room as if she were trying to memorize the upturned faces. "I guess that's really all I have to say, so, thank you."

Gladiola found it hard to follow the Valedictory that followed, and her smile was a bit too bright as Terra received her Interstellar Nurses Corps pin—a silver caduceus rocketing through a black-enameled hole.

It was nearly over now. Suddenly quick tears touched Gladiola's eyes as the lights dimmed and the Lighting of the Lasers began.

One by one, each laser flared and the room was ribboned with ruby light. It was Terra's turn. "My daughter," said Gladiola to the red-eyed woman.

Thumb on the switch, Terra waited for her cue. With a hum, her laser flamed and the room blazed with the lights of the class—except for Bevis Riviera, R.N., Salutatorian of the 29th S.P.O.T, who was having trouble with his laser.

"It's stuck," he hissed in Terra's ear. "The switch— It's stuck."

"Let me try," she whispered back, and applied a fingernail to the reluctant lever. "There," she said, and the laser flamed.

And at that precise moment, Bevis Riviera, R.N. leaned over it to see, and flared his narrow nostrils. The hair that normally emerged from Bevis Riviera's nostrils was very black and very bushy. Now it was very red, each fiber glowing like an overheated wire. For a split second, a look of horror tracked over Bevis Riviera's face. The look repeated itself on Gladiola Tarkington's. "That's my daughter!"

Twin streams of fire issued from Bevis's nose.

Restraint thrown to the wind, the red-eyed woman flung a hand toward the bellowing, stomping Bevis. "And that—" she howled tragically, "that's my son. . . ."

"It isn't as if you meant to, Terra." Gladiola patted her daughter's shoulder firmly, and stared around the auditorium defensively as if daring anyone to say otherwise.

"It was awful," said Terra darkly. "There was Bevis Riviera, stamping and yelling, with flames coming out of his nose. He looked like a dragon."

"Well, yes he did. But it was your quick thinking that put him out. If you hadn't pinched his nostrils shut there's no telling what would have caught. Besides, everybody says he'll be just fine as soon as the tubes come out of his nose." A perplexed frown wrinkled her brow. "Why *did* they put tubes in his nose, anyway?"

"So his nostrils won't grow together. They don't think the hairs will grow back. Ever." A tragic look crossed her face. "Bevis Riviera won't have any nose hairs for the rest of his life. And it's all because of me."

Gladiola's shoulder patting grew more rhythmic. "There, there." Then with a glance toward her side and the missing cloissonné cylinder, she said, "Oh, I wish your father was here."

"Where is he?"

"I had to leave him off at Eternal Rest. His lid was coming loose. Every time his lid turned some of his ashes sifted out. Just like a pepper mill. But they told me PerpetuBond would fix him." Her gaze slid away for a moment. "I hope so. He never wanted to be scattered." Then she looked back at Terra, searching her face. "I'm going to have them add your picture. They make a little curved frame that fits on the case."

"But, Mom, I'm just going away for a while. I'm not—" Terra's eyes met Gladiola's for a long moment. "That's very nice," she gave her mother a quick hug. "I'm glad you want to add my picture."

Suddenly a tall redhead halfway across the room called, "Terra."

"Carmie!" Terra's eyes grew wide as the girl ran toward her. "You came after all. I didn't think you would."

The girl straightened her already straight, dark eyebrows in reproof. "Of course I came."

"But after what you said—"

"I take it back. If going into space is what you want, then I'm happy for you. I really am."

Eyes brimming they stared at each other for a moment, and then the two girls were hugging each other in their first reunion since nursing school.

"I'm going to miss you. You know?" said Carmie.

Terra nodded. "Me too."

Gladiola Tarkington grasped the girl's hand. "Why it's Carmelita O'Hare. I didn't recognize you with clothes on."

Carmie laughed. "I guess you never saw me in anything but a nursing student uniform. Tell me, how do you like your new apartment? Did you get rid of the mildew?"

"Finally. But it took nearly a case of Mil-Die. I really love Subsea now. Of course, I don't have a reef view, but it's nice all the same. Every day this lovely big grouper comes to the kitchen port. I'll tell you he gave me a start at first, but now he's company. Why he—"

"Terra!" came a bellowed female voice. "Where is Terra Tarkington?"

Terra looked up in horror. The voice belonged to Bevis Riviera's mother.

The woman rushed toward her. Red eyes brimming, she clutched Terra's shoulders. "The doctors say his nose isn't fit. They won't let him go out to space with his class. 'Not till the next class,' they said. 'Not for six months.'" Raising her red-rimmed gaze to the ceiling she said in a hushed tone, "Thank *God* his nose isn't fit." She gave Terra a crushing hug. "Bless you. Bless you." Then with a vigorous parting squeeze, she turned and sped away.

A stricken look came into Terra's eyes. "Oh, Carmie. I not only destroyed Bevis Riviera's nose hairs, I destroyed six months of his professional life."

Brows lowered, Carmie looked at her intently. "I suppose you did. But there's nothing you can do about it now. You'll feel better after some cake and punch." Hand on Terra's shoulder, she aimed her into the line of people headed for the reception.

As the three moved toward the Parasitic Diseases of Aliens Room, none of them noticed the narrow-faced man behind them, nor his covert glance in Terra's direction.

The reception line crept up a hall lined with alien skeletons, both exo and endo, and turned the corner.

Just ahead of the two chatting girls, Gladiola followed the crowd around the bend and froze. A six-foot-tall creature, vaguely blue and reptilian, stood in her path. She gave it a brave, if tremulous, smile. Her smile wavered when the blue-gray snout opened, showing a double row of sharp teeth. Not daring to take her eyes from it, she slowly backed away.

The creature hissed.

"Oh God, oh run, oh God!" Gladiola wheeled and dashed full-tilt into Terra's arms.

"It's all right, Mom."

Her breath grazed Terra's ear; her voice dropped an octave. "Oh no, it isn't."

"It's a holotext."

"Oh God, a *what*?"

"A holotext. It's not real."

9

Gladiola peered cautiously over her shoulder at the creature, then back at Terra. "Are you sure?"

"Of course I'm sure. It's an Aldeberan. From the Bull Run."

"The what?"

"The Bull Run— In the constellation Taurus. Sometimes the I.N.C. sends nurses to the hospital outpost there, so we had to study the beings in that system."

"Oh, Terra—" Gladiola raised shocked eyes to her daughter's and shook her head. "You're not going *there*?"

"No. We're all going to Cygnus. The whole class."

The press of people pushed them ahead. With a quick backward glance at the hissing holotext, Gladiola was swept into the Parasitic Diseases of Aliens Room, darkened for the occasion and decorated with misty electronic nebulae overlaid with the insignia of the Interstellar Nurses Corps.

A large cake shaped in the likeness of a swan and emblazoned with the single word, CYGNUS, was flanked by two enormous bowls of acid-green punch, one with the discreet message, "Without."

A man in uniform stepped up and clapped his hands for attention.

Gladiola caught Terra's eye. "Are they cutting the cake now?"

"No. They're cutting the orders."

Clyde Debien, natty in his I.N.C. Assistant Administrator braid, waited for everyone's attention before he spoke. "Ladies and gentlemen, this is the moment we've waited for—the call to space." With a flourish, he pressed a button on the terminal at his elbow. "I will now issue the assignment orders from I.N.C. Central."

A computer voice spoke: "Avery, Linda-Laura."

Linda-Laura Avery, new uniform rustling, stepped forward.

The machine spat out a plastex I.D. card which Debien caught expertly and read: "Linda-Laura Avery. Called to the service of her fellow beings in the system of Cygnus."

The computer, sensing the end of the applause said, "Bonanno, Adolph," and disgorged another I.D.

"Adolph Bonanno," said Debien. "Called to the serice of his fellow beings in the system of Cygnus."

Terra nudged Carmelita. "Isn't this exciting?"

"I suppose so. In a cut-and-dried sort of way."

One after another, the class was called to space.

The computer spoke again: "Tarkington, Terra," and deposited a card in Clyde Debien's outstretched hand. "Terra Tarkington, called to the service of her fellow beings in the system of—" A puzzled look spread over his face, followed by an extended pause. Then, turning quickly, he shoved the card back into the machine and tapped out a new code. The computer burped and in a few moments extruded a new card.

"Terra Tarkington, called to the service of her fellow beings in the system—" Another pause while before the eyes of the assembled the plastex I.D. card bent like a stick in the wind and began to melt.

Debien stared helplessly as a blob detached itself from the card and fell onto his shoe. "Uh— We, uh, we'll just have to do that one over, heh-heh." With a shade more vigor, he stabbed the computer keys again.

This time nothing happened. Nothing at all.

Debien attacked the keys with a touch of despair as two hundred friends and relatives of those called to the service of their fellow beings looked on.

Nothing happened.

"It, uh, seems to be hung up." He turned a tremulous smile toward the assemblage while his thumb urgently worked the REENTER key.

Nothing. Nothing but a malevolent glow on the stage of the terminal.

The room was quiet now. So quiet, that when the machine spat out a new card, everyone jumped.

Debien seized it with relief. "Terra Tarkington, called to the service of her fellow beings in the system . . . Taurus."

"Taurus?" Terra looked from one to the other in disbelief. "The Bull Run?"

"The Bull Run!" echoed a dozen shocked voices.

"They're sending me there?" Terra's eyes were very wide. "Alone?"

Gladiola caught at Debien's arm. "My little girl? Going to live among alien beasts and crocodiles?"

With a little shrug, he nodded and a sheepish grin slid over his face.

At the back of the room the narrow-faced man quirked thin lips in a half-smile. But no one noticed in the commotion as Gladiola Tarkington threw up her hands with a little shriek and fainted dead away.

Chapter 2

Barbizon Hotel For Humanoids
Avenue of the Stars
Moontana
Moon 000456222, Sol
June 18

Gladiola Tarkington
45 Subsea
Petroleum City
Gulf of Mexico 233433111 United Earth, Sol

Dear Mom,

Well, here I am on the moon. This time tomorrow I'll be tucked in my starship cabin and ready to leap to Taurus—there to take my place amid the diseased and traumatized of the Bull Run.

It's going to be all right, Mom. Really, it will.

You shouldn't worry so. Everybody at Satellite Hospital won't look like the holotext you saw. The personnel list shows only seventy-eight percent of the employees are Aldeberan. Twenty-one percent are from Hyades IV and they look sort of human. I know that doesn't leave much, but the hospital is really big. The "one percent—Other" is sure to include lots of people from Earth.

Besides, Aldeberans aren't really crocodiles. They aren't even reptiles, exactly. I mean, they are in a sense, but appearances aren't everything. Anyway, Aldeberans are really picky about what they eat, so I won't be in any danger at all.

I can understand how you feel. I used to think they were odd-looking, too, but the last day at school I found myself thinking the strangest thoughts. I was in the O.B. of Aliens Room watching "Aldeberan Dislocated Yolk

Syndrome and Other Obstetrical Emergencies" when somehow I knew that I was meant to go to the Bull Run.

It's hard to explain, but it was as if I were part of a greater plan—a grand design. I had to ask myself, "Who am I, but a fly in the face of destiny."

I'm going to be fine.

> Your loving daughter,
> Terra

The narrow-faced man stared at the intercepted letter. The plan was working, he thought in satisfaction. A few hours more and the Tarkington girl would be on her way to the Bull Run. At a casual flick of his fingernail, the letter vanished and his wrist reader again displayed the time and date.

Stepping off the conveyer into the dimly lit bowels of Hyades IV, Dieter Diderot moved toward the public altar. Feigning interest in the howling sacrifice, he slid into the shadows of a flame-licked column and scrutinized the passersby with a pale and professional eye. At last satisfied that he had not been followed, he turned toward the pitted alleys of the City of Twelve Evils.

The rhythmic thud of scaleflails signalled the approach of Hyadean zealots. Falling back, he waited. He could see them now: humanoids wearing the scales and tails of the Order of Blooded Persecutionists, at least a dozen of them weaving through the narrow street. The scaleflails rose in volume. Diderot narrowed his narrow eyes as the Hyadeans raised their noseflaps in unison and then snapped them shut with a hollow "flup." Just as he feared—they were in ecstasy, and highly dangerous; they were not to be messed with. He slid into the entry of an illicit bathhouse and let them pass.

An eye, not human, appeared at the doorway. "Soap," whispered the pusher. "Terran soap. Very good quality. For you, cheap."

He moved away.

A gray-green tentacle snaked out of the shadows and hooked around his neck. Whirling, he found himself staring into a gaping maw studded with yellow teeth. The tentacle crept toward his upper arm and squeezed his meager biceps. "Not much to you, is there?" sighed the maw.

Dieter Diderot licked his narrow lips and turned his cold gaze on the hooker. "Let go."

"Just one little bite?" it whined. "I pay top rates."

An almost imperceptible movement and a wicked light-knife gleamed in Diderot's hand.

The tentacle retracted. "Tough, aren't you? I don't like tough." The hooker pursed its maw. "I'd spit you out, tough thing." As if in punctuation, it spat glutinously and oozed away.

Diderot came at last to a folded crevice of rock in a shallow crater. Placing his hands on the smooth stone, he spread his fingers apart.

In a moment, the rock panel glowed and became a translucent screen. A pair of claws, scaled and faintly blue, appeared and assumed the same position as his hands.

"Divided—" whispered Diderot.

"—We s-s-stand," came the hissing reply.

Diderot braced himself. The crater dropped away, lowering him to a dim vaulted chamber.

Fendeqot's yellow eyes burned into his.

Unflinching, he met the Aldeberan's gaze. Though human, Diderot had the inhuman ability to outstare his slit-pupiled reptilian adversary. And adversary he was. Fendeqot, Chief of Divisions of KABBAGE, had once been his superior. They were equals now, but Diderot trusted no one.

And no one trusted Diderot. He was a turncoat, a former operative of the Galactic Intelligence Agency. Now he pledged his flimsy fealty to KABBAGE—the KBG for short—the covert arm of the Sectorites.   —For ideological reasons, he had said.

Covert activity, once unknown to the rest of the galaxy, was Earth's most successful export. The concept was embraced enthusiastically, and soon any government without its secret arm was deemed hopelessly provincial and probably uncivilized. The shakeout that followed the early diversification of clandestine power groups had left two major foes:

The KBG, the galacticazation of an old Earth force, used the closed system—or cell—to divide and conquer. Rigid control of information, surveillance, and the setting of faction against faction were its methods.

The GIA, growing throughout the galaxy from its Earthly rootstock, was dedicated to the open system—or as some called it, the open-maw system—designed to efficiently swallow entire cultures, masticate them, and disgorge them into neat, pre-digested heaps.

Diderot leveled his pale gaze at the Aldeberan and smiled thinly as he remembered the day SEPTUM had named him Chief of Subdivisions. Fendeqot had blanched at the news, and then turned indigo with rage. From under half-closed lids, Diderot studied the Aldeberan. The big lizard wasn't stupid—and that added zest to the game. Fendeqot was all too aware of the shift of power. Just one more coup, he thought, just one, and the Aldeberan was finished.

As he stared down Fendeqot, he whispered the KBG motto, "Kabbage blugo garkahtas." KABBAGE: Eye—or "Eyestalk" as some versions of the sub-Standard dialect had it. "Big Kabbage is watching you," he said again with a menacing smile.

Fendeqot's tail scurried nervously back and forth. "You've programmed the s-s-subject?"

Diderot nodded curtly.

Fendeqot licked his right index claw which was ingrown and throbbed quite horribly. "And, uh, who *was-s-s* the subject, did you s-s-say?" he asked with elaborate casualness.

You'd like to know that, wouldn't you? thought Diderot. Aloud, he said, "*My* subdivision, I believe. I report only to SEPTUM."

Fendeqot's pupils contracted to a thin verticle line. "Of course-s-s."

"Divided—" prompted Diderot.

"—We s-s-stand," came the Aldeberan's quick reply.

"I'm ready to report—to SEPTUM."

Fendeqot's jaw fell open in feigned boredom and exposed a double row of teeth. When the gesture, designed to strike terror into the brains of lesser beings, failed to have perceptible effect, the Aldeberan flared his nostrils, turned, and hissed softly at an inner door. It slid open and they stepped inside. The Coordinator of Communications looked up from her console and wrinkled her nose expectantly.

"Mrs-s-s. Wiggs-s-s," said the Aldeberan, "we need a patch to S-S-SEPTUM."

Mrs. Wiggs's long ears quivered in the stream of hisses. "How many to speak?"

"One," said Diderot with a glance toward Fendeqot. She nodded and leaned primly over her console, furry little pseudopaws poised over the keys and buttons. In a few moments she looked up at Diderot. "We're ready now." A semi-sentient scentplant in a hollowstone pot rolled away and the wall slid open to reveal a small windowless cell. "You may enter the chamber."

When Diderot stepped inside, the door slid shut and the

scentplant, with much groaning and rustling of its stems, rolled back into place. Mrs. Wiggs looked up at the Aldeberan. "Solo," she reminded.

With a spiteful lash of his tail, Fendeqot turned and headed for the outer door. It was only after it locked behind him that Mrs. Wiggs reached for her communications console and with a deft motion of her little pseudopaws turned up the chamber pot.

Dieter Diderot looked up at the featureless walls of the chamber. As the lights dimmed a nervous shiver ran up his spine and scrabbled at the nape of his neck.

A harsh breath broke the silence.

Purple light, flaring as the breath grew in volume, died, and flared again. SEPTUM. The supreme head of the KBG. No one knew his face; no one knew his location. SEPTUM—no more than a disembodied voice—yet to incur his wrath meant death.

"Divided—" said Diderot in a small voice.

Twin spurts of light pulsed blood-red: "—WE STAND."

"Chief of Subdivisions, Diderot, reporting."

SEPTUM began the Sectorite catechism: "WHAT IS THE RESULT WHEN THE WINDOWS OF THE GALACTIC MANSION ARE OPENED?"

"Ill winds blow through, sir."

"AND WHAT IS THE RESULT WHEN THE PARTITIONS OF THE GALACTIC MANSION ARE REMOVED?"

"The roof falls in, sir."

"DAMN RIGHT." Light blazed in his eyes. "BEGIN YOUR REPORT."

Blinking, Diderot shifted his gaze. "Psychological testing of the Tarkington girl proved—"

"HUSH!"

Angry orange streaks shot into Diderot's eyes, and a foul and sulfurous odor, indicating SEPTUM's disapproval, assaulted his nostrils.

"NEVER SPEAK THE GIRL'S NAME. SHE HAS NO NAME. SHE IS ONLY AN INSTRUMENT—A FINGER ON A TRIGGER."

"Of course." Diderot tried not to breathe. "Uh, psychological testing of The Finger proved that our preliminary assessment was correct. She is exactly suited to our purposes."

16

"NEVER SAY 'SHE!'" boomed the irate voice. More orange streaks and sulfur suffused the cell.

"Right, sir. It—The Finger—is exactly suited to our purposes."

"CONDITIONING?"

"A complete success. It suspects nothing."

"PHASE ONE IS COMPLETE?"

"Complete. The Finger will be on its way to Satellite Hospital Outpost in a matter of hours."

A rosy light mingled with the odor of violets and exotic pastries suffused the cell. Diderot felt a surge of exhilaration at SEPTUM's approval.

"YOU WILL NOW HEAR YOUR INSTRUCTIONS FOR PHASE TWO. PAY ATTENTION. . . ."

As the door to Communications locked behind him, the tip of Fendeqot's tail twitched back and forth in agitation. He considered his status: not privy. Locked out of SEPTUM's council. His pupils narrowed until his eyes were yellow mirrors. Then, with a sidelong glance in each direction, he slid toward a small closet, opened it, and closed the door stealthily behind him.

His pupils dilated in the dim light of the closet. A thin exposed pipe ran from a vat suspended from the ceiling. Fendeqot's claw traced the pipe to a bend where it disappeared into the wall. The pipeline, designed to carry nutrient solution to the scentplant, passed through the inner wall of the communications cell.

His claws ticky-tacked along the top of the pipe feeling for the plug he had left there. It was gone. Dismayed, he leveled his yellow stare at the juncture of pipe and wall. He would have to do without it.

Seizing the elbow of the pipe, he twisted, then let go at once as sharp pain throbbed in his ingrown claw. He tried again, more cautiously this time, and was rewarded by a gush of nutrient solution from the vat. An index digit stabbed into the upstream section of the pipe staunched most of the flow.

Oblivious to the nutrient solution dripping onto his chest scales, Fendeqot leaned forward, and tipping his head, applied his earhole to the pipeline.

"YOU WILL NOW HEAR YOUR INSTRUCTIONS FOR PHASE TWO. PAY ATTENTION. . . ."

17

Chapter 3

Galactic Spaceways—Concourse C
Interstellar Spaceport
Moon 0004562221, Sol
June 19

Carmelita O'Hare, R.N.
Teton Medical Center
Jackson Hole Summation City
Wyoming 306548760 United Earth, Sol

Dear Carmie,

I'll be boarding Galactic Spaceways' Flight 409 in just a few minutes, so this will be short, but I had to let you know the latest developments.

I just met the cutest guy you ever saw. His name is Augustus. He's a detail man for Bluggway & Son Pharmaceuticals and he's going to be on the same flight! Of course, he's not going all the way to Taurus and we're going to be sleeping most of the flight, but we'll be awake for seven hours before the ship jumps.

Augustus has been to space before. He's a very sophisticated traveler and he says he's going to make my first trip "out there"—that's what he calls it, "out there"— a memorable one.

First we're going to the lounge for Moon Maidens. Then we're going to look at the stars. Augustus says we won't bother with the observation ports. He says they're for tourists. He knows a private place where we can observe the wonders of the galaxy away from the madding crowds.

Augustus is an amateur astronomer. He says there are things out there I never dreamed of, and if we're lucky *he might even show me a little-known nebula shaped like an Archimedean screw.*

Here's to Archimedes.

Yours, out there,
Terra

Nostrils pinched in a grim line, Fendeqot emerged from the closet. Dabbing absently at the scentplant nutrient solution dribbling down his chest, he glared at the inner door that led to the communication chamber. Diderot would be coming out soon.

In his zeal to hear everything, Fendeqot had pressed too hard and too long against the pipe. He rubbed at the painful indentation around his earhole as he sifted the information he had gleaned from the pipeline: The Finger was on its way. And Phase Two—The Trigger—was about to begin. But who was The Finger? And what could possibly connect it to Phase Two?

Only SEPTUM knew—and Diderot. Diderot, the upstart. As Fendeqot stared at the inner chamber door, his pupils contracted to thin, unreadable lines.

Outwardly, Fendeqot appeared quite calm, but dangerous hormones were pulsing through his body. Scales rose and quivered at the nape of his neck. An attack was coming on, he thought darkly. He had to get away. He had to get away before someone saw.

Turning abruptly on his tail, he strode out of the room on legs so knotted with tension that the scales on his thighs stood on end and rubbed angrily against each other as he walked.

The street outside KABBAGE headquarters was dark, illuminated only by yellow pools from the lamps that burned night and day in the inner depths of Hyades IV. The thick muscles in his jaw clenched and released in rhythmic thrusts. He had to hurry; the attack was imminent now. He sensed that it would be a bad one—even worse than the one he had had three years ago when the Interstellar Revenue Service auditor disallowed ninety-seven percent of his travel and entertainment deductions.

He turned into a narrow doorway and faced the hotel clerk. The clerk, an Aurigan dragon, looked up. Fendeqot stared back with ill-disguised contempt. The dragons were degenerates: exploiters of every known vice in the galaxy. To a casual glance they looked like pure-blooded Aldeberans, and it was this that was so disturbing to Fendeqot. He wanted desperately to leave, to turn his tail on this travesty of flesh and scale, but he did not dare. The attack was too close.

"A room," he said in a voice husky with the hot flow of hormones.

The clerk sniffed. As he caught Fendeqot's altered scent, he waggled his tongue suggestively. "Not much time, is there?" After extracting an exorbitant deposit for an hour's rent, he thrust his snout toward the back. "In there." Then with a silky little hiss, he turned away as a hooker, purring with delight at the Hyadean locked in its tentacular embrace, oozed toward the desk.

In the shabby room, Fendeqot struggled against overpowering urges. Not yet, he told himself. Not yet. With a great effort of will, he withdrew a small device from the pouch slung around his hips. Switching it on, he quickly checked the room for scanners. It wouldn't do for anyone to see, anyone to hear. Satisfied that he was quite alone, Fendeqot leaned back on his tail, closed one set of eyelids, and surrendered to the attack.

In a rush of blood that turned his snout and eyelids a gelid blue, Fendeqot allowed the image of Diderot to surface. There it was—branded in his brain, the flat alien face, smiling its flat alien smile.

The rage shuddered through Fendeqot and erupted in the most violent tantrum he had had in years.

It began with a generalized stamping of his feet and a high-pitched shriek that was echoed by a howl from the room next door. (The room next door housed the hooker and the Hyadean, and the Hyadean had begun to regret the hasty liaison.)

Fendeqot's shriek was followed by a vigorous lash of his tail and a steamy hiss. A stream of invective followed: "S-s-skinbag . . . round-eyed s-s-skinbag . . . mis-s-s-begotten, mis-s-shapen s-s-son of a rotting, blas-s-s-phemed egg . . ." When, through the mad haze of emotion it came to Fendeqot that Diderot had indeed not hatched from an egg at all, he redoubled his vituperative efforts: "Vile viviparous-s-s villain . . . s-s-stumptailed, white-bellied, jelly-bag . . ."

Under the assault of Fendeqot's tail, a lamp crashed to the floor to the accompaniment of sundry howls and thumps from the next room.

"Clawless-s-s *cuticle*," shrieked Fendeqot. In emphasis, he raked at the wall with his extended digits (which by now were quite blue) and shrieked again at the damage to his ingrown claw. Thrusting it into his mouth, he danced first on one foot, then on the other, and whacked his tail belligerently against the heat register. This was followed by a series of bounding jumps, heel grindings, and generalized scale flappings. "Jelly-bag, jelly-bag, *jelly-bag!*"

His jaundiced gaze fell on the netbed next. With a howl, Fendeqot attacked it as if it were his adversary's frail, gelatinous body. Snatching it from its frame, he shredded it with a single horrid swipe of his toenails. Wadding the remains with a vicious curl of his tail, he sailed it against the wall where it was answered by another thump, a strangled yelp, and the hooker's aggrieved voice saying, "But, you promised . . ."

Promised. Fendeqot glared murderously at the wall. He had been promised the Subdivisionate. It was to be his—completely under his control. But that was before the jelly-bag alien came on the scene and ingratiated himself with SEPTUM.

The hateful face of Diderot rose in his mind again. Chief of Subdivisions, indeed! Even now the skinbag was beginning Phase Two. It was intolerable. Never before had SEPTUM assigned two consecutive phases to the same operative. It was against everything the KBG stood for. Next thing, and the vile flat-face would know as much about the Grand Scheme as SEPTUM did.

Suddenly it struck him with the violence of a hammer. Of course. That was Diderot's plan: He was going to trick SEPTUM into revealing the Scheme. When he had it, SEPTUM would fall.

And so would he. . . .

The thought rang in his brain like a death knell. He was going to be let go long before his retirement plan matured—and he had no job skills. Shuddering at the bleakness of his future, he drew his tail over his toes the way he used to when he was three and his mother scolded him. Then flinging himself onto the floor, thrusting his snout from left to right, Fendeqot began to hold his breath.

At the Aldeberan Esthetics Center in the Megamart on Hyades IV, Qoqedd Qotemire, wife of the Chief of Staff of Satellite Hospital Outpost, fought against the moment of panic that always preceded her treatment.

"Relax-s-s-s," said the scaler who though very young knew her job quite well.

At the scaler's admonition, Mrs. Qotemire gave a faint hiss and let herself be manipulated into the prescribed position.

With a quick motion, the scaler expertly flipped Mrs. Qotemire onto her back.

The panic rose to a crescendo. Helpless. She was utterly helpless on her back. The tension was mingled with embarrassment. She had always hated for anyone to see her like this. Anyone except for Curtiz, of course. Although she couldn't see her belly in this dreadful position, she knew she was blushing. Hot with shame, she could imagine it: translucent scales growing bluer by the moment for the scaler to see—for everyone to see. Stealthily, she glanced from side to side to see if anyone else had noticed, but the dozen other clients hanging in a dozen other nets were obviously too self-engrossed to pay any attention.

As the scaler's claws skittered over her chest and belly, Qoqedd felt the familiar lassitude creep over her. First her arms flopped quite obscenely outward, then her legs. Finally her tail—a lovely tail, if she did say so herself—uncurled and, with a jaunty little flourish, relaxed.

The scaler's clever claws played a ticky-tacky little rhythm on her chest and Qoqedd felt a delicious surge of drowsiness. Her snout went limp and her jaw fell open. A trickle of anxiety made her wonder about the state of her teeth. Were they presentable, or were there brown and grizzly traces of her mid-morning crunchy stuck between?

Qoqedd knew that deep down in the depths of her being she was enjoying her treatment, but perversely she flared her nostrils and tried to say, "The things we females have to go through to be beautiful," but her tongue was too relaxed and nothing came out but a disgracefully slurred hiss.

With her client now prepared, the scaler went to work in earnest. Reaching overhead among a thick nest of implements, she seized a scraper and began to plane Qoqedd's belly scales to a fashionable adolescent thinness, trimming carefully around the little convexity on the lower abdomen—the plump, round protrusion of which Mrs. Qotemire was so proud, for Mrs. Qotemire was with egg. The scaler, of course, was not allowed to groom a gravid convexity. That was left to the blazer who with consumate skill would carve graceful arcs of fertility

22

into the overlapping belly plates before turning Mrs. Qotemire over to the colorist for tinting.

Deeply relaxed now, Qoqedd creened a little cree of pleasure at the thought of the egg, her first. If it were female, she thought, she would call it Chune-yon after the obscure mythological heroine who with a single telling hiss fought off an ice monster. Not that Qoqedd cared a cracked rock about mythology, but it was fashionable these days to give your first a heroic name. If she had a male, he would be Chune-yore—and *that* to Eddeqedd Fleshqot who had gone on and on about how much she had to spend to buy the name Chuggnapp. And serve her right, too, the hateful thing.

Qoqedd was nearly asleep when the netbed began to move on its conveyor. Off now to the blazer, she thought lazily. She hoped it wouldn't take too long. If the blazer didn't dawdle, there might be time to see that new fortuneteller before the meeting. On the other hand, she *did* want the blazer to do her best. It might be worth missing out on the seer if she looked extra nice for the "Preservation of Our Illustrious Culture and Mythos" meeting this afternoon. If she didn't look her best, Eddeqedd Fleshqot would be the first to notice.

The trundling ride in the netbed rocked her back to somnolence until the faint scent of something vaguely foreign and disturbing caused her to start awake. She looked up, not at the familiar snout of the blazer, but into alarming round eyes and a narrow, primitively flat face. An alien, she thought in alarm. And worse, a human alien. She had always tried to be nice to them in a distant sort of way, but she had never expected one here.

The face, awful in its flatness leaned over hers. A hand—a *hand*—reached toward her face and raised one of her eyelids. An altogether dreadful human voice spoke then: "You said she'd be sedated."

Alarm turned to sheer panic. With a mighty effort of will, Qoqedd Qotemire flailed her tail and raked at the smashed-in face with outflung claws.

The man's thin lips split open in a howl of pain. Suddenly something wet and smothering wrapped around her snout and covered her nostrils.

Then there was nothing but a thick, sweet odor that smelled not bad at all, that smelled, in fact, something like mashed plumps. . . .

* * *

"It is-s-s time to arise-s-s-s," said the colorist.

Qoqedd Qotemire found herself lying on her side. With a little sighing hiss, she got up and shook her head as if to dislodge the remnants of strange and frightening thoughts.

Her eyes narrowed to slits as she tried to recall what it was that disturbed her, but the memory was wisps and fragments, disappearing even as she tried to grasp them.

Clucking in pride, the colorist aimed her at the reflector.

Turning, Qoqedd gazed at her newly carved belly. Nostrils widening in delight, she praised the scaler, the blazer, and not the least, the colorist. Then turning this way and that, creening little crees of pleasure, she admired the play of light on her gravid convexity. Beautiful. Really beautiful, she thought.

And wouldn't Eddeqedd Fleshqot be blue with envy?

Fendeqot could not hold his breath any longer. Try as he might, his lungs rebelled, and tongue lolling, he gasped weakly at the stale air in the room. He wasn't as young as he used to be, he thought grimly. His wind was going.

He tried to hang on to the remnants of his rage, but it was fading with every breath until nothing was left but the cold rags of fear.

Knees wobbling, he sat up and looked around at the shambles of the room. The floor bore deep scars from its tail-flailing; the walls were gouged. And the netbed was nowhere to be seen. Vaguely, he wondered if he had eaten it in the heat of emotion.

Groaning, Fendeqot leaned back against the remains of the heat register which hung at a crazy angle from the wall. The bleak thought came that he was going to lose his breakage deposit. Worse, it was going to take a whole bottle of Qotaflap's Scale Repair to mend his ruined tail.

The face of Diderot still leered from his mind. Diderot. Nemesis. With the successful completion of Phase Two, there would be no way to stop him. No way at all.

If Diderot *successfully* completed Phase Two. . . .

A yellow gleam came into Fendeqot's eye and glistened like a drop of golden bile. There *was* a way—he saw it now—a foolproof way. His terrible jaw fell open and a poisonous laugh came bubbling up from deep in his throat. The Finger might be on The Trigger, he thought balefully. But the missile was going to be aimed at Diderot's flat face. . . .

On the frigid surface of Hyades IV, persistent winds skimmed and buzzed through the ice harp fields that wrapped the north end of Central Sector Zoo and Arboretum. The north end was the terminus of the self-guided tour, and the visitors, who were invariably wrapped to the eyeballs in Hyadean snuggies—good for forty-below in the wind, had by then a viable interest only in the Visitors' Center ahead. Most paid little attention to the Ice Klarrp's Cave. And if a few spotted the narrow opening at the rear, they probably thought it led to yet another galactic specimen.

In a way, it did. The chilly annex housed the office of DISSECTOR, a covert operation of Clandestine Services, Galactic Intelligence Agency.

Jesus "Zeus the Zapper" Zapata, Director of DISSECTOR and former human, howled in rage. "What's this! What's this!" He rotated his right hand—the one that repels—toward the audio plug emerging from his temple; the central hand—the one with the Swiss Army knife attachment—clicky-clacked his belly button in an agitated way. "What's this I'm hearing?" he demanded.

In answer, Klapto, GIA Chief of Countercounterintelligence, quirked his nose flap in the Hyadean Attitude of Respectful Questioning. Cuthbert Cuthbert, spy, raised his eyebrows.

"Well, dammit, *say* something," bellowed The Zapper. This was followed by a rafter-shaking lion roar emanating from Zapata's midsection. The roar came with such force that it fluttered the Black Watch-plaid scarf marking the line of demarcation between his fleshy chin and his metal middle.

Cuthbert Cuthbert turned up his collar and raised woebegone eyes to the icicles hanging from the ceiling. He hated Zapata and he hated the lion roar. At times, he was sure that The Zapper had ordered it just to devil him. He sighed; he could see his breath. "We can't hear what you're hearing, sir. If you'd amplify—"

"Sly aren't you, Cuthbert?" The Zapper raised his left arm.

The little spy braced himself, but it was too late. With an angry hum the arm activated, propelling Cuthbert at an alarming rate toward Zapata. When the thin metal band that circled his neck clicked into the cyborg's iron grip, he let himself go limp. The arm retracted, drawing Cuthbert with it until his hound eyes were uncomfortably close to The Zapper's narrowed ones. "I asked you a question. I asked you if you're sly. You think you're sly, don't you, Cuthbert?"

"If you say so, sir."

"I *do* say so. You think you're sly. But you're not sly enough. You'd have to stay up *nights* to be as sly as I am. Isn't that *so*, Cuthbert?" This last was followed with a bone-rattling shake.

"Yes sir. That's so, sir."

"You really think, do you, that I'm going to *reveal* sensitive GIA information to *you*?"

"No sir. I wouldn't think so, sir."

"Damn right." The Zapper's right arm rose.

Cuthbert Cuthbert again tried to brace himself. Again it was too late; it was always too late. The Zapper's repellent arm slammed him across the room and back into his chair.

It was surely karma, thought Cuthbert. He must have been unimaginably evil in a former life to be used so in this one. He mused on the nature of the evil, failing utterly to come up with one vile enough to condemn him to the life of an indentured spy. He sighed again and watched his breath curl in the chilly air.

The Zapper's gaze slid toward his right temple where the audio jack emerged. Eyes narrowed dangerously, he listened. Then with a creak he turned on Klapto. "Why aren't we on top of things? Why aren't we?"

The Hyadean raised his noseflap in an elaborate gesture of conciliation. Its elegance was lost on Zeus the Zapper.

"Stop all that flapdoodle and give me a straight answer. KABBAGE has infiltrated the Interstellar Nurses Corps. Prissing Sectorites in the I.N.C.! Do you know what this means?" he bellowed. "This means they can go anywhere—do anything—in the name of medicine. And where are *we*? Where in the hell are *we*?"

Klapto's noseflap puckered in perplexity. "But sir, we *are* in the I.N.C. It's always been one of our front organizations."

"Cretin! Don't you think I prissing know that? I want to know from you why the KBG kidnapped the wife of the prissing Chief of Staff of Satellite Hospital and genetically altered her prissing *egg*!"

With an alarming clatter of his midsection, The Zapper swiveled toward the hapless Cuthbert. His eyes narrowed to slits. "Why do you suppose they did that?"

The little spy gazed intently at the wall and searched his mind for inspiration. "I suppose, sir, that the KBG had a nefarious purpose in mind, sir."

"Oh, you do?"

Cuthbert's eyes widened at the low and dangerously gentle tone of The Zapper. "Yes sir, I do, sir."

"And I suppose that what you have in *your* mind"—his voice raised forty decibels—"is a foul and malodorous, prissing *void!*" A particularly shattering lion roar followed. "Of *course* the KBG has a nefarious purpose in mind, cretin. The question is what?"

"I couldn't be sure, sir."

"I couldn't be sure, sir," mimicked The Zapper. "What *can* you be sure of, Cuthbert?"

"I'm, uh, not sure, sir."

"I will tell you what you can be sure of, Cuthbert. I will e-nun-ci-ate so that you can understand. You can be sure that KABBAGE altered that prissing reptile egg for a prissing good reason. It is up to you, Cuthbert, to find out prissing *why*."

If nothing else, Cuthbert Cuthbert knew his cues. He leaped to his feet. "Yes sir. I'm going now, sir." With as much speed as he could muster, he headed for the door, only to be plucked to a halt in mid-stride by the irresistible left arm of Zeus the Zapper. "Semper clandestinus."

"Semper clan, sir. Semper clan."

"One last thing, Cuthbert. The only good reptile egg is a dead reptile egg."

Then the relentless right arm raised, propelling Cuthbert Cuthbert, indentured spy, onto the frozen floor of the Ice Klarrp's Cave. Legs and arms flailing, Cuthbert rode his rump into a cluster of the little beasts, who, frigid with delight, affectionately nuzzled his ears and nose with a dozen long and lapping frozen tongues.

Chapter 4

Cargo Hold
Galactic Spaceways Flight 409
June 19

Lonzo Leaf, Sub-sector Chief
Interstellar Nurses Corps
Step Sister Plaza
Pleiades III 555777666

Dear Chief Leaf:

I wish to enter a formal complaint regarding Galactic Spaceways Flight 409. You can only imagine my dismay when the flight attendant looked at my ticket—which was issued by the Interstellar Nurses Corps and which I, Terra Tarkington, accepted in good faith—and sent me to the boarding area for semi-sentient beings, pets, and other carboniferous cargo.

According to the flight attendant, Flight 409 has been booked for months and months. She said I was lucky to get any accommodations at all.

I don't feel lucky, Mr. Leaf.

Have you ever spent seven hours in a barred cubicle with a Pleiadean clawed chat on one side and a howling wirefur on the other? I do not think it is fair of the Corps to put me up with an oozing vegetative growth across the aisle instead of a person with whom I could have had Moon Maidens in the lounge and who promised to show me the wonders of the galaxy.

I realize that it is too late to rectify this grievous situation, Mr. Leaf, because the ship is about to jump and two people with tranquilizer guns are coming down the

*aisle now. But I want you to know that I'm not happy at
all with my accommodations.*

> *Yours in a joyless environment,*
> *Terra Tarkington*

As the shrouds of a dream fell away, Terra stirred and
looked up. A large flap of mottled skin was hanging just above
her nose.

The skin flap quivered. "Good morning-evening, I say to
you in your native tongue," said a gravelly voice. "Good
afternoon."

"Good night!" Eyes wide open now, she stared up at the
face attached to the skin flap.

"Welcome-hello-howdy. I am Clahkto." The skin flap rose,
and arching in the middle, exposed a pair of flat nostrils
underneath. Below them, a lipless slit gaped open and
displayed an uneven row of grayish teeth.

Terra stared transfixed at the grisly sight.

"Smiling-grinning I am doing, in your native custom,"
intoned the voice. "Hi there-greetings-how are you now?
Welcome-hello-howdy to Satellite Hospital Outpost." Abruptly, the skin flap ceased its waving about and retracted in
creased accordian folds.

Satellite Hospital Outpost? She stared around the
featureless cargo cubicle of the starship in bewilderment. It
wasn't possible that she'd reached the Taurus system already. It
didn't seem like more than an hour since she'd fallen asleep.
But the safety webbing had fallen away, and the ticket on her
left wrist pulsed first yellow, then red, with the message,
FLIGHT TERMINATED. And someone had removed the
vegetative growth from across the aisle.

Disoriented, Terra stared at the creature. With its face
rearranged it looked vaguely familiar. Slowly recognition
dawned. "You're a Hyadean." Its—his—appearance was easier
to handle now that the skin flap was in repose.

"Yes-affirmative-correct, I am indeed Hyadean. And you
are Earth-porpoise."

"Person. Earth-person."

"Not porpoise?"

She shook her head.

"I have made a mistake in your language. Haha-hoho."
The skin flap rose again most disconcertingly and quivered

29

above the lipless, open mouthhole. "I am laughing-smiling-grinning in your custom."

Terra tried to smile back, but her lips trembled when the Hyadean's bulbous liver-colored tongue emerged and glided over the gray teeth. "You really don't need to smile on my account."

The Hyadean blinked. "I have practiced smiling-grinning very hard for you. Am I doing it wrong?"

"Oh, no. You do it very well," she said uncertainly.

"You would not mind if I stopped?"

"Oh, no. I'd be happy for you to stop. I mean, I *like* your smile, and all that, but, uh, maybe it's not good for your face."

The skin flap retracted at once. "It *is* an effort," he admitted in obvious relief, quite forgetting himself, and speaking in Standard. Then remembering his instructions— *"Though the newcomer may speak Standard, greetings in the alien's native tongue will comfort it in its new surroundings,"*—he reverted at once with a "Come now. We must hurry-hustle-run." Extending a somewhat human hand, he tugged at hers.

"Why?"

At a warning squawk that came from somewhere behind her left ear, the Hyadean yanked harder and pulled her into a narrow passageway. "Got to get off now before the ship jumps. Quick-hurry-run." Dragging Terra behind him, he raced down a labyrinthine corridor through a series of doorways that whooshed shut behind them.

After a prolonged sprint, they came to a curving green-and-beige hallway. "We are in the satellite now."

Terra leaned against the wall and tried to catch her breath when the Hyadean tugged again. "This way, hurry-rush." They dashed off again and stopped before a large port in the satellite's bulkhead.

Terra looked through the port. The starship that had brought her from Earth hung like a huge silver whale in a black sea. As she watched, the snakelike tubeways that connected ship to satellite retracted and disappeared. Signal lights flashing from the outpost station played over the pale hull. Red turned to amber and the ship slid away until it was no bigger than a pale eye in the sky.

"You watch now," said the Hyadean. "You watch the jump."

The lights turned blue and the ship seemed to shimmer for a moment. Then a wink, and abruptly it was gone.

"It won't be back now. Not for months-years-long time."

Clinging to a railing that seemed designed for claws instead of hands, Terra stared through the port. The black of space seemed to stretch out forever, shrinking her to nothing in the immensity of it. She searched the sky for a glimpse of the sun, but it was lost in a thousand alien stars. Blinking, she raised a quick hand to her face so the Hyadean wouldn't see the sudden moisture in her eyes.

Terra looked around in bewilderment. Satellite Hospital Outpost seemed to have as many skins as an onion. After negotiating half-dozen or so levels, the Hyadean had deposited her in an inner layer distinguished from the others by its color—bile green—and by a small group obviously waiting for someone.

"Goodbye-so long-see you later," said the Hyadean in a parting attack on Terra's native tongue. With a jaunty wave of his flap, he vanished through a curved doorway.

Terra glanced from one to the other of the group. Each one wore the insignia of the Interstellar Nurses Corps; each one wore a travel bracelet like her own. None were human. And all of them were staring back at her.

"Well," she began uncertainly, "here we are." She launched a bright smile toward the others.

A slim young Aldeberan leaned back on her tail and tapped her companion's earhole with a slim claw. "What is-s-s it?" she hissed softly, with a sidelong look at Terra.

"A Hyadean," said the other Aldeberan knowledgeably.

"But it has-s-s no flap," said the first.

"Birth defect."

Another of the group, this one, in truth, a Hyadean, creased her noseflap in disdain. "Provincials," she sniffed to Terra. "Do you see the purple background on their insignia? They're not nurses. They're kitchen help." Then turning to the group she said, "Don't you recognize a human when you see one?"

"A human?" asked the slim Aldeberan with a doubtful swish of her tail.

"Of course." The Hyadean sniffed again. "I've certainly dissected enough of them to know what I'm looking at." She

31

shook her flap at Terra. "You just stay with me and I'll take care of you."

Terra wasn't sure whether to be grateful or not.

In a few minutes, a thick-trunked Hyadean showed up to claim the kitchen help who trailed after him into the bowels of Satellite Hospital. Moments later, a cluster of assorted aliens wearing armbands inscribed ORIENTATION arrived and took away the rest of the little group—except for Terra.

She waited alone for what seemed to be hours when suddenly an overweight Aldeberan with the words NURSING SUPERVISOR carved on her chest scales appeared.

The hefty Aldeberan Supervisor primly curled her tail and looked down her snout at Terra accusingly, "Your orientation per-s-son is-s-s not here."

Terra, not finding a ready reply to that, smiled hesitantly.

"I s-s-suppose you'll be wanting to s-s-see your quarters-s-s." Not waiting for an answer, the Supervisor pinched her nostrils in an aggrieved way and marched toward the slidleator. "Follow me."

The slidlelator whisked them to sixteen and opened to a hallway that was neither buff nor brown, but somewhere in between. Terra looked around. "Is this level for humans?"

The Aldeberan's unbelieving stare was slowly veiled by a membranous blink. "We could never give over an entire level for two beings-s-s."

"Two! Only two humans?"

"Three now. Counting you." With a sweeping whisk of her tail, the supervisor headed toward an open door down the hall from which came a series of moaning squawks and muffled scufflings.

Abreast of the room, the Supervisor pulled herself up in disapproval. Inside, her back to the door, a young Aldeberan clicked green-painted claws over her head and thumped her tail in a suggestive way to the rhythm of a recorded reptilian voice singing, ". . . fat, sleek"—thump, scrape—"shiny, s-s-sexy tail . . ."

"Hah-h-h!" came the shocked hiss of the Supervisor.

The Aldeberan girl froze in mid-thump and looked cautiously over her shoulder. Her yellow eyes moved from the Supervisor to Terra, then back again. "Oh. I guess-s-s I'm late."

"Indeed," said the Supervisor. Then to Terra. "This-s-s is

Dandde QotQot. She is-s-s your orientation pers-s-son." With a parting whisk of her tail, designed to show disdain of all present, the Supervisor turned and strode away.

Dandde extended her pointed little tongue in greeting. "I'm s-s-sorry. I should have met you. I forgot." Thumping her tail absently to the squawking singer she stared at Terra. "You're a human," she said by way of conversation.

Terra nodded. "And you're an Aldeberan."

Opening volleys out of the way, they looked at each other uncertainly.

"We don't s-s-see many humans-s-s here."

"I don't suppose you do," said Terra with a wistful smile.

"We have Hyadeans-s-s though." Dandde's voice rose in optimism. "And you are a Hyadeanoid."

Terra blinked. "I, uh, never thought of myself in just that way."

"Oh, yes-s-s," said Dandde in a comforting tone. "You are definitely Hyadeanoid." Tail and feet combining to form a tripod, she leaned back next to a three-dimensional picture of a broad-chested Aldeberan male signed with the legend: *For Dandde—who makes my tail throb.* "I'm a nurse-s-s, too. I work in Malignant Fungi, but I'm off today. You s-s-start tomorrow."

"In Malignant Fungi?"

Dandde QotQot's shoulder scales rose in a faint shrug. "I don't know where they're going to put you. The other human female was-s-s a float nurse-s-s at firs-s-st, but it didn't work out. Her s-s-skin shriveled up from all that liquid s-s-so they had to trans-s-sfer her."

Terra's brow furrowed for a moment before she said, "I think maybe they didn't tell us everything back in nursing school."

Dandde nodded in sympathy. Then springing forward, she said, "I'll show you your room."

Terra's room proved to be three doors down. It was murky beige and empty except for a netbed and a desk at a height designed for a tail-reclining Aldeberan. There were no chairs. The small room leading off from it was a mystery at first.

"This-s-s is where you wash." Dandde dug a claw into a little opening in the wall and out popped a rubbery nozzle-like device. Next to it was another nozzle that proved to be a dryer, and a ball-shaped object that began to whirl and buzz when

Dandde touched it. "Buffer," she said, running it lightly over her scales.

"What's that?" Terra was staring at a small, rimmed hole in the floor. It was filled with dark liquid.

Dandde blinked. "The depository. That is-s-s where you"—she paused discreetly—"deposit."

Terra stared at the rimmed hole in dismay. "I, uh, don't know if I can do that—there."

"Very s-s-simple." Dandde flung her tail back, tripod fashion, and balanced over the aperture. Then with a sudden look at Terra, she thrust her snout into the air and closed her eyes in the Aldeberan picture of acute embarrassment. When she opened them again, she was most careful not to stare at Terra's backside and thus draw attention to physical frailties and absent appendages. Then, as inspiration struck, Dandde said, "Just telescope your parts like all Hyadeanoids."

"Well," said Terra doubtfully, "only half of us humans have, uh, telescoping parts."

Dandde blinked. "The other half?"

Terra nodded.

"Well," said Dandde, "you'll think of s-s-something. It's-s-s time to eat now. Come on." Then brightly, "We're having a Pleiadean dinner: boiled blebs-s-s and tuberoid muck s-s-suckers-s-s."

"Welcome to the Bull Run," said Terra.

Chapter 5

Satellite Hospital Outpost
Taurus 14, North Horn 978675644
Nath Orbit
June 29

Carmelita O'Hare, R.N.
Teton Medical Center
Jackson Hole Summation City
Wyoming 306548760 United Earth, Sol

Dear Carmie,

Well, you were right. Go ahead. Say "I told you so," and get it over with. "Join the Interstellar Nurses Corps and see the galaxy. . . ." Oh, Carmie, why didn't I listen to you? I've been on Taurus 14 for ten days now, and there is absolutely nothing to do except work. The worst thing is there's no male homo-sape for just light years— unless you count Dr. Kelly-Bach and he's old. Carmie, he's really old. He has liver spots and his neck hangs in folds like that preserved turkey we had in anatomy lab in school.

There are only three homo-sapes on this whole tin can: Dr. Kelly-Bach, me, and Olga Ludowicki. And Olga is bitter—really bitter. She says the only reason she's a nurse is that she broke her toes when she was ten and ruined her ballet career. Carmie, if you could see Olga, you'd know why she broke her toes. It was from the sheer weight of her legs. If you ask me, Olga's fracture was ballet's gain.

I can hear you thinking, Carmie: "At least you have your work." Let me tell you something. Nursing here is not your run-of-the-mill thing. Remember how we giggled and laughed all through Alien Physiology? I'm not *laughing now. This morning I had to prep an Aurigan's belly for surgery. You may not remember this, but Aurigans are all belly. There was Mrs. Redondaltff lying there on a megabed like some vast termite queen. I had to use seventeen prep kits. And the surgery—a horror. Dr. Qotemire (he's Chief of Staff) operated, and he had the vilest temper you ever saw. He's just as sarcastic as he can be and when he gets really mad, he hisses and lashes his tail around the room. I almost tripped over it right in the middle of the operation.*

It's enough to make you hate Aldebarans, except for Mrs. Qotemire. She's really nice. She's pregnant, and she and Dr. Qotemire are very nervous over it. It's kind of sweet once you get over the idea that she's going to have an egg instead of a baby.

Well, I really have to run. I've got so much to do when I'm off duty. Tonight after supper I can watch reruns of old holos in the rec hall and drink bogus beer. Seriously, if a man doesn't turn up on this Bull Run soon, I think I'll go stark star crazy. There is a light on the horizon though. Rumor has it that we're getting three Marines in for observation. Boy, do I plan to observe.

Love,
Terra

Cuthbert Cuthbert felt horribly conspicuous. It was the outfit that did it: The cape was very wide at the shoulders, and flared out in thick black folds to his ankles. It was covered with silver stars and arcane symbols that flashed and winked at every step. The cap was a tall, black cone designed to fit a reptilian head both narrower and deeper than his own.

The cap was a torment to Cuthbert. It was made of memoflex that clung tenaciously to its original dimensions. Fore and aft it gaped enough to admit his fist; port to starboard it gripped his temples cruelly.

Even now, the cap's rightful owner, Horfutz Vladeqot, was dozing in the service lounge of the Hyades Hilton. A spritz of Brain Drain (which Cuthbert had purchased at the Spy X-Change, and which was nearly empty) had done the trick, leaving Vladeqot tilted peacefully back on his tail over the depository.

Disrobing the tall Aldeberan had brought a sweat to Cuthbert's brow, partly because of the fear that he might be discovered, partly because Vladeqot's massive tail, emerging from a split in the back of the cape, had anchored the hem quite effectively against the floor. At last Cuthbert got it loose and put it on along with the hateful cap. He tried to pry loose Vladeqot's wand, but it was too tightly clutched in the Aldeberan's claws.

Cuthbert pulled out a spraytube of Mus-L-Mush, guaranteed to relax the tightest of grips. He had the spraytube threaded halfway up the Aldeberan's nostril when he stopped and reconsidered. The service lounge was tiny, and the idea of a Mus-L-Mushed Aldeberan tilting out of control and pinning him under a hundred-plus kilos of scale and tail was not appealing. "To hell with the damned old wand," he muttered. He would do without it.

Withdrawing the unused Mus-L-Mush, he tucked it under the voluminous cape and strode away to the service slidleator. The cape was much too long. It followed Cuthbert in rustling protest. Like a recalcitrant trailer, it turned in tighter arcs than he did, and snagged on furnishings and doorways. And when he tried to unsnag it, the malevolent garment wrapped around his feet and legs. Sighing, Cuthbert hitched the cape around his waist and stepped into the empty slidleator.

The ceiling of the slidleator impacted with the tip of his cap and flattened it. The cap, responding to the memory of its shape, thrust upward and formed an irresistible bond with the ceiling that locked Cuthbert in place like a vise. Wedged as he was in the slidleator, Cuthbert raised his woebegone gaze toward heaven and questioned his fate.

It had seemed like a good idea at the time to sign up for Spy School. And his term of indenture was just for five years after graduation. He had been a conscientious student. Hadn't he done well enough in dirty tricks and covert surveillance? Hadn't he done precisely what was expected of him? He had betrayed his roommate on schedule; he had planted careful seeds of disinformation in the cafeteria. Why then did the GIA send him to the ass end of the Galaxy to serve under a demented cyborg?

That Zeus the Zapper would destroy him if he failed seemed sure; he had told him so—and Cuthbert had an unwavering faith in the Zapper's prediction.

The slidleator came to a stop, and Cuthbert with much bending of his knees and tugging, managed to extricate himself. As he stepped out, the memoflex cap reestablished its shape with a pop that echoed deep inside his ears.

He was in the Aldeberan Annex now. The doorways to the rooms were wider here to accommodate the broad haunches of the guests. Turning in a broad sweep to allow for his cape, Cuthbert Cuthbert made his way to the suite which housed Dr. Curtiz Qotemire and his gravid wife Qoqedd.

Qoqedd Qotemire reclined on her haunches and slowly buffed her tail while her husband watched from across the hotel room.

He had always loved to look at her tail. Now it coiled plumply around her body and gleamed a soft blue in the light. There was something so sensuous about the way she sat, head tilted, delicate claws holding the buffer, working it over the swelling inner curve where tail met haunches that in spite of himself and the fact that they were late, Qotemire felt his chest scales quiver and rise.

With a quick look to be sure she hadn't seen, he pressed them down and took a quick lick at his frozen euphoric. He hated Convivialities and medical conference Convivialities were the worst. He remembered the last: the crushing boredom of scale-to-scale contact in a stuffy pair of rooms; the sight of a colleague, half-murked on double lassitudes, playing tailsies with a run-down actress; the terribly significant conversation with the terribly earnest, terribly plain, young researcher with chipped tail lacquer and bad breath; and the ghastly encounter with a thick-scaled matron who contrived to brush against his chest and hiss thickly in his earhole, "Call me Huss-s-s Huss-s-s." Qotemire's nostrils triangulated at the memory and he diminished the euphoric with a vicious thrust of his tongue.

Qotemire stretched and his tired muscles creaked with the movement. He had put in a full morning of surgery before he met Qoqedd at the shuttle, and he had spent the rest of the afternoon on the boring trip to Hyades IV. He hissed faintly and lapped at the remains of the euphoric. That was the trouble with Satellite Hospital: it took half a day to get away and then when you arrived, where were you? He looked around the room again. It was a suite. One of the best the Hyades Hilton had to offer. The wide, curving window offered a moonlit view of the equatorial ice-harp fields shivering in the wind. Hyades IV was terrific—if you liked frostbite.

Qotemire hated cold. It seemed to him that Xavierqot could have picked a better place for the conference. Someplace where the sun was more efficient and a person could get in a few rounds of whackit, he thought wistfully. Failing that, he could have picked the interior. The absurd thought of a respectable medical conference in the underground City of Twelve Evils caused a low laugh to burble in his throat.

With a downward thrust of his tail, he levered himself to a standing position in an attempt to hurry Qoqedd along. They were already late and Xavierqot took tardiness as a personal affront.

Oddly, Qoqedd seemed reluctant to leave.

"But you love Convivialities-s-s—" Qotemire began, when a chime chimed and the outer door spoke: "Someone is here, Dr. Qotemire, Mrs. Qotemire."

He looked up in surprise. They hadn't been expecting anyone. "Who's-s-s there?"

"Rune Service," came the muffled voice.

Qotemire stared at Qoqedd who rolled her yellow eyes coquettishly and drew her tail over her toes. He might have known. She couldn't go anywhere without having her fortune told.

Qoqedd quivered her nostrils in that clever little way she had when she wanted to be indulged. "Why don't you go ahead? I'll be along s-s-soon."

Hissing faintly in defeat, Qotemire said to the door, "All right."

With another chime and a click, the door said, "Someone is coming in now, Dr. Qotemire, Mrs. Qotemire."

A human in a grotesque cape and ill-fitting cap stepped over the threshold and impaled the cap in the doorway. With deep knee bends and disjointed bobbings, he disengaged himself. As he entered the room, the cap regained its pointy shape with a discernable pop. "Who called for Rune Service?"

Superstitious spiddlepot, thought Qotemire with ill-disguised distaste. Indicating Qoqedd with a thrust of his snout, he turned tail and strode out of the room without a backward glance.

As the door shut behind Qotemire, Cuthbert Cuthbert breathed in relief. With the husband gone, his job would be much easier.

Qoqedd Qotemire stared at him in open curiosity. "I never had a human s-s-seer before."

39

"Would you like to see my union card?" he asked, praying she would say no. It wouldn't do to show it to her—not with its picture of Horfutz Vladeqot's toothy snout.

"Oh, no. It's-s-s fine that you're human," she said uncertainly.

"We'll need the Basin of Portents."

"Oh, yes-s-s. I'll get it." She found it next to the hotel copy of *Cosmic Truth* (placed there compliments of the Hyadean Society). Filling the shallow bowl with water, she set it on a low platform in front of Cuthbert.

He reached into an inner pocket of the cape and drew out a handful of chiropods and another object which he carefully palmed. With swooping passes of his hands—here the wand would have come in handy—and a gutteral "Hah" and a "Hi-Yah," he sprinkled freeze-dried chiropods on the water.

Qoqedd watched in fascination as the little animals absorbed the water and thrust random limbs into configurations of strange and mystic letters. "What does-s-s it s-s-say?"

> "*Idd*-dy, iddy-iddy
> Biddy-biddy, biddy-biddy,
> Umlaut, umlaut. . . ."

intoned the seer.

Qoqedd slid her inner eyelids down in wonder. "I never heard that one before. What does-s-s it mean?"

"Look closely." Cuthbert's hands circled mystically—and palm down—over the soggy chiropods.

Qoqedd obediently lowered her snout and gazed into the bowl.

"Closer." He pointed to a clump of chiropods. "It means—"

Her nostrils flared in anticipation. "Yes-s-s?"

With a half-turn of his hand, he aimed the nozzle of the Brain Drain at her open nostrils and gave the tube a quick squeeze with his thumb.

"O-o-o-oh," said Qoqedd as if she had received a sudden revelation. Then her snout thrust toward the ceiling and began to circle slowly. As her eyelids slit shut one by one, her upper body followed the circling motion of her snout in increasing diameters until she came to a stop decidedly off-center.

At a poke from Cuthbert's index finger, she gave a little snoring hiss and toppled over on her back.

Cuthbert had to work fast. The effects of the Brain Drain wouldn't last long, and he didn't want to use the last squirt in the tube. He might need it to get away. It made him horribly nervous to run out of Brain Drain, but it made him even more nervous to have to ask Zeus the Zapper for a refill chit.

He threw open the cape and felt for the buttons on his work shirt. There were three of them, large and opaque gray. He gave each a half-turn. As he did, neurons fired, miniscule crystals responded, and the three tiny, living computers activated.

The top button glowed darkly and Aleph—that was his name—surveyed the prostrate Qoqedd Qotemire. "Let's get humping, Cuthbert." Aleph, who was descended from a renegade strain of *E. coli*, was not your most refined button. Aleph believed in action and brute force. Cuthbert didn't like him much, but he had to respect his guts.

Beth, the middle button, was the intuitive one. Hers was a patrician strain of *Serratia marcescens*, a very old line indeed, and she never forgot it. Yet if she treated Cuthbert with a touch of condescension, it was tempered with kindness. He suspected she felt sorry for him.

Gimbel, who resided near Cuthbert's waist, was another story. He was a bacillus (acetoethylicus to be exact), but there was a touch of yeast about him that disturbed Cuthbert. He was sure that Gimbel indulged in self-abuse on the sly. Gimbel denied it, of course, claiming it was nothing more than a temporary derangement of metabolism, but during those times when his voice slurred and his perceptions skewed it was clear to Cuthbert that Gimbel was into auto-fermentation.

Sober, Gimbel was an indispensable member of the team. It was his job to mesh Aleph's raw data with Beth's random intuition and come up with a workable synthesis. Today, he greeted his activation with a jaundiced flare of his button and an acid "It's you again" to Cuthbert. Know-nothing peripheral, Gimbel thought darkly.

Gimbel resented being awakened. God knows, he needed his rest. Without it, he might come down with something. The fear that an alien virus might invade his cells and take over his nuclei chilled him to the marrow of his mitochondria. Although the buttoncase protected him, there was no safeguard against the Cuthbert-peripheral's carelessness. At any moment he could be whacked against something, scraped, scarred. All it would take was a tiny crack and, then—infection. And the Hyadean Blight, the Eastern strain, was going around. (According to his calculations, the chance that he would crack his button and subsequently catch the Hyadean blight, Eastern strain, was 1 in 1E09.)

The risk, however tenuous, was real enough to Gimbel. You couldn't argue with the figures, he reasoned, and at 1 chance in 1E09, it was undeniably possible. At the hideous thought, sequestered juices began to flow through his little body and bathe each neuron with the warm glow of ethyl.

Beth glowed a warm pink that shaded into red and said, "Let's begin."

Cuthbert lifted a scale at the edge of Qoqedd's gravid convexity (which on the occasion of the medical conference Conviviality was decorated with cobalt to accent her delicate color and yellow to match her eyes). He touched the tip of a probe to the underlying skin, and at the touch, the slender probe burrowed unerringly toward her egg. The resistance changed as the tip encountered the partially calcified shell and the probe began to spin. In a moment it had drilled through.

The probe's minute sensors began to send streams of data to the waiting computers. Aleph, whose memory was prodigious, retrieved the bulk of the data, while Beth, sampling at random, noted condition of egg tooth, sundry enzymatic secretions, scale maturation, and tail-length. Gimbel compared the data to the norms for unhatched Aldeberans in an attempt to find the KBG's genetic alterations.

"What did they do to it?" asked Cuthbert.

Now if Gimbel had not indulged in self-pollution, or perhaps if he had been in a more positive frame of mind, he might have noticed the odd, but very minor change pinpointed by Beth's intuitive sampling. As it was, he glowed orange—which was the equivalent of a shrug—and said, "We're wasting our time, Cuthbert. We have a perfectly normal unhatched Aldeberan here."

And if Cuthbert had noticed the faint slurring of Gimbel's words he might have asked Aleph and Beth to store the data for further study. Instead, only one thought was going through Cuthbert's mind: the particularly murderous look on Zeus the Zapper's face when he had said, *"The only good reptile egg is a dead reptile egg."*

42

But it wouldn't do to wipe out the egg then and there. It would rouse suspicion. He needed a time bomb. . . .

Later, Qoqedd Qotemire woke with a blink to find herself leaning against the wall. Balancing unsteadily on her tail, she wheeled around. The room was empty. How was it possible that she had dozed off in the middle of a reading?

Soggy chiropods still floated in the Basin of Portents. She stared at them in puzzlement, and tried to remember what the seer had said, but though she tried, nothing came to her except the feeling that this reading had somehow been especially portentous—perhaps the most portentous of them all.

Then with a wistful hiss and a little shrug of her tail, she went off to join Curtiz at the Conviviality.

Chapter 6

Satellite Hospital Outpost
Taurus 14, North Horn 978675644
Nath Orbit
July 1

Carmelita O'Hare, R.N.
Teton Medical Center
Jackson Hole Summation City
Wyoming 306548760 United Earth, Sol

Dear Carmie,

Remember the Marines I told you about? They were Marines, all right: Capellan Marines. We had to put them in the starboard tanks in smelly old ammonia solution. Dr. Qotemire was a pain. He wanted me to check the filtration every fifteen minutes and check vital signs, too. If you think it's easy checking vital signs on Capellans—well,

*think again. My hands look like diaper rash from all that
ammonia. Did you know that Capellans will eat only
Capellan plankton? Well, I didn't either. Could I help it if
dietary sent the wrong plankton? I, in good faith, gave
them what dietary sent. Well, you should have heard Dr.
Qotemire—"This-s-s is-s-s very serious-s-s nurse-s-s." Dr.
Qotemire is getting harder to live with every day. He got
so mad over the plankton he turned bluer than a ten-
credit note. There's no telling what he'll be like next week.
Mrs. Qotemire is due then.*

*I can't tell you what a disappointment it was about
the Marines. The closest thing to humans that we have
here are the people from Hyades IV. They really look
passable except for the creases where their noses ought to
be, but their reproductive habits aren't like ours at all.
Not at all! Look it up, Carmie. I'm not going to repeat it
here.*

*On top of the trauma over the Marines, I discovered
yesterday that I'm not going to get out of this chicken
outfit in two years like I thought. When I signed up they
told me it was for two orbits, but they didn't mean Earth
orbits. Do you realize it takes twenty-seven Earth months
for this tub to get around Nath? I am in despair. I'll be an
old woman before I get off. An old, celibate woman.
Carmie, I'm desperate. The other night I dreamed about
Dr. Kelly-Bach.*

> *Yours in despair,*
> *Terra*

Terra stared up at the winking sign over the wide doors.

MALIGNANT FUNGI
Attention All Personnel
Enter Through Decontam-port Only

Well, it *had* to be better than all that ammonia in the
Marine ward. She hesitated only a moment before she went
through the entrance port.

The showers were ahead. Terra stripped and tossed her
clothes onto what seemed to be a bench. As soon as it sensed
their weight, the surface of the bench began to move and her

clothes glided toward the wall where a door opened and swallowed them up.

A sign glowed from the door.

ALL GARMENTS AND ADORNMENTS ARE NOW
ENTERING RECYCLE
RECONSTITUTED PERSONAL WEAR MAY BE
RECLAIMED AT EXIT PORT

There seemed to be no turning back.

As she stepped into the shower room, a dozen nozzles sought her out and began to spray her with a foul-smelling disinfectant at a temperature better suited for heat-loving Aldeberans than humans.

Sprinting through, she sloshed through a trough awash with more hot smelly fluid that splashed over her feet. The trough gave way to a short aisle that ended at a blank wall with no discernable exit.

Suddenly a voice came from the wall: *"Foot covers must be worn at all times in Malignant Fungi areas. Toe claws must be clipped to avoid puncturing foot covers."*

Scarcely had the wall delivered its message than Terra heard a high-pitched mechanical whine near the floor and the wall extruded a pair of whirling blades that rapidly approached her toes. After a moment of frozen horror, she leaped backwards and landed in the trough again.

Ankle-deep in disinfectant, she glared at the wall. "I'm not an Aldeberan."

After a moment's hesitation, the wall retracted its toe clippers and spoke again: *"Hyadeans must scrub under all flaps and apertures."* This was followed by an array of brushes and scouring devices that oozed from the wall and began to whirl noisily.

"I'm not a Hyadean."

"What?"

"I said"—she raised her voice over the din—"I'm not a Hyadean."

"Well, what are you then?" asked the wall.

"A human," she yelled, "I'm a human."

"A what?"

"A hu-man."

"My data does not include hu-mans," said the wall. *"My*

45

data indicates hospital personnel are seventy-eight percent Aldeberan, twenty-one percent Hyadean, one percent Other."

"Other, then. I'm an Other."

"*Oh*," said the wall. "*Never mind.*" It swung open with a little whooshing sound. "*You may proceed to Drying and Buffing.*"

Drying and Buffing was a windy hazardous tunnel that terminated in a door labeled DRESSING AREA. The dressing room was featureless except for a battered old garment dispenser that took up the greater part of one wall.

The dispenser creaked and belched up a sterile package containing a pair of foot covers and a surgical mask apparently designed to accommodate an Aldeberan snout. There was nothing more.

Terra stared at the package in dismay. "I'm not an Aldeberan," she told the dispenser. "I'm an Other."

The dispenser had nothing to say.

"I can't go out there like this," she told it. It was all very well for Aldeberans; they didn't wear much anyway, but at least they were covered with scales. "I can't go out there like this," she said again. "I'm not used to it."

The dispenser had nothing to say. In fact, no amount of pleading, poking, or shaking seemed to have any effect on it at all. Close to tears, Terra stared at the foot covers and the surgical mask. She was wondering how to attach them for maximum modesty when the door opened and Dandde Qotqot—dried, buffed, and toe claws neatly clipped—walked in.

"Oh," said Dandde, "you're on Malignant Fungi now." She looked down her snout at the foot covers and mask. "Humans-s-s usually wear more than that."

"It won't give me any clothes," said Terra. "It won't even talk to me."

"You have to give it a whack." Dandde swung her tail vigorously and whanged the dispenser in its midsection.

From somewhere deep inside came a click, and the dispenser said, "*Waiting.*"

"I'm an Other," said Terra. "I want some clothes."

"*Small, medium, or large?*" asked the dispenser.

"Small, I guess."

Another click and the dispenser disgorged a tiny package.

When Terra opened it, a white gown the size of a handkerchief fell out.

Dandde's gaze went from the gown to Terra, then back to the gown. She narrowed her yellow eyes and said thoughtfully, "I really think you're going to need a medium."

Clad in a size medium, Hyadeanoid-type gown, Terra followed Dandde out of the dressing room into a short hallway that ended in a small alcove shaped like half a hexagon. There were three locked doors labeled with glowing letters: The door on the left bore the label ISOLATION WARDS, the right door, MF-ICU, the middle door, SURGERY.

"*Name?*" asked the alcove.

"Qotqot," said Dandde.

"*Assigned to Surgery.*" Then sensing the presence of another being, the alcove asked again, "*Name?*"

"Tarkington."

"*Assigned to Surgery.*" The center door clicked and slid open.

Inside, the O.R. supervisor looked up. "Ah yes-s-s, the human. S-s-still on orientation." She consulted her notes. "Tarkington to observe Qotqot today." Then to Dandde, "You begin in O.R. 2. Laparotomy with exploration of the gizzard on Mrs. Shushuus, a fifty-year-old Nath Two female. Dr. Qotemire will open. Dr. Creeebo will explore the gizzard."

"Have you ever s-s-seen a Nath Two patient?" asked Dandde.

"Just a holotext," said Terra, recalling the image of a two-meter-long being that resembled a glistening earthworm. "They're miners, aren't they?"

Dandde bobbed her snout in assent. "Primitives-s-s. They find rare minerals-s-s by taste and s-s-store them in their third s-s-stomach. They can s-s-stay in the mine for weeks-s-s. When they come out, they regurgitate the ore."

Terra frowned as she tried to remember what she had learned about Malignant Fungi in the Nathian patient. All that came to her was M.F. in the Aldeberan and Hyadean. She knew it caused a profound suppression of the immune system, and that the patients had to be kept in reverse isolation to prevent superinfection. Try as she would, she couldn't seem to remember anything about Nathian diseases at all. Strange, she thought. She distinctly remembered that "LESSER KNOWN

47

ALIENS, DISEASES OF" had been one of the SleepTeach units at school.

Operating Room 2 was detached from the rest of the suite by a double gate. Between the gates, the floor was corrugated as if it had the ability to telescope into accordian folds. When they stepped inside, Terra caught her breath. Although the room wasn't particularly wide, it was incredibly long—maybe the longest room she had ever seen, certainly the longest operating room. Equipment stretched endlessly along the walls, but there was nothing in the center of the room.

"Why—" she began. But Dandde interrupted, "Here comes-s-s our patient now."

The gates clanged open and the conveyor bearing Mrs. Shushuus began to roll in—and in, and in. Terra's eyes widened in awe at the glistening gray mass that looked for all the world like a Brobdingnagian sausage. When the first ten meters of Mrs. Shushuus rolled by, and a quick estimate indicated there was at least that much more to come, Terra concluded that the Nathian holotext back at school had to have been a one-to-ten scale model.

The conveyor finally came to a halt and with a series of hissing groans, lowered the patient to floor level. Normally round, Mrs. Shushuus was somewhat flattened due to her sedation, but even so, Terra had to stand on tiptoe to see Dandde on the other side of the conveyor. "What do we do now?"

"We have to find her gizzard."

Terra looked first left, then right. There didn't seem to be any features that distinguished head from tail from mid-section. "How?"

In reply, Dandde tossed her a soni-scan. "You can hear it. I'll s-s-start down here. You try over there. It could be anywhere along here."

Terra stuck the soni-scan's audio in her ear and tried to remember what she had learned about gizzards. She touched the sensor to Mrs. Shushuus's glistening hide, and suddenly it was as if she stood in the middle of a howling storm. Wind shrieked in her ears. Concluding she was hearing the passage of air through what served as Mrs. Shushuus's lungs, Terra moved downstream.

Bowel sounds were next: great sloshing waves of bowel sounds, unending alimentary riptides and breakers. Terra stared at the slick, almost featureless hide as if she suddenly realized for the first time how truly alien it was.

"What am I doing here?" she whispered. Then a grin. Obvious. Listening to Mrs. Shushuus's oceanic bowel sounds. Just like listening to a conch shell. She remembered being five years old and hearing an ocean trapped in a shell. Her quick smile wavered. The conch was curved and warm from the sun. Inside it glowed as pink as a morning sky. And suddenly she realized that she wanted very much to hold it again, just for a little while.

"Over here," said Dandde.

When Terra applied her sensor to the opposite side she heard the clash of fair-sized rocks churning in Mrs. Shushuus's gizzard. But a half-meter lower, and the sound grew muffled, and it disappeared somewhere near the floor. "M.F.?" she asked.

"Yes-s-s. Loaded with it."

"How are they going to operate down there?" Mrs. Shushuus obviously needed to be turned over, and that was just as obviously impossible.

"That's-s-s why we have her here. They can't operate on a patient this-s-s big on land. We'll move to the center of the s-s-satellite and do a flip. Have you ever been weightless-s-s before?"

Terra shook her head. "Is that when we turn her? Out there?"

Dandde chuckled—or at least it sounded like a chuckle to Terra. "No. Too much mass-s-s. We flip the O.R. around her." Dandde reached for a nozzle and pulled it out of the wall. "Help me prep her. There's a prep hose behind you."

Terra glanced over her shoulder and found the prep set. She snapped a scrubber on the end, and started the hose. Pink disinfectant foam spread out from the brush as it glided over the Nathian's gizzard area. Like nursing in a carwash, thought Terra, wondering what the rest of her class was doing out in Cygnus. Not any thing like this, she was sure. But things could be worse, she reflected. What if she had to give Mrs. Shushuus an enema? She glanced toward the remote terminus of her patient and sighed. Things could be a lot worse.

The gates clanged again and Dr. Qotemire and the Hyadean anesthesiologist came in followed by the O.R. Supervisor who carried a small box. She set it on a table behind Terra, clicked it open, and said to her, "Have you met Dr. Creeebo?"

"No, I haven't." She turned around in time to see a pair of black feelers emerge from the box followed by a chitinous little head. Terra had never seen anything quite like Dr. Creeebo before, although it seemed to her that her mother had squashed beings similar to him when they had the audacity to invade her kitchen. But similarities aside, there were significant differences: Dr. Creeebo was much larger, and he was wearing a handkerchief-sized gown.

"This-s-s is-s-s Tarkington," said the Supervisor.

Dr. Creeebo extended a feeler in her direction.

Not knowing what else to do, Terra touched the end of it with the tip of her finger.

Dr. Creeebo's feeler flipped hastily away.

"Hah-h-h," hissed the Supervisor in alarm. "You must excuse-s-s Tarkington. She's-s-s new."

"Of course," said Dr. Creeebo stiffly, drawing himself up and straightening his gown with several of his limbs.

"Schedules-s-s. Schedules-s-s," reminded Dr. Qotemire. "We need to move now."

The O.R. Supervisor did a quick retreat. As soon as the gates shut behind her, Dandde flipped a switch and O.R. 2 began to glide toward the weightless center of Satellite Hospital.

When O.R. 2 began its flip, Terra grabbed onto a light stalk for support. The light stalk popped out of its container at the touch and she bore it away. Aware of her resemblance to a buoyant Statue of Liberty, she dropped the light stalk which obediently bobbed along beside her like a trained dog.

Mrs. Shushuus seemed to revolve under her—or was it the room? She couldn't be sure. In fact, she wasn't even sure that Mrs. Shushuus was technically below, but her mind rejected the idea that she might not be. Terra wasn't ready to think about Mrs. Shushuus being overhead, even if the laws of gravity were temporarily repealed.

Although the light stalk seemed to be in synchronous orbit with Terra, her gown wasn't. When the horrified realization came, her hasty attempt at decency somersaulted her within centimeters of Dr. Qotemire's head. Qotemire, deep in consultation with Dr. Creeebo, who was clinging to his

50

shoulder, fortunately didn't seem to notice. Nor did Dr. Creeebo, who didn't seem to be having any trouble with his gown.

When Terra gave her garment another tug, she noticed a tab on it that she hadn't seen before. In desperation, she gave it a yank. The gown, discreetly molded itself to her body, but the motion of the tab-pulling catapulted her toward the far end of the O.R. where she found herself aimed just above—or was it below—the anesthesiologist, who pursed his flap in the Hyadean Attitude of Alarm at her uncontrolled approach.

She managed to find a handhold on the wall and cautiously began to make her way back to the distant Dandde who seemed to be using her tail as a rudder.

Suddenly, Terra was aware of a tickling nausea. She clamped a hand over her mouth. Deep breaths, she thought. For a moment the deep breath helped, but her exhalation jetted her toward the looming bulkhead of Mrs. Shushuus.

With only instants remaining before impact, Terra felt claws close around her middle as Dandde guided her back toward Mrs. Shushuus's gizzard. "Why don't you s-s-stay here and watch," she suggested as she deposited Terra just above— or was it below—Dr. Qotemire, and hooked her to a tether.

She had a perfect view of the operation there. Between bouts of nausea, she saw Dr. Qotemire swing the laserblade in a wide arc that laid Mrs. Shushuus open. There wasn't any blood, only vats of yellow-gray blobs of fat oozing out from between ropy blackish tendons. Dandde, equipped with a device that resembled a horn of plenty, suctioned up the blobs as quickly as they emerged.

Deep below the layers of fat, Terra could see the dark, pulsing gizzard.

"I'm going to s-s-stop the gizzard now," said Dr. Qotemire, apparently for Terra's edification. He plunged two long probes into the incision, laying one on either side of the organ. "S-s-stand back."

He turned on the current and the gizzard shuddered to a halt.

When Qotemire withdrew the probes, he liberated a blob of grayish fat from its moorings. It rose like a giant greasy amoeba and lazily aimed itself in Terra's direction.

She shut her eyes and took a quivering breath. When she opened her eyes again, the blob was gone—swallowed up by

Dandde's horn of plenty. Then Terra blinked in amazement. With clinging nips of his pincers, Dr. Creeebo was crawling toward the edge of Mrs. Shushuus's incision.

"Are you ready?" asked Qotemire.

"Ready." Twitching his feelers in a way that seemed to signify acute embarrassment, Dr. Creeebo removed his gown.

Anchored to the edge of the incision by his hind pincers, Dr. Creeebo swayed in black and chitinous nakedness. He clutched a tiny laserblade. Terra's eyes widened in horror as she remembered what the O.R. Supervisor had said. *"Dr. Qotemire will open. Dr. Creeebo will explore the gizzard."*

Releasing his hind pincers, Dr. Creeebo plunged head-first into the quagmire of glistening fat, and with a vigorous kick of his bristly little legs, disappeared inside the cavernous Mrs. Shushuus.

Terra shuddered at the end of her tether. "I'm going to throw up," she said to herself. "I am. I know I am."

And the only thing that kept her from it was the sure and certain knowledge that if she did, it would float.

Satellite Hospital Outpost
Taurus 14, North Horn 978675644
Nath Orbit
July 2

Carmelita O'Hare, R.N.
Teton Medical Center
Jackson Hole Summation City
Wyoming 306548760 United Earth, Sol

Dear Carmie,

I am just not cut out for the pioneer life. I'm just not suited for it at all. When I heard from you I wept bitter tears. But I'm happy for you. Very happy. I hope you both enjoy. But when you and Mbotu laugh together, think of me, Terra Tarkington, exile from life.

I won't tell you what I saw in surgery this morning. There are some things that a sensitive human being is better off not knowing. But I can tell you this: If you ever

52

come to work on the Bull Run, you mustn't let them put you in Malignant Fungi.

At the end of work today I had a conference with Mrs. Pernaldeqot, who is the Director of Nurses, and we decided that both of us would be happier if I worked in obstetrics for a while. Carmie, I would even be happy with the Capellan Marines—with a hundred thousand Capellan Marines—if it meant that I would never ever have to work with Dr. Creeebo again.

I am going to bed now. I have a sick stomach.

> Yours at the end of a very bad day,
> Terra

Chapter 7

Satellite Hospital Outpost
Taurus 14, North Horn 978675644
Nath Orbit
July 9

Carmelita O'Hare, R.N.
Teton Medical Center
Jackson Hole Summation City
Wyoming 306548760 United Earth, Sol

Dear Carmie,

Let me fill you in on my exciting existence. I returned yesterday from a twenty-four-hour pass. I went to Nath II (that's the only place we can go for a twenty-four-hour pass) and had an exciting tour of the robo mines. But the real highlight was a trip to the home for aging Aurigans. There they were, geriatric bellies all shriveled up, lying around watching the same old holos we see up here. Carmie, I am going mad.

Mrs. Qotemire went into labor last night and had her egg this morning. Dr. Qotemire was just ridiculous about the whole thing. Technically, Dr. Kelly-Bach was supposed to deliver her, but Dr. Qotemire kept interfering until I was afraid Dr. Kelly-Bach would have a stroke. Mrs. Qotemire kept hollering "O-o-sss, o-o-sss, o-o-sss," which, as you might gather, translates as "ouch."

When the egg came, Mrs. Qotemire was hysterical. She kept saying, "Is-s-s it all right? Is-s-s it cracked? I know it's-s-s cracked," until Dr. Qotemire picked it up and showed it to her. But she couldn't focus her eyes because of the sedation, so she kept on hollering. Dr. Qotemire stuck it up right under her snout and waved it around. "It is-s-s perfect. It is-s-s good egg." Then he dropped it. It's a good thing I was around to catch it in a receiving blanket. Honestly. You'd think it was the only egg ever laid.

Well, after I weighed it (1480 grams), and taped on the I.D. bracelet, I put it in the incubator. You know, Carmie, that's what was so depressing. I couldn't help but think about the babies in the incubators back on earth— little arms and legs waving around, little mouths crying, faces. Instead, there lay the Qotemire egg—it's sort of a magenta color—with absolutely no personality at all. It really got to me.

You know what's worse? After it hatches, it's going to look like Dr. Qotemire.

Now for the rest of the news: Dr. Kelly-Bach is beginning to look good to me. Think of me, Carmie, in my darkest hour.

Bleakly yours,
Terra

Dieter Diderot raised his narrow face to the blue pulsing light in the KABBAGE communications chamber. The smell of ozone hung in the air.

SEPTUM's voice boomed. "BEGIN YOUR REPORT ON PHASE TWO."

"Phase Two is proceeding on schedule. The Trigger has been laid."

The chamber flashed a neutral gray. "AND THE FINGER?"

"The Finger is in attendance. It suspects nothing."

A rosy glow mingled with the odor of melons. "WELL DONE, DIDEROT. WELL DONE. . . ."

Outside the chamber, Mrs. Wiggs attended her KABBAGE patch while the scentplant, unhappy at being disturbed, muttered and gnashed its little limbs.

Beyond the inner room, sequestered in the closet, Fendeqot raised his earhole from the pipe. In the dim light, nutrient solution glistened on his chest scales and a greenish-yellow glow suffused his eyes.

The Finger is in attendance.

So it's there, he thought. The Finger—whoever that was—was there, in Satellite Hospital. The GIA was going to welcome the news. . . .

Satellite Hospital Outpost
Taurus 14, North Horn 978675644
Nath Orbit
July 16

Carmelita O'Hare, R.N.
Teton Medical Center
Jackson Hole Summation City
Wyoming 306548760 United Earth, Sol

Dear Carmie,

Junior Qotemire hatched yesterday. Wonder of wonders, he doesn't look much like Dr. Qotemire. I suppose he will later on, but right now he's kind of cute. There was a big ceremony over the hatching, a sort of combination welcoming ceremony and circumcision. Junior Qotemire didn't like the circumcision part. He just wouldn't stop hissing. But when that was over and they gave him the ceremonial wafer to eat, he just chewed and crunched with his little bitty teeth. Everyone was there and made a big thing over him, especially all the Aldeberan nurses. After it was over, Junior Qotemire was all tuckered out and went to sleep with his little tail curled over his belly. He's really very sweet.

Now the disgusting news. Dr. Kelly-Bach and Olga Ludowicki are in love. The fossil and the ballet machine.

*They walk around holding hands and kissing. Couldn't
you just vomit? Lucky for me I'm not that hard up.*

Bravely,
Terra

P.S. Carmie, I can't lie to you, a friend. I am hard up.

Terra

Zeus the Zapper swiveled so abruptly that he nearly
stripped his gears. He raised his left arm and glared at the
rapidly approaching Cuthbert. "Didn't I tell you to kill that
prissing reptile egg?"

The metal band circling Cuthbert's neck clanked into the
outstretched hand of the cyborg. "Yes, sir. You did, sir."

"Then explain to me, Cuthbert—if you can—explain to
me why I have just been told that Chune-yore Qotemire was
circumcised this morning."

Partly due to the pressure on his windpipe, and partly
due to mortal dread, Cuthbert was at a loss for words.

"Do you think it is *desirable* to circumcise a dead reptile
egg? Do you think it is even *possible* to circumcise a dead
reptile egg?"

"No, sir," he managed to say. "I don't, sir. But I did, sir."
He dragged in a shaky breath. "I infected it with a deadly
disease. It's going to work any day now."

The Zapper narrowed his eyes to slits and pressed them
uncomfortably close to Cuthbert's own. "It had better,
Cuthbert."

"Yes, sir. It will, sir."

"It had certainly better, Cuthbert, because that circumcised reptile is The Trigger to SEPTUM's scheme. And I have
just learned that The Finger for that trigger is now—even as
we speak—in Satellite Hospital." Although somewhat mol-
lified at the news of Chune-yore Qotemire's imminent demise,
The Zapper followed his statement with a medium shake (just
to keep Cuthbert on his toes) and a bellowing lion roar.

Zapata's voice dropped to a gentle, almost pleasant tone.
"It would be to your advantage, Cuthbert, to find out the
identity of The Finger." Abruptly, the volume rose to normal.
"Isn't that *so*?"

"Yes, sir. That would certainly be so, sir."

"Now then," said the Zapper, "what is all this or*dure*
about a chit for more Brain Drain?"

Satellite Hospital Outpost
Taurus 14, North Horn 978675644
Nath Orbit
July 19

Carmelita O'Hare-Mbotu, R.N.
Teton Medical Center
Jackson Hole Summation City
Wyoming 306548760 United Earth, Sol

Dear Carmie,

I know you and Mbotu will be very happy together. If you decide to have children and they need an honorary maiden aunt—well, you know where I am.

There isn't any good news from the Bull Run, so here goes with the bad: Dr. Kelly-Bach and Olga Ludowicki are going to be married and I am to be the maid of honor. Can you beat that? Now the real corker—Dr. Kelly-Bach took me aside and said that due to our circumstances he ought to offer to "service" both me and Olga, but due to his age and general condition he didn't think he was up to it. Oh, nausea. He then went on to say that he was taking a new kind of Aldeberan tonic and if it worked he'd let me know.

If that wasn't enough of a blow, I went into the nursery this morning and found out that something is wrong with Junior Qotemire. All the Aldeberan nurses had left him in a panic and there was Junior Qotemire alone. He was very pale, sort of baby blue instead of medium blue, and listless. Dr. Qotemire is in a state. It seems that they're afraid Junior has copper-storage disease and they're running a bunch of tests. Something is depleting the copper in his blood, and he's very anemic. They have him in strict isolation and no Aldeberan is allowed near him because C-S disease is contagious as hell to them. It looks like Olga and I will have to stay with him around the clock. Dr. Qotemire just haunts the nursery. Everytime I look up, there he is on the other side of the plexi window. Poor little Junior Qotemire—treated like a leper.

It's just as well that I have to work double shifts. It

helps keep my mind off my other troubles. I found myself thinking seriously about this guy from Hyades IV yesterday. If you looked up their reproductive habits, Carmie, you know what that means—certain death.

> *Yours fatalistically,*
> *Terra*

Chapter 8

Satellite Hospital Outpost
Taurus 14, North Horn 978675644
Nath Orbit
July 21

Carmelita O'Hare-Mbotu, R.N.
Teton Medical Center
Jackson Hole Summation City
Wyoming 306548760 United Earth, Sol

Dear Carmie,

Oh joy. Oh sweet, sweet joy!

I'm still at work, but I had to drop everything and tell you what just happened: There is a man on the Bull Run. A human, real, homo-sape man. I thought I was hallucinating at first. I was feeding Junior Qotemire when in walked Dr. Kelly-Bach with this big beautiful guy.

"Well, hello," he said (I remember his every word), "I'm Dr. Brian-Scott. I'm going to be replacing Dr. Kelly-Bach."

It's too much to believe, Carmie. Dr. Kelly-Bach—bless him—is actually going to retire in a few months.

Junior Qotemire isn't doing well, but I'm sure Dr.

Brian-Scott will pull him through. I have a feeling that Dr. Brian-Scott can do anything he wants to.

Deliriously,
Terra

Terra was singing a lullaby to Chune-yore Qotemire. He was wrapped in a double layer of blankets, and though what was exposed looked decidedly reptilian, when she closed her eyes and cuddled him, she was able to imagine that he was human.

And it was all right even when she looked at him. All babies are cute, she thought. Well, maybe not *all* babies; maybe not the babies of the Nath II miners. When the image came to her of a newborn giant gray sausage filling the nursery, she devoutly hoped that Mrs. Shushuus wasn't pregnant.

Terra liked Chune-yore much better now that he was hatched. And it was sweet the way he wagged his little tail in time to the song. She was so absorbed in him that she didn't hear the footsteps behind her. When the voice came, she jumped.

"I forgot something."

She whirled around, which proved so unsettling to young Qotemire that he nipped the end of her finger. "Oh. Ow!" And then when she saw who it was, "Oh! Dr. Brian-Scott."

He reached out and absently rubbed Chune-yore Qotemire's scaly little head, but he was looking at Terra. A little smile played around his lips as if he were in the middle of a delightful dream. "Just thought I'd take another look at my patient here," he said staring deep into her eyes. His were startlingly changeable, first blue, then blue-gray, now blue with flecks of green. "How is he?" he asked, looking at her.

"Oh, he's fine." His eyes were blue, she decided, definitely blue. Then her own widened at what she had said. "I mean, he's not fine. He's sick."

He looked down at Chune-yore Qotemire then as if he were seeing him for the first time. "Let's take another look at him."

She laid him down, unwrapped the blankets, and took off his diaper. "His color is awful, and his respirations are up. He seems listless to me."

Brian-Scott nodded and stretched Chune-yore's little arms out to their full length. When he did, the little Aldeberan tried feebly to pull away, but the exertion proved too much.

Each panting breath depressed his sternum. "Flaccid. And he's retracting more. We're going to have to give him some oxygen."

He extended Chune-yore's tail and released it suddenly. Chune-yore didn't care for the maneuver. He hissed and curled his tail. "Good Mandelqot reflex, though," he said, pointing to the coiled tail. As the hand again approached his nether parts, Chune-yore opened his little jaws and displayed a double row of tiny teeth. "Look. He's trying to terrify us. Cute little guy."

When the examination was over, Terra gave Chune-yore a fresh diaper, rewrapped him in blankets, and installed the oxygen setup, while Brian-Scott recorded his notes. When he finished, he didn't seem to want to leave. Instead, he looked at Terra wth a bemused expression on his face as if he wasn't quite sure she was real. "Have you been in the nursery long?" he asked by way of conversation.

She shook her head; she couldn't take her eyes off of him. "They wanted me in Malignant Fungi, but this is better."

"Yeah." He was looking at her lips now, as if he found them of extraordinary interest. "You want to watch out for the toe-claw clippers they have over there."

"Uh-huh," she said faintly. His hair was dark and thick. She liked the way it swept across his brow. It was definitely a noble brow.

His gaze lingered on her mouth. "Uh, what do you do around here for amusement? I mean, after work."

Somehow she was finding it hard to breathe. "Not much." His eyes were extraordinary. Deep blue with flecks of green. "I write a lot of letters. I study some."

"Study," he said, as if he were repeating something profound.

"Uh-huh." He really had a marvelous smile—a little lopsided—completely marvelous. "I don't know as much as I should about some of the lesser-known aliens. Like the patients from Nath II."

"Tell you what," he said, seizing her hand, holding it between his two broad palms. "I'd be happy to give you a few pointers"—he looked down at her hand as if to reassure himself that it was really a hand instead of something with scales and claws; he squeezed it gently—"about the lesser-known aliens. If you'd like me to, that is."

"Oh, yes," she whispered. He was a real person. She was

touching a real, gorgeous, human person. "Oh, yes," she said again, "I'd love it."

"I would never have thought about having a picnic here," said Terra looking around at the deserted hospital level. They were in the new Rehab section still under construction.

"This is going to be the Aldeberan area," said Brian-Scott, clutching their picnic box with one hand and Terra's shoulder with the other.

"What's that?" She said, pointing to a low, shiny tank that was tilting decidedly off-center.

"That's an Enzyme-Ma-Tic. It fills with heated enzyme solution, and then the whirlpool comes on. It's for tail sprains, caudal trauma, strains—things like that." With gentle pressure to her shoulder, he aimed her down a corridor.

"Where are we going?"

"It's a surprise," he said with a quick grin.

At the end of the hall, he said, "Wait here." He ducked inside for a moment and shut off the lights, then taking her hand, he pulled her into the room. "Dr. Qotemire showed it to me this morning. It's terrific, isn't it?"

They were standing in a large bubble of a room that took Terra's breath away. From all sides, from overhead, a million stars pierced the darkness. It was as if they had stepped into space itself. In the moment of disorientation that followed, Terra clung to Brian-Scott for support.

"We're in a blister at the outer edge of the satellite," he said, wrapping an arm around her. "Observation port."

Terra stared up at the stars that slowly wheeled by as the satellite spun on its axis. "It's beautiful."

"Isn't it." Then disengaging his arm, he said, "Let's have that picnic. I even brought a tablecloth." He opened the box and whipped out a thin silver sheet about two meters square. When he pulled a tab at one corner, the sheet puffed into a thick cushion that more resembled a mattress than a table-cloth.

One of the moons of Nath II slowly swung into view, washing them both with a pale light. He reached out. She took his hand, and mesmerized at the scene, slowly sank down onto the plump surface of the tablecloth.

"It isn't much," he said, opening the box. "Pudgies and beer."

"It's wonderful."

He handed her a pudgy. "How did you end up here, Terra?"

"I'm not sure. The rest of my class went to Cygnus. I really don't know why I'm here."

Without taking his eyes from her, he took a slow swallow of beer. "I'm glad you are."

"Why did you come to the Bull Run?"

"I thought it would be the experience of a lifetime—a chance to practice medicine and learn about alien cultures all at once." He gave a rueful little grin. "I'm a little disappointed with the Aldeberans though. I guess I expected something different."

Terra was amazed. "You don't think they're different?"

"Oh, they're physically different all right, but— Well, you take Dr. Qotemire for example. He's so . . . middle class. You know, concerned with his game of whackit, his social standing, that kind of thing. But Dr. Creeebo—now *there's* an alien," he said in admiration.

Terra couldn't agree more on that point.

Nath II began to gleam through the port, showering them with silver light. "The ways of some of the lesser-known aliens are fascinating."

"Are they?"

"Take the Nathian miners, for instance. Do you know how they find ore?"

"They taste it, don't they?"

He nodded. "Do you know how they communicate?"

She shook her head.

"By taste too. It's very interesting." He touched her cheek and leaned toward her. "They hold their mouths together. Like this. . . ."

Overwhelmed by the intensity of Nathian communication, Terra shut her eyes. When the demonstration ended, she caught her breath. "I had no idea."

"Now the inhabitants of Capella Pornatha—"

"You mean, the beings with the horny excrescences?" It was a whisper.

He nodded. Then he smiled an altogether devastating lopsided smile, and leaned toward her again. "The inhabitants of Capella Pornatha have an even more interesting way to communicate. . . ."

* * *

It was very late when Terra got off the slideator. As she made her way through the darkened corridor to her room, a misty smile flitted over her lips.

Inside, she began to sing softly to herself as she undressed. She twirled each garment overhead with abandon and sailed it across the room. Then wriggling into a comfortable old flannelite dowdy, she flung herself into the net bed.

But she couldn't sleep.

Getting up again, she reached for her notebook, and when its light came on, she began to write:

> *Satellite Hospital Outpost*
> *Taurus 14, North Horn 978675644*
> *Nath Orbit*
> *July 21*

She considered this beginning and the hour of the night and changed the date.

> *July 22*

> *Gladiola Tarkington*
> *45 Subsea*
> *Petroleum City*
> *Gulf of Mexico 233433111 United Earth, Sol*

> *Dear Mom,*

> *It's horribly late.*

She deleted the word "horribly," substituted "deliciously," and continued the entry:

> *. . . but it's been a lovely evening.*
> *Today I met a fellow professional who is human. His name is Dr. Brian-Scott Brian-Scott, and he is going to teach me all about lesser-known alien beings.*
> *I can't begin to tell you all the things he's already taught me about the strange and wonderful ways in which they communicate. . . .*

Terra woke before false sunrise to the echoes of her own voice speaking in her dream. What was it? What was it she said?

She tugged at the edges of the dissolving dream, and blinked as the words came back to her. And as they did, a new emotion stronger than any she had ever felt before quivered deep inside her. I'm in love, she thought in wonder. Really in love.

It was amazing. All the feelings she had called love before had just been shadows of the real thing. She nibbled a nail and shivered at the disturbing thought. She had never felt like this before. She wasn't used to it. It was all a jumble of good feelings mixed with the scary idea that somehow, in the night, she had been robbed of all her defenses and what was left was naked and vulnerable.

Maybe it was just that she was coming down with something.

She felt her brow tentatively, half in the hope that she would discover some malaise that would go away with treatment, half in the fear that she might.

Her forehead felt cool to her touch.

It's probably just loneliness, she told herself. She couldn't really be in love. She was just deceiving herself.

Wasn't she?

Of course she was. If there were loads and loads of men to choose from— She stared at the wall anxiously, but instead of its plain buff surface she saw the faces of all the men she had ever known, ever seen, ever imagined—a sea of faces, an ocean, blurring, fading away, until there was only a single pair of eyes, as changeable as the sea, looking into hers. Blue. Now blue-green. Then blue touched with gray.

Uh oh, she thought, and touched her forehead again. This time her hand brushed through her hair and came to rest at the back of her neck. She cradled her head against her arm as if to prevent it from flying apart from all the thoughts that tumbled inside. She wanted to cry and she wanted to smile all at once. And she wanted a doughnut.

She suddenly, desperately, wanted a doughnut. It seemed to her that nothing else would stop the strange, trembly feeling she had deep inside. She giggled at the idea of trying to describe doughnuts to the hospital kitchen help; they'd think she was sick. And maybe in a way she was. It's a lot like low blood sugar, she thought analytically. Being in love obviously caused metabolic changes.

It was disconcerting to think that her metabolism had

been altered during the night without her consent. It made her feel out of control. Frowning, she tried again to imagine a series of different male faces. Again, a single pair of changeable blue-green eyes met hers. She sighed, and a little smile crept over her lips.

Suddenly she caught her breath and sat bolt upright. What if he was thinking the same thing about her? What if he was comparing her to every girl he had ever known? She could be just another face in a sea of faces. The horrible thought streaked through her like an electric bolt. In response, she scrambled up so fast that the net bed tipped ungraciously and dumped her onto the floor in a nest of bedclothes.

She stared blankly around the room for a moment, and then she began to laugh. "Head over heels," she said out loud. "I've really fallen in love."

When Terra stepped into the nursery, she caught her breath. He was there—leaning over Chune-yore Qotemire's tiny bed, frowning, saying something to the Aldeberan nurse.

With a sharp hiss, the nurse backed away from the crib, and hurried out of the room.

Brian-Scott's troubled gaze followed her to the door. Then his eyes met Terra's.

They were beautiful eyes. Just like they'd looked on her wall, only bigger. Big enough to fill the whole Galaxy, she thought. Suddenly stricken with shyness, she looked down and studied her fingernails.

"Hi," he said, and followed it with a marvelous asymmetrical grin.

"Hi."

Suddenly he was looking at her strangely. "I, uh—" Then his eyes slid away and he stared at a tray of instruments as if they consumed his interest.

"Yes?"

He looked back at her intently, and his gaze came to rest on her lips. "I wish I had a doughnut," he said abruptly.

"Do you?" she said in wonder. "Really?"

He nodded. "All of a sudden, I really miss them. I think I could eat a dozen."

"That's wonderful," said Terra. "So could I."

He gave her a startled look. Then he grinned again, and little crinkles touched the corners of his eyes, but the smile faded and he leaned over Chune-yore Qotemire's crib. "We've got real trouble here."

Terra took a quick step forward. "What?"

"There's no doubt. It's C-S."

"Copper Storage disease?" Her eyes widened. Terra looked toward the door the Aldeberan nurse had so abruptly left by, then back at Brian-Scott.

He nodded. "It's contagious as hell to Aldeberans. They'll have to stay out of the nursery."

"Are you sure it's C-S?"

He handed her the chart. She scanned the test results, then looked down at the infant Aldeberan. He lay on his stomach with his rump in the air and his little tail emerging through a hole in his diaper. "Poor little thing," she said.

At her voice, Chune-yore gave a faint cry. Terra patted his back and he cuddled his tail next to her hand as if he took comfort from her touch. "Is he going to die?"

The bleak look in Brian-Scott's eyes turned them to the gray of a winter sea. "If he stays here," he said, "he surely will."

Satellite Hospital Outpost
Taurus 14, North Horn 978675644
Nath Orbit
July 23

Carmelita O'Hare-Mbotu, R.N.
Teton Medical Center
Jackson Hole Summation City
Wyoming 306548760 United Earth, Sol

Dear Carmie,

It's all over for me. My heart aches and my liver throbs with grief. I am to be exiled.

Yes. It's true.

I don't know how to set this down. Tears keep blurring my eyes and my mind falters. Junior Qotemire has C-S disease. He's got to be transferred and I have to go with him. He's got plenty of copper stored in his liver, but not in his blood. The disease depleted an enzyme that he needs to make hemocyanin. That means he's slowly suffocating. They're sending him to Hyades IV tomorrow, but they can't hope for a cure—just a sort of half-life on the oxygenator.

Dr. Qotemire asked for nurses to volunteer. That meant Olga and me. Well, Dr. Kelly-Bach just wouldn't hear of Olga going, so who did that leave?

I couldn't make up my mind right away. I was too shaken. I went into the nursery and looked at Junior Qotemire. I wanted to hate him. I nearly did, I think, but he reached out with his little pale snout and hissed softly against my hand. I picked him up then and held him. I cried until I was dry, and all the while Junior Qotemire curled up in my arms and licked off the tears with his little pointed tongue.

Well I couldn't let him die, could I?

So I volunteered. I volunteered to leave beautiful Dr. Brian-Scott and to go and live among the Hyadean IVs. My mind is unhinged. Instead of Dr. Brian-Scott, I will have Junior Qotemire to comfort me—Junior Qotemire and the males of Hyades IV who have creases instead of noses and whose embrace is death.

My heart aches, Carmie. My spleen pulsates. Weep for me.

Yours in exile,
Terra

Chapter 9

Central Hive
Hyades IV 354657687 Hyades
July 27

Carmelita O'Hare-Mbotu, R.N.
Teton Medical Center
Jackson Hole Summation City
Wyoming 306548760 United Earth, Sol

Dear Carmie,

Hyades IV is beautiful. I love it here.

But I do miss Junior Qotemire a little. He's still back on the Bull Run—and doing fine.

After I volunteered to go with Junior Qotemire, he improved. Really improved. His color perked up and his blood picture got better.

But it didn't last. The next morning he was sick as ever and due for transfer to Hyades IV that afternoon.

Dr. Brain-Scott was in a state. He was positive that we had overlooked something that could be important about C-S disease. He dialed printouts of the whole chart and just pored over them.

I was in a state too, as you might imagine. Outwardly I was calm, but inwardly I was a seething mass of raw emotion. Then while I was dressing Junior Qotemire, Dr. Brian-Scott hollered at me. Well, Carmie, he startled me so that I forgot to pull Junior's tail through the diaper hole.

"Did you put this note in the chart?" He stuck the printout under my nose and pointed.

I looked at it. It was a nurse's note about Junior Qotemire licking the tears off my face. Well, sitting there

68

in cold print it really looked ridiculous. I had to admit it was my note. I could have died of embarrassment.

Dr. Brian-Scott looked long and hard at the chart and then at Junior Qotemire. Then he said to me, "Cry."

Well, Carmie, I was on the verge of tears anyway, and I just broke down and sobbed. I couldn't seem to stop.

Then he did the strangest thing. He stuck a test tube up to my face and collected the tears. I just didn't believe it. I was so astonished I stopped crying.

He reached for another test tube and said, "Don't stop."

Did anyone ever tell you to keep on crying? It has a positively dehydrating effect. I couldn't squeeze out another tear.

Dr. Brian-Scott called dietary and ordered an onion. Stat. When it came, he sliced it with a scalpel from the circumcision kit and poked it in my face. Well, you talk about tears. . . . And they weren't all from the onion either. By then I was mad. Who did he think he was anyway? Storming around sticking onions and test tubes in my face.

Then he held me by the shoulders and said, "Keep crying, Terra. It may be the only chance that little guy has."

He collected six test tubes. He sent one to the lab. Then he fed the other five to Junior Qotemire.

It was like a nightmare, Carmie. Here was the man of science feeding my tears to Junior Qotemire. It was like an old horror holo. . . . And pieces of onion all over the floor.

But it worked.

After a while, Junior Qotemire's color improved.

Dr. Brian-Scott says it was because of mucin in my tears. Do you believe it? When Junior Qotemire digested the mucin, it broke down into the amino acids that he needed to synthesize his depleted enzyme. The lab made up buckets of amino acid soup for Junior Qotemire, so I won't have to take the onion shift anymore.

Dr. Qotemire was delirious with joy. He insisted— absolutely insisted that I go for R and R to Hyades IV. And Carmie, he insisted that Dr. Brian-Scott go too! When he got on the shuttle, Dr. Brian-Scott said to

69

me (I remember his every word), "That was awfully unselfish of you to cry for Junior Qotemire."

You know what else he said, Carmie? He said, "I know that a girl like you, who could be so unselfish about Junior Qotemire, would always give of herself in other ways too."

Isn't that sweet?

> *Unselfishly yours,*
> *Terra*

SEPTUM's voice reverberated through the scentplant's pipe with what seemed to Fendeqot to be an overlay of anxiety. "THE TRIGGER?"

"It nearly died," said Diderot, "but I managed to cure it."

"THEN THE DOOMSDAY PROJECT IS SAVED—" A pause. "UH, FORGET YOU HEARD THAT, DIDEROT."

Another pause. "Forget what?"

"THAT WILL BE ALL."

Fendeqot scrabbled at the pipe connection. He had to get out before Diderot emerged. With a final poke, he shoved the connector home and cracked open the closet door.

Too late. The door to the inner chamber opened and Diderot and Mrs. Wiggs stepped into the room. They spoke for a moment, then Diderot left.

Fendeqot's relieved breath cut off at once. Mrs. Wiggs was headed for his closet.

Trapped.

The door swung open and Mrs. Wiggs jumped back with a little squeal of dismay at the sight of the big Aldeberan with the wet and glistening chest. "Oh, my! How you startled me."

"Just, uh"—then as inspiration came to him—"s-s-seeing that the s-s-scentplant had a bite." He seized the valve that supplied the nutrient solution and gave it a twiddle.

Her whiskers quivered. "Why, that's very thoughtful of you, Mr. Fendeqot. I thought I was the only one who cared about the poor little thing."

"Oh, no." Fendeqot strode briskly out of the closet.

"But I always give it something before I go home," she said doubtfully. "We don't want to overfeed."

"You're right, Mrs-s-s. Wiggs-s-s. I won't do it again."

"Well anyway, it was very kind of you." Pulling out a pair of gloves from her pink shoulder pouch, she stretched out her little pseudopaws and put them on. "Time to go home and turn on the safe light in case any of our beings want to come in from the cold." She looked up at Fendeqot and gave a little gasp. "You've hurt your earhole!"

"Oh, no. It's-s-s fine."

Mrs. Wiggs, ear laid low in sympathy, reached out and touched the side of his head. "But you have. There's a terrible indentation all around it."

Fendeqot winced at her touch; it had been a long session at the pipe. "It's-s-s nothing. It comes-s-s and goes-s-s." He leaned toward her and lowered his voice. "Ringworm."

Mrs. Wiggs retracted her pseudopaw at once and stared in faint horror at her glove.

"It's-s-s not contagious-s-s now," he said quickly. "Burnt out case-s-s."

"I'm so sorry, Mr. Fendeqot." Her eyes misted and turned to a soft rose pink. "I had no idea." Then with a look at the time, she said, "I really must be closing up now."

"I have a little work to do," said Fendeqot. "Why don't you go on? I can lock up." In emphasis, he strode to his desk, leaned back on his tail, and opened his project report.

A faint look of horror crossed over Mrs. Wigg's face. "I'm afraid we couldn't do that, Mr. Fendeqot. You know it's against SEPTUM's regulations."

He considered bullying her; Mrs. Wiggs was easy to bully. But he thought better of it and followed her to the door.

Outside, he said goodbye and strode away. Then slipping into a darkened doorway, he watched until she disappeared. When he was sure she was gone, he went back to the cratered entrance of KBG headquarters and spread his claws over the stone. Fendeqot had made it his business to crack the entrance code and its variants which changed each day. He used it now, half-whistling, half-hissing the seven pitches through his pursed snout. A moment later the crater dropped away and lowered him into the darkened chamber.

Fendeqot moved to the inner room and turned on the lights. Ignoring the dozing scentplant, which thrashed and muttered at the disturbance, he hurried to Mrs. Wiggs's console.

Within minutes, he had his patch to the GIA.

Cuthbert Cuthbert poked a finger under his tight metal collar in a vain attempt to relieve the pressure, and shuddered at the memory of The Zapper's pig eyes, glazed with an awesome madness that transcended rage. He was lucky to have survived.

He looked around his grim little room. It was as dismal as his life. The only spot of color was the large holograph of Zeus the Zapper on the wall. The holograph stirred, as it did periodically, and The Zapper's eyes narrowed: "I see you, Cuthbert. Lying around again, are you?"

Cuthbert shuddered, and wished for the thousandth time that he had a way to shut off the holograph and escape the hated face. He wanted desperately to run away and hide in a remote crevice of the galaxy. Only the knowledge that The Zapper would beam onto his collar and track him relentlessly kept him from it. He had tried to remove the metal indenture band once. Just once. The Zapper had known it, of course, and when he finished expressing his displeasure, Cuthbert knew it would never do to try that again.

So what did that leave him? Success or suicide.

At the moment, success seemed elusive. He had no idea why the little Qotemire reptile had survived. And he was still half-deaf from The Zapper's lion roars that sandwiched the awful words, *Doomsday Project*. He contemplated the alternative: He could kill himself. Regretfully, he concluded that suicide was unnecessary. If he failed again, The Zapper would surely do it for him.

There was nothing left to do, but to carry on. Sighing, he tweaked the three buttons on his work shirt.

Aleph responded first with a brisk, "Stepped in it again, didn't you?" While Beth glowed a pale and silent pink that Cuthbert knew was a rebuke.

The three computers were, after all, incapable of error, as they constantly reminded him. Failure was his, and his alone.

Gimbel came on last with an angry orange flare and a mumbled curse.

Hungover again, thought Cuthbert. Aloud, he said, "We've got a problem. The KBG has a Doomsday Device. The Trigger survived, and we don't know the identity of The Finger. Our orders are to destroy Satellite Hospital and all beings on board. . . ."

The Covert Arts Building stood on the outskirts of the City of Twelve Evils. Clutching his precious chits, Cuthbert stepped up to the door which responded with a sharp "Look this way."

Light blazed into his eyes. A moment later the door matched his retinals to one Cuthbert Cuthbert, indentured spy, and slid open.

He made his way past Archives where a grizzled old agent was reading a chapter of his memoirs to a group of retired confreres. He passed the door marked OPERATIVES CLUB. The sound of music punctuated with laughter came from the room, and he glanced toward it wistfully. He wasn't allowed in there, of course; he had to content himself with the meager appointments of the Indentured Club.

Winding through a maze of passageways, he came at last to the Spy X-Change. He passed the assortment of candy bars and shaving gear and went directly to the back where he rang for the D.D.T. After sundry creaks and groans (for the Dispenser of Dirty Tricks had not been lubricated recently) the machine rolled out. It extended a clamper and examined the chit Cuthbert handed it. "Aurigan Plague spores, eh? Pan-Galactic strain. What vector?"

"Hyadean snuggies," said Cuthbert.

"In that case," said the Dispenser, "you'll need Spore-Tite. Its innards rumbled and in a moment it produced two packages and handed over the first. "Good stuff, that Spore-Tite. Makes the spores stick to any surface." Still holding the last package, it hesitated, "You *do* know, don't you, that this stuff has to be kept cold. Let it out in a warm place and—" Here the Dispenser gave out an ominous croaking sound.

Cuthbert nodded. It wouldn't do to spray the spores down here. But on the frigid surface of Hyades IV it would be safe enough—until the snuggies hit the warmth of Hospital Satellite.

Tucking both packages into an inner pocket, Cuthbert pulled out another chit and headed for the alcove designated CHAMELEON.

"What disguise?" asked the vendor.

"Hyadean IV," said Cuthbert.

"Entire body disguise?"

"Just face."

"Chit, please." He handed it over. After a moment's scrutiny, the vendor disappeared for a few minutes and came back with a flat package and a little vial of Stickem-Up. Sliding them toward Cuthbert, he said, "That's your noseflap there, and brow rolls. Directions are inside."

The last chit was for six Hyadean snuggies—one outright

sale, five loaners. Clutching the mound of snuggies, Cuthbert headed back to his dismal little room.

Cuthbert stared into the cracked reflector next to his bed. The Hyadean noseflap hung down to his chin. The brow rolls were good though, he thought, but the Stickem-Up was irritating his skin.

He stared at the limp noseflap in dismay. It would never do. He stared at the directions again:

HYADEAN NOSEFLAP, MODEL HU-2112

Apply a thin line of Stickem-Up to the inner upper edge of Hyadean Noseflap, Model HU-2112. Let dry. Attach center of Noseflap to bridge of nose. Holding carefully to avoid contact with Stickem-Up, extend each edge of Noseflap over cheekbones. Attach, smoothing from bridge of nose outward to avoid a wrinkled appearance.

Well, he had done all that. He read further:

The Hyadean Noseflap, Model Hu-2112, will assume a lifelike expression upon appropriate muscular action of the face beneath. (See Figure 1.)

Figure 1A showed a human face with the noseflap removed. The nose was pinched; the lips were extended vigorously showing top and bottom teeth. Figure 1B showed the same face with the noseflap in place. It was labeled HYADEAN ATTITUDE OF PEACEFUL CONTEMPLATION.

Raising the flap, Cuthbert screwed his face into an approximation of Figure 1A, and then lowered the flap to view the results. Not bad. But he wasn't sure how long he could keep it up.

The HYADEAN ATTITUDE OF FORCEFUL PERSUASION required a thrust-out, upcurved tongue, while the HYADEAN ATTITUDE OF WARM SINCERITY called for an underlying grin that resembled the *risus sardonicus* of advanced strychnine poisoning.

An hour later, Cuthbert stripped off the noseflap and the brow rolls. He was exhausted, and his face hurt. He took a final look at the pictures on the passenger roster of the morning shuttle, memorizing the features of the two who were headed to Satellite Hospital: Tarkington, Terra R.N. and Brian-Scott, Brian-Scott M.D. Then pulling off his work shirt, he flung it onto the floor and flung himself into bed as the holograph of Zeus the Zapper stirred, narrowed its eyes, and said, "I see you, Cuthbert. Lying around again, aren't you?"

In the dark, a faint glimmer came from the bottom button on Cuthbert's work shirt. Within moments it flamed to a spiteful orange as Gimbel activated himself and looked out. Appalled, he saw how far he had been flung across the room— tossed willy-nilly by the Cuthbert peripheral.

He could have been cracked on impact. Cracked and then invaded by the billions of vile bacteria and opportunist viruses that waited on the floor. (Gimbel calculated the odds of his being cracked and invaded by floor germs at 17 in 1000.) Shocking. He was quite right to deactivate his off switch.

Gimbel had, in fact, poisoned his biological off switch with a particularly potent squirt of alcohol. It was bad enough to contemplate being cracked and infected, but to be cracked and infected while deactivated—and therefore helpless—was unthinkable.

The proximity of the Aurigan Plague spores (Pan-Galactic strain) made him especially nervous. Gimbel had favored a neat, and remotely controlled, explosion of Satellite Hospital. Obviously the safest way. But no, he thought grimly. Nothing would do the Cuthbert peripheral but plague. "It can't look like sabotage," he had said. "We don't want to tip off the KBG."

Don't we? thought Gimbel darkly. He had made up his mind. For too long he had been abused by the GIA and the insensitive Cuthbert peripheral. It was time to act.

As Dieter Diderot walked through the dark streets of the City of Twelve Evils, his wrist terminal gave a beep. His eyes narrowed as the message begun to scroll:
. . . *This is Gimbel*. . . . *GIA*. . . .
When the message ended, Diderot stared into the shadows and tried to think. Was it a trick? It might be a trick of Fendeqot's. Yet, could he afford to ignore it? The Finger *was* going to be on board that shuttle in the morning.

The Aurigan Plague was the deadliest in the galaxy. It was like Zeus the Zapper to come up with something like that. Diderot's fingers crept nervously to his neck as if to prove to himself that the old GIA band of indenture was really gone. It had been a year since he defected to KABBAGE, yet there were still times when he could feel the metal collar constrict around his throat.

Aurigan Plague. There was only one thing in the galaxy that could combat its spores. One thing—if there was time. But could The Finger survive it?

The shuttleway of Hyades Interstellar Freeport was crowded with assorted beings trying to make the morning launch. Vendors, noisily hawking their wares from the alcoves that lined the wide passage, offered intricately carved nephrites (found only in the diseased kidneys of Lesser Lepans from the Outer Banks), Hyadean snuggies, irradiated bananas, and other interstellar delicacies and treasures.

Ensconced in a rental alcove near Customs, Cuthbert Cuthbert stared at the clot of passengers. "Where? Where are they?" he asked his top button.

"Keep a cool one, Cuth," said Aleph, who had been activated for the occasion, and who had tapped into baggage processing. "They've checked their luggage. Watch Gate 7."

Gate 7 clanged open and disgorged a rowdy group of Disctech students, who rolled away in all directions to the dismay of their rotund advisor; five Freeport attendants wheeling an elderly Aurigan matriarch on a megatran; a disgruntled Aldeberan; and a shabby Minipodian with unkempt fur and dents in his glubbers. Finally he spotted them—the Tarkington girl and Brian-Scott. "Last chance," howled Cuthbert brandishing a snuggie at arm's length. "While they last."

Under cover of the snuggie, Cuthbert allowed his aching face to relax and his noseflap fell limp. Then as the two came close, he cranked up a painful grimace that he hoped translated into the Hyadean Attitude of Optimistic Bargaining, and flapped the snuggie in Terra's face.

"Cheap," he said. It was extremely difficult to hold the attitude and speak at the same time; it came out "cheat."

"Bargain," he amended.

"Oh, look," said Terra. "They're so pretty. I wish I could afford one."

"You can."

"No. I really can't."

Cuthbert adopted the Hyadean Attitude of Brilliant

Ideation. "Tell you what! If you'll tell all your friends where you bought it, it's yours at half-price." He studied her pupils the way he had learned in Advanced Interrogation 302; she was interested, he was sure.

Terra caressed the smoke-gray snuggie. "It *is* awfully nice. But—" She looked up at Brian-Scott. "What do you think."

"Just slip it on," urged Cuthbert. He held it out.

"Well— I guess it wouldn't hurt to try it on."

In a flash, Cuthbert draped it over her shoulders. Drawing back he assumed what he hoped was the Hyadean Attitude of Esthetic Appreciation—he was not altogether clear on its subtle differences from the Hyadean Attitude of Rising Lust—and said, "Beautiful." Then to Brian-Scott, "Isn't she beautiful?"

"Very nice," said Brian-Scott in such a way as to suggest that he wasn't altogether clear about the differences between esthetic appreciation and rising lust either.

"I don't know," said Terra doubtfully. "Even half-price is more than I ought to spend." She slipped it off and handed it back.

Panicked, Cuthbert cranked up his face in the Attitude of Painful Confession and leaned forward. "I'll tell you the truth. This is last year's model. I'll let you have it at the closeout price. Seventy percent off."

"Seventy?"

Her pupils were definitely larger now. "Of course," said Cuthbert craftily, "the Aldeberan lady asked me to hold it for her, but who knows when she'll be back? Unless of course—" He looked up significantly as a group of Aldeberans stepped through Gate 9.

Terra, following his gaze, stared at the approaching group, then back at the Snuggie. "I'll take it."

Cuthbert's bizarre underlying grin hoisted the noseflap into the Hyadean Attitude of Warm Sincerity. "You'll enjoy it," he said, "for the rest of your life."

With her Snuggie on one arm and Brian-Scott on the other, Terra moved toward the boarding gate. She glanced down at the snuggie as if it were too good to be true, and said, "That was the strangest looking Hyadean I ever saw. Do you think it was palsy of the nose crease?"

"Uh," said Brian-Scott absently. He was looking at the

uniformed Customs Inspector just ahead who crooked a finger in their direction.

"Let's have the snuggie, please," said the pale-eyed, narrow-faced man after a perfunctory look at their tickets.

"What for?" asked Terra.

"Weighing and measuring. All Snuggies in excess of a kilo or longer than ninety centimeters are subject to tax. Put it in there." He indicated an elongated box with his thumb.

When Terra dropped the snuggie into the opening, the box swallowed it with a click. A minute later, the snuggie, packaged neatly and sealed with an official-looking port emblem, emerged from the other side. "You're all right. No tax." He handed her the package. "Don't open it until you get to Satellite Hospital."

Clutching her boxed snuggie with one hand and Brian-Scott's with the other, Terra headed toward the gate. "Strange," she said, "I never knew that snuggies were taxed like that."

"Uh," said Brian-Scott, staring ahead at another Customs Inspector just outside the boarding gate.

"Twice?" asked Terra incredulously.

The new Inspector raised an eyebrow. "What's this twice?"

"Why back there—" Terra turned and pointed. But the narrow-faced Customs man and his weighing and measuring equipment were nowhere to be seen.

Chapter 10

Satellite Hospital Outpost
Taurus 14, North Horn 978675644
Nath Orbit
August 4

Carmelita O'Hare-Mbotu R.N.
Teton Medical Center
Jackson Hole Summation City
Wyoming 306548760 United Earth, Sol

Dear Carmie,

This may be the last time you hear from me. I am doomed. Just as beautiful Dr. Brian-Scott and I were beginning an ardent alliance—Armageddon.

Yes, it's true. When I signed up with the Interstellar Nurses Corps, I signed my life away. I am writing to you from a plague ship. There's been no official word, but where there's steam there's a reactor (to coin a phrase).

I hadn't been back from Hyades two days when I learned that I had returned to a nest of pestilence. All of the Aldeberan nurses are hissing about it, but they keep lapsing from Standard into their native tongue so it's hard to get any details. I asked one of the Hyadean orderlies about it, all he'd do was shake his head and wiggle the flap where his nose ought to be. He wouldn't say a word, Carmie, and he's a terrible gossip. When Glockto is at a loss for words, it is serious.

I did find out that old Dr. Kelly-Bach, who is chief epidemiologist, is stricken. His wife, Olga the Grim, is sure to be next. And after Olga? Well, we have been in close proximity. Very close. She's even borrowed my clothes (and she still has my new snuggie). It's perfectly *clear to me, Carmie: I am going to die. And I don't even know what the symptoms are yet.*

When you read in the medical journals of the disease that decimated Nath Outpost, think of me and weep.

Yours in dissolution,
Terra

Satellite Hospital Outpost
Taurus 14, North Horn 978675644
Nath Orbit
August 4

Gladiola Tarkington
45 Subsea
Petroleum City
Gulf of Mexico 233433111 United Earth, Sol

Dear Mom,

Everything is fine here, but boring. I just got back from a week's pass. I'm afraid I was terribly extravagant; I spent the week on Hyades IV and bought a snuggie. I can't wear it on the ship, of course, because Hyadean snuggies are good for forty degrees below zero, but it will come in handy back on Earth if I ever get there.

Don't worry about the plague.

Love,
Terra

Dandde Qotqot leaned back on her haunches and stared at the wall just above Terra's head.

"You're not telling me everything," said Terra. "I know you're not."

The tip of Dandde's tail ticked at the floor, the way it did when she was nervous.

"When you said 'some beings' are immune, you didn't mean human beings, did you?"

"Well . . ."

"Well?"

Distressed, Dandde nibbled at the tip of a claw, blunting it rather badly.

"Talk to me," Terra begged. "You're supposed to be an

expert in all this. You're the one who works in Malignant Fungi."

In answer Dandde rose and handed her a text. "Look up Blugonian Fungus-s-s," she said. Then lowering her snout mournfully, she paused for a moment at the door and said, "I'm really s-s-sorry, Terra."

"Don't go," said Terra. But it was too late. Eyes wide, Terra opened the text and in a voice that was not quite steady, asked for Blugonian Fungus.

The text responded with a dirge-like musical theme. "General? Or Species Specific?"

"Specific."

"Which?"

"Human," she said in a small voice.

"*Blugonian Fungus in Humans*," answered the text. "Press button for illustrations."

Terra hesitated for a moment. Then she pressed.

Pictures began to flash from the text, and as they did, Terra stared, finger frozen on the button, horror frozen on her face.

Satellite Hospital Outpost
Taurus 14, North Horn 978675644
Nath Orbit
August 5

Carmelita O'Hare-Mbotu R.N.
Teton Medical Center
Jackson Hole Summation City
Wyoming 306548760 United Earth, Sol

Dear Carmie,

I told you that I was going to die, but it is much worse than that. Much worse. I am to be flayed alive—victim of an insidious and malignant fungus.

We still don't have any official word, but that's because the official word has to come from Dr. Kelly-Bach, and he is in awful shape. Poor Dr. Kelly-Bach is still up and around, ministering to the sick; but his mind wanders, and his heart is not in his work. Carmie, you should see him. He has to wear thick gloves to keep from scratching his hide off. Olga tells me she has to restrain his hands every night, because if she didn't, he would

*wake up in the morning with most of his epidermis gone.
The look in his eye is terrible, Carmie. Sort of maddened.
And he moans and sighs a lot.*

*There is no known cure, Carmie. None. And it is
definitely contagious. Only this morning, I found Olga
smearing the end of her nose with a local anesthetic, but
she said it didn't help much. To make matters worse,
Glockto, the orderly, came in about then and begged some
for his crease.*

*Carmie, it is so depressing that I am nearing
catatonia. Just when Dr. Brian-Scott and I were devel-
oping such a fulfilling relationship, disaster strikes. We
will be cut down in our prime.*

*I know that if he is stricken first, I will stand by him.
But what if I'm first? Would he want me if my skin were
gone? They say that beauty is only skin deep, but that's a
lie, Carmie.*

*There is only one consolation: All the texts tell me
that Blugonian Fungus, though incurable, is the only
known preventative for the deadly Aurigan Plague (Pan-
Galactic strain). I am finding it very difficult to take
comfort from that fact.*

*There is only one thing left to do. I've got to figure
out a way to get us off this tub.*

> *Machinatingly yours,*
> *Terra*

> *Satellite Hospital Outpost*
> *Taurus 14, North Horn 978675644*
> *Nath Orbit*
> *August 6*

Gladiola Tarkington
45 Subsea
Petroleum City
Gulf of Mexico 233433111 United Earth, Sol

Dear Mom,

*I'm not sick. I never said I was sick. I don't see why
you're worried, because I'm fine.*

*The Hyadean snuggie does not carry disease. The
only diseases we get around here come from the patients.*

*I have applied for a transfer, but they said I couldn't have
it until Olga Kelly-Bach's skin grows back.*

> Your loving daughter,
> Terra

"Destination?" asked the slidleator.

"Staff Emergency Room," said Terra.

"Are you in pain? Would you like to lie down?" A tab
emerging from the ceiling of the slidleator lit up with the
legend: PULL FOR NETBED.

"No. I'm fine. So far," she added darkly. "I'm going to
work."

"Oh," said the slidleator. It trundled her off, not bothering
to speak again until it came to a stop. "Staff Emergency."

Since the Aldeberans were relatively immune to Blugonian Plague, the Director of Nurses reasoned that only they
should work in the nursery. Non-stricken Hyadeans and
Others were floated to areas that needed covering.

It was quiet in Emergency. It was too quiet. The calm
before the storm, thought Terra. She stared up at the glowing
Morbidity Report. Sixty-seven percent of the Hyadean staff
were afflicted, and with the Kelly-Bachs stricken, fifty percent
of the humans.

And here she was in Staff Emergency where all the new
cases first came. Terra's lower lip quivered as she stared up at
the report. It seemed inevitable that the human plague tally
would soon hit seventy-five percent. It made her itch to think
about it.

There was only one other nurse assigned to the S.E.R.
today, an overweight Aldeberan male named Haldeqot who
thrust his snout in the door, saw there were no patients, and
waddled off for a prolonged crunchie break.

Terra was alone when the first patient came in. The
S.E.R. tech, a skinny little Hyadean, trundled up to the door.
He clutched a carrying case.

"What have you got?" asked Terra.

In answer, he raised the lid.

Dr. Creeebo raised an antenna in a feeble salute.

"He says it started in his anterior vibrissae," said the tech,
holding his noseflap stiffly away as if to breathe the same air as
Dr. Creeebo insured infection.

Terra stared into the box. Dr. Creeebo, usually so careful
about his appearance was wearing a ratty little robe and all his
feet were bare. He looked miserable.

83

"I didn't know it affected Arcturans," said Terra.

Dr. Creeebo tweaked at the stubby little hairs on his upper thorax with single-minded intensity. In horror, Terra saw that he had pulled several out. They were littering the floor of his box.

She glanced up at the Hyadean, then back to Dr. Creeebo. "Dr. Brian-Scott ought to have a look at him."

While the S.E.R. servo made the call to Brian-Scott, Terra checked the standing orders for "OTHER BEINGS, ARCTURAN" and came back with a tiny applicator. "This won't cure anything," she told her diminutive patient, "but it'll make you feel better."

She was painting Dr. Creeebo's anterior vibrissae with ChitiCare when Brian-Scott walked in.

He shook his head and looked grim when he looked into the box. "It's Blugonian Plague, all right." The Morbidity Report, responding to his voice and Dr. Creeebo's condition, amended its display with a red STAFF—ARCTURAN: 100%.

Tucking several samples of ChitiCare into Dr. Creeebo's carrying case, he sent him back to his little room with orders for strict rest.

When the Hyadean tech left with his patient, they stared at each other. "There's nothing more we can do?" asked Terra.

He shook his head. "We can offer them rest and fluids, and some pain relief."

"If we stay here, we're going to catch it, aren't we?"

He nodded. "You ought to leave the satellite, Terra. While you can."

"What about you?"

He started to speak, then shrugged as the S.E.R. console interrupted: *"Incoming message."*

The Communications tech came on. "Consultation request coming in from Pleiades II."

The Comstage darkened and two spots began to glow. The spots resolved into a pair of multi-faceted eyes set in a shiny, greenish face. "Prayer we send from the Great Ovum to Star Egg. The Mother is unclutched. Oh, help us, Star Egg, to unclutch the Mother." This was followed by a fervent twiddle of a pair of jointed feelers.

"What does it mean?" asked Terra.

"The 'Great Ovum' is Pleiades II," said Brian-Scott. "That's what the natives call it."

"But who are they praying to? Who is Star Egg?"

"We're Star Egg. The Satellite. They're asking us for help." He furrowed his brow and said, "I think 'the Mother is unclutched' means she can't lay her eggs."

"It's a mission of mercy, isn't it?" Then a speculative look came into Terra's eyes. "You and I can't just let her lie around unclutched, can we? That would be terribly unprofessional."

Satellite Hospital Outpost
Taurus 14, North Horn 978675644
Nath Orbit
August 7

Carmelita O'Hare-Mbotu R.N.
Teton Medical Center
Jackson Hole Summation City
Wyoming 306548760 United Earth, Sol

Dear Carmie,

Well, they wouldn't let me transfer off this tin coffin, but I've beaten them at their game. I volunteered for special assignment on Pleiades II, and Dr. Brian-Scott is going too. It seems that one of the Pleiades II Mothers is sick. Her egg production slowed down to zero, and we have to find out why. The Pleiades II population is on the decline anyway, and they can't afford to lose a Mother. It sounds like an interesting case, and it sure beats terminal pruritus.

Olga is a mass of excoriation, and it is better not to describe the condition of poor Dr. Kelly-Bach. I really fear for his sanity, Carmie. He is so testy, you just can't stand to be around him.

We thought the Aldeberans were immune; but just this afternoon Dr. Qotemire came into S.E.R. to reattach Dr. Creeebo's central vibrissa, which Dr. Creeebo really can't do without. And during the surgery, one of Dr. Qotemire's tail scales fell out. He seemed awfully distressed about it, and the Aldeberan nurse who was assisting him turned such a pale blue that I thought she would faint. I'm getting off this tub just in time, Carmie. It's one thing to see the disease in humans and Hyadeans, but it's altogether something else to contemplate Dr.

Qotemire's defoliation. I don't think I could bear that. It's hard enough to look at Dr. Qotemire when he's in health.

Terra

P.S. How's this for an intinerary? Tomorrow we take the shuttle to Hyades IV and then the express to Pleiades II. Our port of entry is Seven Sisters—the only Pleasure Dome in light years! We'll spend the night at the Kubla Khan and then off to see our patient.

Yours in anticipation,
Terra

Satellite Hospital Outpost
Taurus 14, North Horn 978675644
Nath Orbit
August 7

Gladiola Tarkington
45 Subsea
Petroleum City
Gulf of Mexico 233433111 United Earth, Sol

Dear Mom,

My skin is fine. You worry too much. I worry about your worrying about me.

They won't let me come home, Mom. They're sending Dr. Brian-Scott and me to Pleiades II to see a patient there. But don't be concerned. It's probably not true what they say about the Seven Sisters Pleasure Dome.

Much love,
Terra

It was a long ride on Express to Pleiades II. Terra leaned back in her seat and slept until an odd sound woke her. She blinked awake and looked around. There wasn't anything unusual to be seen, only the other passengers and Brian-Scott dozing beside her.

Shrugging, she leaned back again and in a few moments was nearly asleep when the sound came again. It was a low, repetitive shoop-shoop of a sound that increased both in volume and speed. Then it suddenly stopped.

She looked around suspiciously. Nothing.

The third time she heard it, she gave up on sleep and was adjusting her seat when a low and drawn-out "Oh-oo-ooh" came from Brian-Scott. Startled, she reached for his arm. He stirred in his sleep and moaned again. Shoop-shoop. She froze in dismay as Brian-Scott's shoulders began a rhythmic scratching against the back of the seat. Shoop-shoop. Shoop-shoop. The scratching rose to a crescendo and culminated in another groan loud enough to wake him.

He gave her a vacant glance. "Guess I dozed off." His fingertips began to claw at his knee—shup-shup—and his shoulders moved again—shoop-shoop.

Eyes widening in horror, he stared down at his hand, scratching as though with a will of its own, up one thigh and down the other until it came to its clawing finale on his other knee.

Terra caught her lower lip between her teeth.

Shoop-shup. Shoop-shup.

Brian-Scott avoided her gaze.

And then in tacit agreement that it was better not to speak of unspeakable things, they both stared straight ahead with tragic looks on their faces until the express arrived at Pleiades II.

"Oh, please," begged Terra. "You've got to stop. Everyone's watching us." She glanced nervously toward the two customs officials who fixed them with hard, suspicious eyes.

Brian-Scott gave a little moan and said between clenched teeth, "I'm trying to. I really am. See?" He clasped his hands together and squeezed. "I won't do it anymore. I promise."

"If you can just hold out for a little while," she whispered. "When we get to the room you can scratch all you like."

Desperation touched his eyes and his fingers clenched tighter.

"Oh," she said. "It's really awful, isn't it? Think of something cold—something icy numbing your skin. Maybe if you concentrate—"

He squeezed his eyes shut.

"Does it help?"

He shook his head in misery.

"Well then, don't think about your skin at all. Think about something else."

"I can't help thinking about my skin," he said through tight lips. "I'm thinking about my skin right now. I'm thinking especially about the skin on my eyelids." His clenched hands began to shake. "I'm going to die, Terra. I know I am." A wild hope sprang into his eyes. "And then I'll be dead—and I won't itch."

She searched his tormented face. "I wish I could help. Maybe you could think about music—or waves crashing on a beach." She bit a knuckle as a third official, then a fourth, joined the first two and stared in their direction. "They're talking about us. I know they are."

He thrust a little finger into each ear and began to vibrate with such violence that his face jiggled.

"Oh, stop!" pleaded Terra in horror. "You'll poke holes in your eardrums."

"They itch so bad," he said. "Oh, Terra, I can't stand it." With a final shudder, he extracted his fingers and clasped his hands again, squeezing so tightly that his knuckles threatened to pop through the skin.

"Don't think about sounds then, think about—think about smells." As his nose began to twitch she said quickly, "No— Don't think about smells either." She cupped his hands in hers. "You really shouldn't clench your fingers so hard. You'll cut off the circulation."

"Terra, look," he whispered.

She started in horror as two huge beings completely covered in bulky, white decontam suits marched toward them and pulled out disruptors. "They're aiming at us!"

"Maybe they'll shoot us," said Brian-Scott with a tinge of hope in his voice.

In answer, one of the looming figures spoke: "Follow us, or die."

"Inside," said the being in the decontam suit and marched them into a small Floatel room on the periphery of the Seven Sisters Pleasure Dome.

The door clanged shut behind them with such force that the floating room began to bob and sway. The lock sealed.

Terra hammered at the door. "Come back. Let us out."

"THAT WILL DO YOU NO GOOD," said the door. "I HAVE ENGAGED QUARANTINE MODE. NO LIVING BEING CAN ENTER OR EXIT."

With a groan, Brian-Scott fell onto the jelly bed and began to scratch as if his life depended on it.

"Quarantine? Prison, you mean." Terra stared in despair at the door. "What happens now?"

"I HAVE NO IDEA," it said. "I COULD BE IN-STRUCTED TO CHANGE MODES AT ANY MOMENT. PERHAPS I WILL GO INTO DISINFECTANT MODE; I COULD IRRADIATE THE CONTENTS OF THIS ROOM. THAT'S WHAT I DID THE LAST TIME."

"Terrific." Terra sank down on the other side of the bed that sloshed in rhythm with Brian-Scott's scratching. She was going to be sick. It wasn't enough to be arrested and imprisoned in a pest-hole, she thought in despair. Now she was going to be seasick.

The thing to do was to look at the horizon. She lay back on the jiggling jelly bed and stared bleakly through the single elliptical port of the swaying room. Beyond was the gray vista of a singularly uninviting shallow sea. Pleasure Dome, she thought. She wanted to cry.

The jelly bed gurgled and sloshed in time to frantic clawing. "Do something, Terra," pleaded Brian-Scott. "Do something."

"What?" What could she do? He was the doctor. "Do you want me to rub your back?"

"Anything." Then as she began, "No— That's worse." Bent in a frightful contortion, he clawed at his shoulder blades. The motion shuddered through the jelly bed and transferred itself to the room.

The room was pitching now and the jelly bed was yawing in an especially nauseating way. "Do you want me to sing?" she asked in desperation. "I could sing to you."

"Yes. No— Multiplication tables."

"What?"

"They always made me sleepy." Slosh.

Watch the horizon, she told herself. She fixed her desperate gaze on the choppy iron-gray sea beyond the window. "Two times two is four"—pitch—"oh . . . Two times three is six"—yaw—"oh . . ."

As he listened in fascination to Terra's rendition of the multiplication tables, for a moment Brian-Scott forgot to scratch.

Chapter 11

Pleasure Dome
Pleiades II 456765453 Pleiades
August 10

Carmelita O'Hare-Mbotu R.N.
Teton Medical Center
Jackson Hole Summation City
Wyoming 306748760 United Earth, Sol

Dear Carmie,

Have you ever been quarantined in a Pleasure Dome with a man with the itch? Believe me, it is no fun. No fun at all.

But that's not the bad part:

Pleiades II Health said we could visit our patient outside the dome because there's a lot of fungus out there anyway, and the natives are immune to most of it, including the Blugonian plague. So a few minutes ago, the door went into Eviction Mode and told us we were to leave. It said, "Do not attempt to return or you will be executed." Then it opened the porthole and said we have to crawl out and wade to shore.

Can you imagine, Carmie? Here we are on a mission of mercy and that's the treatment we get. I can't wait to get out of here and I would leave right this very minute only it's raining out—and there doesn't seem to be much shore to wade to.

If I were not the dedicated professional I am, I wouldn't bother to help the Pleiades Mother. But as you know, Carmie, I am dedicated to the end.

Besides, we don't have anyplace else to go. They won't let us board the express because we're contaminated. And there isn't any cure for Blugonian Plague,

Carmie. We are doomed to wander the hostile surface of Pleiades II—perhaps forever.

> *Yours into the wilderness,*
> *Terra*

Terra squished through the mud that passed for dry land and stared out across the water. From here, the Pleasure Dome was no more than a bubble floating in a gray sea under a drizzly gray sky. "We may never be dry again," she said.

Between scratches, Brian-Scott stared inland. "Over there," he said. "It looks like a road."

For want of a better plan, they chose a direction and slogged down the unpaved road for several kilometers with nothing but the sound of the rain and surf to accompany them. They stopped at a slight rise. Off to the left, a mushroom-shaped pillar squatted at the side of the road. It bore a sign: PRESS FOR SLIDE. A pale button gleamed just below it.

"What's that?" asked Terra.

Brian-Scott scratched his head. "Let's find out." He pressed the button and waited expectantly, but nothing happened.

Terra plopped to the ground and leaned back against the pillar. "I can't go on another step; there's something awful in my shoe." She yanked and the shoe came off with a little slurping sound. Turning it over, she tapped it on the ground and gave a little shriek at what fell out.

He stared at the green tubelike creature wriggling in the mud. "It looks like something the hospital mess would serve for dinner."

"It is," she howled. "It's a tuberoid muck sucker"—her lower lip began to tremble—"and it was sucking on my toe."

Brian-Scott scratched his instep in empathy. "I guess you picked it up when we waded across the bay. Let me take a look."

She extended her foot.

He reached out, then stopped. He was contagious. He shouldn't touch her. Then he shook his head; it was too late to worry about that now. There was no way that she could have avoided exposure—he had already done that to her, and somehow he was going to have to live with the guilt.

He cupped her little foot gently in his hands. With one finger, he brushed off the muck that clung to it and frowned. "It's red, but it looks all right. The skin isn't broken." He spoke in what he took to be a calm, comforting voice. To his surprise, Terra burst into tears.

"It isn't fair. All I ever wanted was to see the Galaxy and help the downtrodden. And now you have the plague. And I have an alien sucking on my tuh—my tuh—my *toe*."

Distressed, he reached out and drew her to him. "It's gone now, honey."

She clung to him, and he felt her breath against his neck and the warm wetness of her tears. "I know," she whispered.

She held tightly to him for a few moments. Then she looked up and said, "I'll be all right. I will. I promise."

Arms wrapped around one another, they sat huddled in the mud of an alien planet, until what seemed like the distant hum of insects grew louder. They looked up to see a dull green ovoid shape skimming down the roadway toward them.

A moment later, the vehicle pulled abreast and stopped. A pair of multi-faceted eyes stared out at them, and a buzzing voice spoke in Standard: "Are you the beings who called for the slide car?"

"Isn't it a beautiful day?" remarked their driver.

Terra stared out of the egg-shaped car and raised an eyebrow. The rain still drizzled half-heartedly from a lead-gray sky. "Beautiful?"

"We don't get many dry spells here, so we have to enjoy them while we can," he said and twiddled a half-dozen levers with a half-dozen legs. The slide car slowed to a creep over a lumpy terrain of gray-green fungus.

"Dry spells," she said to herself, and shook her head.

The slide car ground to a halt. "This is as far as I can take you."

Suspicion rose in Brian-Scott's voice. "I don't see the Oviporium."

"Neither do I," said the driver cheerfully. He twiddled several of his legs again and the door slid open. The rain fell soundlessly onto a rolling fungoid carpet fissured with a dozen streams running toward a mushroomy forest ahead.

An edge came into Brian-Scott's voice. "Where is it?" His temper was none too even today; during his last itching attack, he had managed to denude his left elbow in less than a minute.

The driver waved an array of arms, legs, and feelers toward the forest. "Through there."

"I'll bet we can't miss it," said Brian-Scott with a baleful look.

The driver seemed interested. "Are you offering a wager?"

Terra stared out at the gloomy forest. "How much to drive us all the way?"

"How much what?"

"Money. Or whatever you use."

The driver seemed amused. "No being can drive you there. Not through Vicious Swamp." He stretched a feeler pointedly toward the door. "You get out now." It was obviously a dismissal.

"Now just a minute—" said Brian-Scott.

In answer, the driver seized another lever. With a sharp whine, the passenger seat rolled outside the slide car and tipped forward abruptly.

"Wow-oh," yelled Tera in a vain attempt to hold on. She found herself dumped unceremoniously into a thick patch of blue-green vegetation, while Brian-Scott rolled ahead until he came to a stop under a giant, fluted toadstool.

The passenger seat retracted and the slide car door closed. "Enjoy your day," said the driver and drove away in a cloud of spores.

Staring helplessly at the retreating slide car, Terra said, "I hate Pleiades II. I really do." She tried to stand up, lost her balance on the springy undergrowth and half-bounced, half-rolled into Brian-Scott. "What are we going to do now?"

He scratched his head—exacerbating a resident itchy place behind his right ear—and said, "I guess our best bet is to try and find the Oviporium."

She stared at the forest just ahead. It was unpleasantly dark in there. But what was the alternative? It would take them days to walk back the way they had come. She scrambled to her feet, broke off a toadstool half as tall as she was, and hoisted it over her head. It made a passable umbrella. "Come on," she said, waggling the mushroom. "There's room for two."

The spongy forest floor grew wetter and degenerated into a shallow lake studded with islands and narrow curving clumps of blue-gray fungus that served as a path. Pale shoots and ruffled ears of fungus towered overhead and spores began to pepper their makeshift umbrella. The air smelled like the inside of an old shoe. After ten minutes of this, Terra began to long for the Pleasure Dome Floatel; after twenty, she thought of having to spend the rest of her life in this place, and she bit her lip.

They trudged on, picking their way over fallen toadstools. It was beginning to grow dark; eerie shadows danced and shuddered in time to the wind. The fungus path was partially submerged now and treacherous. Water filled their shoes and every step threatened to topple them into the black, evil-smelling swamp.

Terra's toadstool umbrella caught on a leathery growth and broke apart as a gust of wind snatched it from her hands. The broken fungus glimmered for a moment in the shadows, then black water swallowed it. Rain rolled down Terra's face and mingled with sudden hot tears. "We're going to die here," she said. "We're going to die of exposure and mildew and the itch."

Brian-Scott looked at her bleakly. Then he managed a faint smile and gave her a kiss. "At least we're together, Terra." They clung to each other for a moment, shutting their eyes as if they could shut out the night and the swamp itself. Then he said, "Let's try and rest. Over there, maybe." He pointed to a curved mound glimmering grub-white in the shadows just beyond a little clearing of spidery dark growths that bent in the rain. "At least it's out of the water."

He stepped up onto the mound and reached out a hand to steady her.

Grateful, she sank down, leaned against his shoulder, and stared blankly at the wispy black shoots bobbing in the drizzle. After a while the rhythm of them grew hypnotic and it seemed to her that the shoots moved with a will of their own—ducking first left, then left again, then right. Drowsily she watched them move: Left, left. Right, left. Up, up, up.

Up?

The spidery shoots seemed to be growing taller. Suddenly hundreds of pale gray pincers sprouted from the undergrowth. Pincers, followed by long grayish mantis bodies with gray-green mantis faces on top. "Welcome to Mothers' Oviporium," said a reedy voice. "Greetings to the Star Egg beings. We thank you for your help." Then the thin voice grew frankly curious, "Is that part of the treatment?"

Terra stared in total confusion at Brian-Scott for a moment. Then suddenly suspicious, she patted the grub-white mound beneath them and a startled look came over her face. "I think," she whispered in his ear, "we're sitting on our patient."

Gladiola Tarkington
45 Subsea
Petroleum City
Gulf of Mexico 233433111 United Earth, Sol

Dear Mom,

Well, here we are at the Oviporium. There's a lot of mildew here, and it's awfully wet outside, but we're staying in the Alien Hive, which is a sort of cave. It's not too bad really, if you can get over feeling like you're inside an ant hill.

We've seen our patient and Dr. Brian-Scott and I are going to start treatment after lunch, if he is still up and around.

I am fine except for my toe which was sucked on by an alien.

Bravely yours,
Terra

Chapter 12

Mothers' Oviporium
Vicious Swamp
Pleiades II 352344480
Pleiades
August 11

Carmelita O'Hare-Mbotu R.N.
Teton Medical Center
Jackson Hole Summation City
Wyoming 306748760 United Earth, Sol

Dear Carmie,

I found out why they call it a Pleasure Dome. The only pleasure that anyone could conceivably have on this planet is under that Dome. Outside, it rains all the time. All the time. Everything is musty and mildewy.

The Pleiades II Mother is in bad shape. When we got here, she was curled up in a kind of spastic ball. We could hardly see her in the dark, so we had to wait till the next day to do anything for her.

Since you've led a sheltered life back on Earth, Carmie, you've probably forgotten your Alien Physiology. The Mother is about three meters long and she looks a lot like a millipede. She's stopped laying her eggs and she seems to be in pain. Of course, it's a little hard to be sure, because she's completely blind, deaf, and dumb.

Before Dr. Brian-Scott could begin to examine her, she began to writhe and her groomers went into a panic. They stood around whimpering and twiddling their feelers while Dr. Brian-Scott stood around and scratched. Then he palpated most of her abdomen and said, "I think it's (scratch, scratch) a mechanical obstruction (scratch, scratch) of the ovipositor."

I thought that was interesting, and I looked at her tail; but Dr. Brian-Scott said I was looking at the wrong end. The Mother's ovipositor is just under her mouth. (Can you imagine, Carmie?)

Then he said, "We'd better (scratch, scratch) put on protective clothing (scratch, scratch)."

He said that when he finished dilating her ovipositor, the eggs would start rolling out. "As soon as they do, she'll start squirting liters of fluid from the pores in her sides to coat the eggs."

So I have to go put on this plasticine suit to keep the juice off me. I'll write and let you know what happens. If you don't hear from me, you will know that I have contracted the Blugonian Plague and later died.

> *Obstetrically yours,*
> *Terra*

The plasticine suit Terra wore crackled unpleasantly, and each step she took echoed inside her helmet with a gurgling, swampy slurp. It smelled funny in there too—oily and acrid—and it was hot. She pulled the helmet off and it fell slackly to her shoulders.

A faint, drizzling rain began to glue her hair to her forehead. She looked up at the sky. The clouds were so low they seemed to balance on the naked limbs of the tall, skeletal mushrooms that edged the swamp.

Brian-Scott followed her gaze to the menacing gray clouds bulging with charcoal. "Be glad we're having a drought—"

"—He said drily," Terra answered with a grin and a sidelong glance.

He plucked at the collar of his suit and muttered, "Hot in here." Suddenly his lips twisted as a spasm of itching came on, and he began to run. Great clots of greenish mud splashed up in his wake and grew more liquid as he reached the edge of the black water. Launching himself in an uncertain trajectory, he plunged in, sank, and slowly emerged with the spidery tendrils of some drowned growth clinging to his silvery helmet.

"Does that help?" asked Terra, wide-eyed at his precipitous plunge.

"No"—he sputtered as a trailing end of the plant slithered across his lips—"but it's something to do instead of scratch."

She watched him in silence for a moment. Then she said, "Do you want to come out now?"

He nodded wetly, and she extended a hand. He took it, swung up, and squished back to the path that led to their patient.

The Pleiadean Mother was surrounded by a dozen fidgety groomers. One of them balanced a tray of instruments on his uppermost limbs and began to lay them out on the back of another groomer who assumed a crouching position and served as an impromptu table.

"Did you ever see instruments like these?" asked Terra.

Brian-Scott gave them a look. "Not since 'M.O.A.G.,'" he said.

"Mo-ag?"

"'Medical Oddities and Antiquities of the Galaxy'—a class I had in med school." He bent over the curving instruments. "These are very old. They've been handed down from Mother to Mother, but now they're only used in rituals." He glanced at the groomers. "Look at them. I doubt they even know what these were meant for."

He pointed. "See the carving on the handles? Those little squiggles show the size of each hatching." He squinted at the faint markings. "You can see how this one's clutches have tapered off. She's got a stricture. Last season the smaller eggs passed through it and the rest were absorbed, but now not even the little ones can get through."

"Which one do you need first?"

He pointed and Terra handed him a large, curved piece the color of old ivory. As he brought it to the Mother's throat, the groomers began to buzz their forelegs in an agitated way. "Uh-oh." He drew back as the buzz grew in volume. "I was right. It looks like we only get one try."

"What do you mean?"

"They don't know what these instruments are for. If I touch her with them and we don't get results right away, there's no telling what they might do."

"You mean, there's no telling what they might do to *us*," said Terra with an uneasy glance toward the groomer to her right who fixed her with an inscrutable multi-faceted stare.

"Are you game?"

Terra nodded slowly. "If you are."

"Here we go then." He slid the rounded tip of the instrument into a depression in the Mother's throat. A moment later, it was buried in her flesh.

Brian-Scott's sudden moan rose over the cacophony of a dozen chorusing forelegs. In horror, Terra watched as he began to dance first on one leg, then the other.

"Gottrscrugge," he muttered through clenched teeth.

"Got to what?"

"Scrudgge. Gottrscrudgge." His fingers clamped the instrument handles as if his life depended on it.

Then as she realized what he meant, her eyes grew wild. "No, please! Don't scratch. Don't let go. Oh, please."

The rhythm of the buzzing forelegs was growing both in volume and menace.

"Got to!" The instrument trembled in his hands. "Help me. Grab hold!"

"How?" Then, "Oh!" as he thrust the handles into her outstretched hands. "What do I do now?" she cried in horror.

His answer was muffled. It came from deep within the fetal ball his body made as he rolled on the ground and frantically scratched the back of his thighs.

"What? What do I do?"

"Pull." Uncoiling, he sprang into an amazing contortion and clawed at his left ankle and right shoulder simultaneously. "Pull the handles apart."

Panting, she tugged against the resisting handles. "They won't move."

His nails pursued a demon itch centered near his spine and radiating torment north and south. "Harder. Pull harder."

Praying that her mute patient would survive the treatment, Terra yanked and felt something tear. Horrified, she stared as the Mother's head splayed back on her neck and her body began to writhe. "I've cut her throat! I've killed her."

Brian-Scott scrabbled up and seized the handles.

"She's going to die. I've killed her."

A white curve bulged just under the Mother's mouth.

"No you didn't," he said. "It's an egg."

The curve grew into a round ball that spurted out of the opening.

The Mother's writhing grew rhythmic. Catching the egg with her anterior legs she began to roll it toward her tail. As she did, fluid pouring out of openings in the side of her body turned the egg to a rich brown.

Another egg emerged. Another. Then they began to roll out in a steady stream.

"It's like an assembly line," said Terra as the coated eggs began to accumulate in a sticky pyramid on the ground.

The syrupy fluid was gushing now, streaming down the sides of the Mother into brown puddles on the spongy soil. "Why does she squirt all that stuff over the eggs?"

Brian-Scott paused in mid-scratch. "It keeps the eggs from rotting. They'd be destroyed by fungus in no time without it."

"Amazing." Then as she stared, her eyes began to widen as a thought came to her. "Do you suppose that juice would do any good for the Blugonian fungus?"

Fingers poised on scalp and hip, he froze.

"What's the matter?" she asked in alarm. He stood completely still, his eyes fixed on the Mother, as if he were hypnotized by the fluid spurting from her sides. Then with a spastic leap he jumped up and began to rip his clothes off.

Stripped to his itchy skin, he splashed handfuls of the brown syrupy mess all over himself. He gave a happy little moan. Sloshing the Mother juice onto his chest he worked it into his armpits with energetic squishes.

"Oh, stop! You've got to stop." It might be poison, Terra thought. He was going to poison himself in a completely unscientific way while she watched. "Oh, don't. You need a patch test first."

His answer was a not quite rational laugh. Then to Terra's abject mortification, he clutched at the Mother in a maddened way, while her keepers twiddled their feelers in a puzzled, yet amiable, chorus. "Oh stop. You're turning brown all over. What if you're allergic?"

He was grinning at her now—a beatific grin that wreathed his stained face and crinkled in brown rivulets at the corner of his eyes. "You've cured me, Terra. I'm cured." He seized her in a bear hug and whirled her in the air while the keepers clicked their feelers in rhythm with this new phase of the treatment. "I love you, Terra. I'm cured and I love you."

"Are you sure? What if you break out? What if your skin comes off?"

"I'm cured. I know I am." Then he laughed and flung an arm toward the Mother. "We're going to get buckets of the stuff—vats of it. And we're going to rid the *Universe* of Blugonian Plague."

"Do you really think Pleiades Health will let us leave?"

"They'll have to," he said with a grin. "We've taken the cure."

Nestled in his squishy embrace, Terra searched his brown

face, and broke out in a happy smile. It was going to be all right, she thought. He wasn't allergic.

She felt like Madame Curie.

Satellite Hospital Outpost
Taurus 14, North Horn 978675644
Nath Orbit
August 15

Gladiola Tarkington
45 Subsea
Petroleum City
Gulf of Mexico 233433111 United Earth, Sol

Dear Mom,

You don't need to come here to see about me. I'm fine. My toe is fine. I really wish you wouldn't call Dr. Kelly-Bach just now, since he's still weak from the plague.

We all took the cure, and Dr. Brian-Scott says that the brown stains may come off in a few months.

In the meantime, I am going to be a student. In view of my interest in the reproductive habits of the Pleiades II Mothers, Dr. Brian-Scott says he is going to teach me all about the most interesting reproductive habits in the Galaxy.

Studiously yours,
Terra

Dieter Diderot's eyes narrowed as the last of the Tarkington letter scrolled across his wrist screen. It had been a close call. Too close. Without his intervention, the Aurigan Plague would have destroyed Satellite Hospital and the KBG's plan with it.

How much did the GIA know? They knew about The Trigger; they had tried to destroy the little Aldeberan and failed. But they were using scattershot tactics against the rest of the satellite—proof they still didn't know the identity of The Finger.

She had to be kept alive—for now. Although Diderot did not yet know SEPTUM's greater plan, he had no doubt that the Tarkington girl was expendable when her work was done.

In the meantime, he had to get her off the satellite before the GIA struck again.

He had to talk to SEPTUM. . . .

"Believe it or not, Dr. Brian-Scott says he likes me brown," said Terra, staring doubtfully in the reflector at the residue of Pleiadean Mother juice still staining her skin.

Dandde Qotqot flattened her nostrils in amazement. Her claws skittered over her belly as if to reassure herself that her abdominal scales were still an unsullied white.

"Well," Terra said defensively, "all the early humans wanted to be brown. The women used to lie around in the sun on their bikinis—or in their bikinis—or whatever, just so they could be tan."

Dandde was horrified. "You mean they ex-s-s-posed themselves-s-s to radiation from a s-s-star?"

"I guess so— They must have. It said so in one of my ancient history books." She faced the reflector and squinted. When she squinted, she didn't look quite so streaky. "Tell me the truth, Dandde. I look awful, don't I?"

Dandde tipped her snout toward the floor and blinked. The gesture wasn't lost on Terra who saw it in the reflector. "I *do* look awful. It's all over your face."

Dandde gracefully changed the subject. "Did you get your mess-s-s-age?"

"What message?"

"Your light was-s-s on." Dandde thrust her snout toward the hall.

Terra grabbed up an oversized scrubbee still damp from her bath and wrapped it into a makeshift sarong. "Let's take a look."

Dandde rocked forward on her tail and followed.

Terra punched the glowing light by her name and the message began to scroll onto the screen. A moment later, she squealed in delight. "I've been promoted! Imagine!" Turning toward Dandde, she stuck her hands on her hips, her nose in the air, and said in mock superiority, "You can call me Prime Clinician, if you please."

Dandde's nostrils flattened. "I can't believe it. Nobody gets-s-s named Prime Clinician unless-s-s they reenlist."

Terra stared at the message as if she expected it to evaporate. "Isn't it incredible? I'm so proud, I could just bust." She erupted in a dance that terminated in a wild spin much to the detriment of her sarong attachment. Clutching the scrubbee, she leaned against the wall and caught her breath. "Wait till I tell my beloved."

"What's-s the other mess-s-s-age?"

Terra blinked and looked up. Her light was on again, but this time the message was for Terra Tarkington, R.N., P.C.:

CALL TO TEMPORARY DUTY:
Above designated, Terra Tarkington, R.N., P.C., will go at once to the Director of Nurses for briefing. Immediately thereafter, she will board the shuttle for Hyades IV where she will report as Prime Clinician in Charge, MediStation Far Out.

"Hyades IV! They're sending me to Hyades IV." She stared bleakly at Dandde. "Away from beautiful Dr. Brian-Scott." She shook her head in disbelief and caught her lower lip between her teeth. "Oh, Dandde— That old saying is really true. Pride really does goeth before fall."

Zeus the Zapper was in an especially foul mood. Fortunately, Cuthbert was a safe distance away from his inflamed boss. He was carefully nursing the single beer he could afford in a corner booth of the Indentured Club when the Algolian bartender extended his prehensile nose and said loudly and nasally through it, "Call for the 'prissing cretin' that works for The Zapper."

A sickly smile wavered on Cuthbert's lips. He raised a tentative finger; he felt everyone's eyes bore into him.

The bartender retracted his proboscis and a moment later extended it toward Cuthbert. This time, it clutched a comset. "Guess who wants a word with you?"

He took the comset and gingerly held it to his ear. "Cuthbert here." First came the metallic sound of gears gnashing and teeth clenching. Then the Zapper's voice boomed in his head: "Is that your idea of a deadly plague, Cuthbert? Is it? What were they supposed to do? Scratch themselves to death?"

"No, sir. It really was deadly, sir. It was Aurigan Plague, Pan-Galatic strain."

There was a malignant pause. "Are you attempting humor, Cuthbert?"

"No, sir. Nothing could be further from my mind."

"Because if you are, Cuthbert. You are going to find that the point of the joke is *you*. Do you get my meaning?"

"Yes, sir. It's perfectly clear, sir." Cuthbert thanked all the fates and providences that he was out of reach of The Zapper's mechanisms at that moment.

"Cuthbert"—The Zapper's voice was diabolically gentle— "are you holding the comset to your ear?"

"Yes, sir," he lied, and snatched the comset away. Even at arm's length, the lion roar was loud enough to cause a dozen pairs of assorted eyes to fix on him and the comset in annoyance.

"Now then—"

"What's that, sir?" said Cuthbert with a cunning born of desperation. "I can't hear you, sir."

"Cretin! Use your other ear," bellowed The Zapper.

Cuthbert tapped his ear with the comset to simulate change. "That one's better, sir. It's definitely better."

"Now listen up. I have just learned that The Finger is going to be temporarily leaving Satellite Hospital." There was an ominous pause. "You are going to check the movements of every prissing being on that prissing satellite. You are going to have *intimate* knowledge of the movements of everyone from the administrator to the janitor. And without fail—without *fail*, Cuthbert—you are going to finger The Finger. Do I make myself clear?"

"Yes, sir!" He snatched away the comset in the nick of time as Zeus the Zapper's parting lion roar left no doubt that the conversation was terminated.

Cuthbert stared at the Satellite Hospital travel agenda. With the help of Aleph, Beth, and a drunk and unrepentant Gimbel, he had narrowed the list to five. Two of these were doubtfuls—discharges going home to distant planets. Tentatively, he removed them from his list.

That left three, but his eye kept going back to one of them: Terra Tarkington, the girl he had sold the snuggie to. She had arrived on the Bull Run shortly before The Trigger hatched, and it was rumored that she was the one who had cured him. Score One. Then, somehow, the Aurigan Plague was mysteriously aborted, and the girl comes up with a convenient cure for Blugonian Fungus. Score Two. Now she was being transferred. . . .

Tarkington was The Finger, he was sure of it. But how could he prove it? He couldn't approach her openly. No one was to know about the GIA's interest in Satellite Hospital.

He stared in gloom at the list. The circumstantial evidence was there, but nothing but hard, cold facts would satisfy The Zapper. What was he supposed to do now? Read her mind?

His eyes widened suddenly and he tweaked his lower button. "Gimbel, who have we got on the telepath list?"

"That's sorting," Gimbel said thickly. "You know I hate to sort."

"You have to. You're programmed to."

Gimbel snorted. "I may have to, but I don't have to like it." Glowing an angry red, he lapsed into silence.

"Have you started?"

"Don't bother me," said Gimbel testily. "I'm working."

Cuthbert stared at the wall and figeted. It was bad enough to be indentured to The Zapper, wasn't it? Why did he have to have an ugly drunk for a computer?

Gimbel's sort yielded only one prospect immediately available. He had been used by the GIA for various and sticky odd jobs in the past, but Cuthbert was unconvinced. The agent was from Hyades II, and reputed to be "difficult." Still, what choice did he have?

Sighing, he picked up a comset and called for an appointment with Ambassador Kronto.

The Hyades II embassy was one of a dozen clustered in a sheltered valley below the Hyades IV ice harp fields. Programmed currents of heated air made Ambassadors Alley—as it was called by the locals—enviably warm. Cuthbert basked in it for as long as he dared before he asked the door for admittance.

The door peered at him for a long moment and then engaged in a hasty conference with another part of its mechanism. Finally it slid aside and he stepped into the thickly padded vestibule.

Wide stairs rolled downward to an empty reception room. Cuthbert, suspecting it was not diplomatic to make himself comfortable without being invited, stood first on one foot, then on the other, while he waited for Ambassador Kronto. When the door finally slid open behind him, he whirled around. "Good morning, Your Competency." But instead of the Ambassador, a pale-blue servo floated into the room.

The servo extended an eye which surveyed him minutely and relayed the vision somewhere into the bowels of the embassy. "Who did you say you were?" demanded the servo.

"Cuthbert. GIA."

"You are human," observed the servo. "Ambassador Kronto relays to me that you are therefore an imposter."

Cuthbert was dumfounded. "There are lots of humans in the GIA."

"This is true. However, the Ambassador tells me that your appearance is inappropriate for the intelligence community of humans. Therefore, you are an imposter. The Ambassador wishes you to know that he is not stupid. He has intimate knowledge of the human intelligence community."

"Based on what?"

"Ambassador Kronto has in his possession top secret tapes which have revealed to him the appropriate behavior and attire of human spies. These tapes include exhaustive material which he has painstakingly decoded. Even the greatest of your people, your Humphrey Bogart, is known to him."

"Our what?"

"Your Humphrey Bogart. The Ambassador wishes you to know that he was not burned yesterday. You cannot pull the woolen over his eyes. You are obviously an imposter. The ambassador orders you to vamoose."

"To what?"

"To vamoose." At that, the servo extended several pairs of arms, clamped Cuthbert in them, and conveyed him up the stairs. The door, which saw them coming, opened, and Cuthbert found himself dumped unceremoniously on the embassy steps.

Much later in the day—after a prolonged conference with his buttons, who had to tap into the vast GIA database for information, and after an impassioned plea with the Spy X-Change vendor for credit—Cuthbert stood again on the Hyades II embassy steps.

When the door slid open again, he strode purposefully toward the steps and rolled down to the reception room.

This time, when the servo appeared and extended its eye, Cuthbert pulled down his snapbrim hat. "Cuthbert. GIA." Leveling his gaze at the servo's lens, he thrust his hands into the pockets of his antique reproduction trench coat, twisted his lips to one side, and said, "Here's looking at you, Ambassador."

And the servo bobbed and jiggled in respect, and said, "His Competency will be with you right away."

Chapter 13

TRANSCRIPT OF A DEPOSITION TAKEN BY THE ROYAL HYADEAN POLICE AND MILITIA FROM T. TARKINGTON, R.N., REGARDING THE CHARGES BROUGHT FOR AND BY THE HYADEAN ALLIANCE AGAINST HER; THE CAPITAL OFFENSE OF MIND SWITCH

DEPUTY SERVO: *Please state your name, occupation, and place of residence.*

My name is Terra Tarkington. I am a registered nurse with the Interstellar Nurses Corps. My permanent base is Satellite Hospital Outpost, Taurus 14, North Horn, Nath Orbit; and I'm temporarily on duty at MediStation Far Out, Hyades IV. And the charges are not true. They're simply not true.

If you want to claim that I am guilty of malpractice or even practicing veterinary medicine without a license, I could understand that. But you're accusing me of Mind Switch and—

DEPUTY SERVO: *Tell us now what transpired with the aggrieved and injured Honorable Kronto.*

How was I to know that the patient was the Ambassador from Hyades II? I thought he was a family pet.

Nobody told me he was Ambassador Kronto. Nobody told me anything.

I was sent here to minister to the diseased and disadvantaged of the Hyades IV Far Out. You've got to admit these people need all the medical help they can get. They're virtual pariahs. If you don't live in the main hives of Hyades II, you're just a forgotten soul. Mired by

107

life into a muddy existence. Sunk into a quagmire of adversity. Swallowed up by—

DEPUTY SERVO: *Would you please confine your remarks to the charge of Mind Switch, and to the patient in question?*

Well! Anyway, these Hyadeans from the Far Out came to the MediStation where I work. My position is Prime Clinician. I check out all the patients first and then teletape to Dr. Brian-Scott for anything I can't handle. And I want to tell you, it requires a lot of me. It's not easy giving first care to the poor and downtrodden of the Far Out. If I weren't the dedicated professional that I am, I could tell you stories that would curl your hair—if you had any hair. Why—

DEPUTY SERVO: *Could we please continue with your version of your encounter with the Ambassador?*

You *don't* have to be rude.

DEPUTY SERVO: *Apologies. Please continue.*

Well, that morning a group of Far Outs came to the MediStation. They were really excited, but I didn't know what they were talking about; none of them spoke Standard.

They were carrying the cutest little animal that you ever saw. He was just a *mop* of silvery wool, with an enormous gold medallion around his neck. I had no idea that he was Ambassador Kronto. I absolutely had no frame of reference. I have studied Alien Physiology and there was *nothing* like Ambassador Kronto on any of the tapes that *I* recall.

Besides, even if I *had* known, I would have done the same thing. Wouldn't you? The poor little thing was suffering. He had a sore paw.

I just can't bear to see animals suffer. I've always been that way, ever since I was a little girl. Once when I was eleven I—

* * *

DEPUTY SERVO: *You were telling us about Ambassador Kronto.*

He looked a lot like a long-haired kangaroo. I don't suppose you know what a kangaroo looks like. The ambassador was sitting on his haunches. He raised one of his front paws to me; it was almost like he was greeting me. That's when I noticed how swollen it was. The other paw looked normal. That is, I suppose it was normal, but the paw he raised—it was his right paw—was in awful shape. It hurt me to look at it.

He didn't whimper at all, not a sound. Well, I *had* to do something didn't I? So, I sprayed his paw with Edemalyse.

How was I supposed to know that the people of Hyades II are telepaths? I mean, it is a ridiculous assumption to expect me to know that his right paw was an hypertrophied esper organ. If I'd known that, I'd never have tried to bring down the swelling.

It wasn't until much later that I found out Ambassador Kronto was on a tour of inspection of the Far Out. But he *was* in pain. They told me later he had a frightful headache.

DEPUTY SERVO: *What happened then?*

It was awful. He started shaking his little paw—the fat one—and he stared at it in the most *intense* way. Then his mouth turned down at the corners and his chin began to quiver. He seemed so distressed that I wasn't sure what to do. So I patted him on the head and said, "There, boy."

DEPUTY SERVO: *You patted the Ambassador on the head?*

I was trying to comfort him. I didn't know that he had a headache then. I didn't know either that it was considered obscene to touch the Ambassador's head.

After I patted him, his eyes got all squinty, and his chin worked up and down more than ever. Then—my heart bled—he took his paw, the one that wasn't swollen, and he rubbed the top of his head in the most pitiful way.

His little paws are short and he had to tuck his head down so he could reach it. It would make you weep to see it.

That's when I put him in the telescanner.

I punched the signal for Dr. Brian-Scott on board the Outpost. I knew I wasn't supposed to use the scanner for animals (I'm not supposed to treat animals at all), but it seemed like an emergency.

Dr. Brian-Scott's face came on the viewer and he said, "What have you got, Terra?"

And I said, "I know it's against all the rules, but please take a look at this little fellow."

Well, it was obvious that Dr. Brian-Scott had never seen anyone from Hyades II either, because when he saw him he said, "Isn't he cute? Turn on the scanner, Terra. I'll see what I can do."

So I turned it on. Then, in about twenty seconds, all the screens went blank. There sat the Ambassador, but with the screens blank, there wasn't anything more to do, so I gave him back to the Far Outs.

Well, you never heard such a commotion. All the Far Outs got these awful expressions on their faces, and they had the most unpleasant curve to their noseflaps.

Then they called the police and I was brought here. So, obviously that ridiculous charge of Mind Switch is untrue. All I did was spray the Ambassador's paw and pat his head.

DEPUTY SERVO: *Are you aware that Ambassador Kronto's mind now resides in the body of Dr. Brian-Scott?*

What?

What about Dr. Brian-Scott? Where is *his* mind? Where *is* it?

DEPUTY SERVO: *Dr. Brian-Scott's mind is now in the much abused body of Ambassador Kronto.*

My beloved? In there? Oh. Oh, no. Oh, no it really can't be so. Tell me it isn't so.

DEPUTY SERVO: *It is so. Is there any further testimony that you wish to give at this time?*

* * *

I think I'd better have a lawyer now.

DEPUTY SERVO: *Explain the term, please.*

Lawyer, advocate, counselor. Attorney, solicitor, barrister. Somebody to *help* me.

DEPUTY SERVO: *The terms do not scan. Somebody-to-help-me scans. Mind Switch is a capital offense. Are you requesting a priest?*

I want to see a lawyer. I want to see the Sol Ambassador. . . . I want to go home.

Terra stared bleakly around the cell. It was the color of old aluminum, and perfectly round. The ceiling was high—at least three meters above the floor—and as she looked up at it, she understood perfectly what all the old books and tapes meant: She was in the can, and it was awful.

She had read about prisons; she had seen portrayals of them on 3V, but all that was a house of a different color, she thought. This was real. It had been bad enough at the Pleiades Floatel, but that had been a room, not a cell, and she hadn't been alone. Since they had brought her here, she had not seen a single being. The deputy servo had been her only company and even it was too busy to come around much.

She leaned back on her bed which had been designed for Hyadeans rather than humans, and laid her head on the flap rest. There was absolutely nothing to do. She had nothing to read and the deputy servo wouldn't even let her have a notebook.

Terra looked up at the single narrow window. It was too high for her to see through. And the fact that it was there, that it was tantalizing her with its hidden view, was more than she could bear, and suddenly the tears came. She wiped them away with the back of her hand. "Stop it," she whispered. Somebody would come. Hadn't the servo notified the Sol Embassy for her? The Ambassador would probably be along any minute. The thing was to keep calm until he got here.

It occurred to her then that the Ambassador might notify her mother as a matter of policy. It was an awful thought. She gnawed a nail and wondered if her mother would believe that she had been seeing a patient when the cell door clanged shut and accidentally locked her in. A tragic look crept over her face; there were some things even a mother couldn't believe.

She jumped up when the door opened, but it was only the deputy servo.

It rolled in and said, "You have a letter." Its chest darkened and the letter began to scroll across it.

> Sol Embassy
> Central Hive
> Hyades IV 875745333 Hyades
> August 16
>
>
> Terra Tarkington
> Central Hive Incarceratum
> Hyades IV 876756333 Hyades
>
> Dear Miss Tarkington:
>
> Ambassador Blasingame has asked me to answer your letter. The Ambassador has also requested that I bring to your attention several things. Perhaps you are not aware of the delicate interstellar politics that are at stake in this matter.
>
> Ambassador Kronto is the envoy of an emerging planet. Their ways are not our ways, Miss Tarkington. The people of Hyades II are warlike. As such, they must be treated with utmost diplomacy until they mature enough to learn that finesse is the better part of aggression.
>
> It would seem that you, Miss Tarkington, have created an interstellar incident.
>
> Although Ambassador Blasingame is sympathetic to your plight, he regrets that there is very little he can do to help you. Any intervention on his part would be interpreted as an affront to the people of Hyades II.
>
> As to your request for defense council, it is obvious that you have little knowledge of the laws of the Hyadean Alliance. In a capital case, the Alliance brings all its forces to bear upon the defendant, while the defendant stands alone. If the defendant can convince the triumvirate of his or her innocence, all is well. If not . . .

I'm terribly sorry, Miss Tarkington.
With regrets, I remain . . .

> *Sincerely yours,*
> *Layton Chung, Embassy Aide*

Terra stared at it in disbelief. It couldn't be true.

The deputy servo restored its chest to its usual opaque gray and said, "It is time now for your recreation. Would you like to go for a walk?" It extended a portion of its squat body. The extension gave a mechanical cough and began to whirr, and Terra saw in horror that it was a treadmill.

"No," she wailed.

"I am programmed to see that you have recreation," said the servo. "We could play chess. I have a master rating, but I could arrange to lose if that would please you."

"I don't want to play chess."

"You have to have recreation," insisted the servo. "I know other games. We could play Hangman. Or would that be in poor taste?"

"Please. Go away."

"Calisthenics?"

She shook her head violently. "Just get me a notebook. And then go away."

"That would be against the rules. Notebooks aren't allowed."

A thought came to her. "I need a notebook. For my recreation."

The servo was on the horns of a dilemma: recreation was compulsory; notebooks were not allowed. It whirred its treadmill gears and blinked its chest screen off and on in a distracted way. "Notebooks aren't allowed," it repeated. "You must have recreation now."

"That's right," said Terra. "And the notebook *is* recreation."

"The notebook equals recreation?" said the servo.

She nodded.

"If the notebook equals recreation"—the servo was thinking aloud now—"then the notebook is no longer a notebook." Looking immensely relieved, it clanked away and came back with a notebook which it formally handed to Terra. "Here is your recreation." Having discharged its obligation, it rolled away.

She held it for a moment before she opened it. At its whispered prompt, she began to speak in a low voice:

Dear Diary,

The tragic and heroic figures of Earth have always kept journals during their imprisonment, so I will too.

Future generations should know of the cruel fate of Terra Tarkington, unjustly accused, imprisoned, and separated from her lover who is shackled in the body of a silver kangaroo.

Poor, beautiful Dr. Brian-Scott. My spleen throbs with grief. If only I could go to him. If only I could get out of here. . . .

She shut the notebook suddenly and looked up at the narrow window. Why not? Why not try? She stared at the shelf over the bed. If she could balance on that she might just be able to reach the window.

Shucking off her shoes, she stood on the bed and grabbed the shelf. The bed's flap rest gave her just the boost she needed, and she was able to scramble up on the shelf.

The tricky part came next. The window was over a meter above the shelf, and to the left. Facing the rough wall, clinging to it as well as she could, she slid slowly upward until her hands found a grip on the right-hand side of the narrow windowsill.

The deputy servo's voice startled her horribly: "What are you doing?"

"Recreation," she said through clenched teeth. "Go away."

"Oh," said the servo.

Relieved, she heard it roll away. She leaned out and her fingers crept along the windowsill. Clinging to it, she swung toward the window. Only one foot was in contact with the shelf now.

The Hyades sunset shimmered through the window. Just below, she could see the grounds and the light fountain of the Sol Embassy . . . shimmering too. She stared at the window in dismay. Power mesh. She'd never get out.

And just as the thought came, the corner of the overburdened shelf gave way. . . .

Dear Diary,

Do you know what you get when you try to escape from a Hyadean incarceratum? Skinned knees. . . .

August 17
1400 hours

Dear Diary,

My trial begins tomorrow. The deputy servo tells me that Ambassador Kronto doesn't have to be there. He's holed up in the Sol Embassy next door. They're keeping him there because the facilities are better for his bodily needs.

I could see the embassy through the power mesh cell window. And if I had wings and were no wider than 5 microns, I'd be out of here in a flash.

The deputy servo tells me that Ambassador Kronto hasn't spoken a word since the Mind Switch. He says that's probably because the Ambassador didn't have any vocal cords in his own body and so doesn't know how to use them now.

Dr. Brian-Scott, my beloved, was brought down from the Outpost. He's being kept at the Hyades II Embassy, and I don't know where that is. Will he ever forgive me?

He probably wouldn't speak to me, even if he had vocal cords. Oh, Diary, I couldn't bear his silent scorn. I couldn't stand to see his whiskers twitch with contempt when he looked at me.

Better . . . death.

The prosecutor fixed Terra with a cold stare and curled his noseflap in the Hyadean Attitude of Disdain. Then turning to the triumvirate, he thrust his fingers into his scarlet vest of interest and said, "Let us consider the plight of the aggrieved Ambassador Kronto. He, on a goodwill mission to our planet, innocently arrives to inspect the Far Out MediStation, when he is wantonly attacked by this person." Here he thrust out his noseflap in Terra's direction.

"I did *not* attack him. You"—Terra twitched her nose back at the prosecutor—"are lying. I—"

"This person," interrupted the prosecutor, "did seize the Ambassador, whereupon she sprayed a dangerous chemical on his esper organ, thereby causing an immediate malfunction."

"It was for swelling. I thought he had swelling. I—"

"Overruled," chorused the three judges. "Overruled."

The prosecutor's noseflap vibrated with the Hyadean Attitude of Respectful Appreciation for Those in Authority. "Not content with the assault on Ambassador Kronto's esper organ, this person"—his noseflap flattened in disbelief—"maliciously and obscenely stroked the Ambassador's head, thus aggravating his headache and causing him no end of public shame. Knowing Ambassador Kronto to be at a serious disadvantage due to his crippled esper organ and his incapacitating headache, this person"—sneer—"thrust the helpless Ambassador into a dangerous machine.

"We can only guess what diabolical thoughts ran through her mind at that time, but one thing is certain: This"—twitch—"*person* was possessed by malice. . . . Malice that drove her to commit upon the vulnerable and injured Ambassador Kronto, *Mind Switch*."

August 20

LAST WILL AND TESTAMENT OF TERRA TARKINGTON

I being of sound mind, do hereby declare the following disposition of my belongings in expectation of my imminent, tragic, and unfair demise.

To my dearest friend and confidante, Carmelita O'Hare-Mbotu, I leave my nursing library, my new make-up set, my Hyadean snuggie, and all the rest of my clothes (except for my new green slither which I look especially good in, and which is to be my burial outfit.) These I leave to her on the condition that she never, ever join the Interstellar Nurses Corps and go among aliens where she will be accused and insulted and probably executed.

To my beloved mother, Gladiola Tarkington, I leave the proceeds of my insurance policy (payable upon my death), and my locket that Daddy gave me, and my journal which is to be published immediately to tell the peoples of Earth of the tragic demise of Terra Tarkington and the grossly unfair and horrendous events leading up to it.

To Dr. Brian-Scott, I leave my love, and my apologies for the fix he is in, and my surro-wool mittens to keep his little paws warm.

To all my other friends, I leave my love and kind thoughts, and my hope that they will remember the unfortunate Terra Tarkington.

Signed: Terra Tarkington
Witness: 0080924 Deputy Servo

Chapter 14

August 21
900 hours

Dear Diary,

I am to be executed at 600 hours tomorrow. This is really unbelievable. Somehow, I know that Fate will intervene in my darkest hour.

The deputy servo isn't as sure. What he said was, "Impossible."

The deputy servo also told me I have one last request. The last request doesn't include release.

Everybody from the ship has been trying to help, but they're not allowed to see me. The deputy servo says there isn't anything they can do.

Layton Chung, the Sol Embassy aide, came awhile ago though. It was an absolutely grotesque scene. He said he had come to give me comfort and then he read poetry to me! He said, ". . . any man's death diminishes me, because I am involved in mankind."

I was furious. If my death diminishes him, what does he think it does to me? I called the deputy servo and had him put out. He kept on reading as he left. ". . . never

117

send to know for whom the bell tolls." *When the door clanged shut, I could still hear him say, ". . . it tolls for thee-e-e."*

I hope no one else tries to comfort me.

I have decided on my last request. I want to see beautiful Dr. Brian-Scott one more time. I know he doesn't look like himself, but I've got to see him.

One more time, my beloved. Then—into the gaping jaws of death.

Light from somewhere down the hall cast the deputy servo's squat shadow into Terra's cell.

Gliding on fat wheels, the servo rolled up to the cell door. The lock clicked once and opened. "Your last request is here to see you."

Terra sat up and the narrow bunk that served as both bed and chair swayed with the motion. Outside, a small, fuzzy shadow appeared. A pause. Then it gave a little leap and she saw that it was attached to a gray-furred creature with a large medallion around his neck.

He fixed her with enormous yellow eyes. Then turning, he gave a long look toward the servo and hopped past it into the cell.

The cell door clicked shut again. Swiveling, the servo rolled away.

A horrible lump grew in Terra's throat. It was bad enough to know that your last human visitor was a silver kangaroo, but it was worse to know that the kangaroo was your beloved. "It can't really be you—can it?"

The little creature's head bobbed on its stubby neck; it was a nod.

She bit her lip and stared at the edge of the bunk and the rough brown fabric of its cover. She took careful note of each wrinkle in the cloth, each tiny peak and valley, because just then she couldn't meet his gaze, couldn't look into those yellow, windowed eyes again. "I'm sorry," she whispered.

A paw crept out and rested on her knee. It was a small paw, much smaller than her hand. Her fingers explored it tentatively. The fur curled in whorls of silver gray as soft as clouds and cobwebs. "I'm sorry," she said again.

Almost imperceptibly, the paw rose, patted gently, slipped inside her hand.

It was too much to bear. If he had hated her she could

have stood that, but it was just too much to know that he still loved her in spite of everything. She looked down at the silvery little paw nestled in her hand and saw it blur with the quick rush of tears.

The other paw reached out and brushed softly against her neck. Then dropping, it caressed her hand with a touch like silk.

Not able to look in his eyes, she stared down at the little paw. It was larger than the first, and in among the silver hairs were thin coiled tendrils. The esper organ. . . .

Her words tumbled out in a rush then, "I was so sure you could help me. I was so sure— I wasn't even thinking about what happened to you. And there you are— All over fur— And you can't even talk to me." She squeezed and patted his little paw as if it were her only link to hope. "What are we going to do? Whatever are we going to do now?"

He reached up and a silver paw brushed her lips as if to silence her.

She looked into his eyes then. Nocturnal eyes like yellow moons at twilight. Alien eyes. But inside something warm peeped out, warm and infinitely comforting.

The little paw moved. Terra stared as the tendrils opened. Then, before she could think about it, she began to fall.

She was caught in a thin, shimmering coil, a helix spinning her downward, inward, into a shadowy cavern—a cavern so vast she caught her breath.

It was enormous. So huge that she was lost inside it. She reached out, in despair for an anchor, but still she fell in the echoing emptiness.

"Where?" she cried. "Where?"

"Here. I'm here."

And suddenly she wasn't falling anymore. And she wasn't alone. He was there with her, reaching for her. Touching.

Something happened then that she knew she would never be able to describe: They merged.

They merged like drops of water, like smooth white cream. They flowed and merged into one being, one single, throbbing sensation. It was music, and vanilla, and warm water and rose petals. And it was so intimate, so delicious, that she—they—wanted to stay there forever.

It was altogether the nicest thing that had ever happened. But it didn't last.

They floated apart, and gradually Terra realized that she

was in the Ambassador's silvery kangaroo body and Brian-Scott was there too. —A way out, she thought with a sudden sharp intake of breath. It was a way to escape.

But suddenly she saw there wasn't room enough for both of them. Not enough room. Not enough air.

She was suffocating. She had to hurry, get out, while she could.

Brian-Scott slipped away. In horror, she realized he was moving toward her body. No, screamed the thought. You can't! They were going to come for her in the morning. They'd find him there instead. They'd kill him.

She clutched at him in a frantic struggle. Panicked, she felt him slide away. Then he was gone.

He was gone and it was her fault. She should have held on, should have, should have. . . .

She looked out of the creature's eyes and saw Brian-Scott hiding behind her own. She reached out, tried to speak, but though her throat worked, she made no sound. I've done it, she thought in despair. I really have committed Mind Switch.

She held up the swollen paw and the esper tendrils uncoiled.

He looked out of her eyes and shook his head.

Through alien eyes she saw her own tear-streaked face, tousled hair, skinned knees. What did he ever see in me? she thought.

Then he was using her voice, calling the servo: "Put him out. I don't want him here anymore."

Moments later she found herself locked in the deputy servo's grip and shoved inexorably toward the outside door.

The Incarceratum door clanged shut behind Terra and she was outdoors. Dismayed, she stared across the wide grounds stretching ahead and tried to think. Just one thing came to her: She had to throw herself on the mercy of Ambassador Kronto.

The decision made, she began to hop toward the Sol Embassy.

Hopping was a little like being on springs. It came to her that it might have been fun except for the seriousness of the occasion and the frightful headache she had. Every leap jarred her head—or rather the ambassador's head—into a lump of pain. And the ridiculous heavy medallion didn't help at all. It thudded against her chest with each bruising hop.

The moving lights of the Terran display shimmered on her fur and dazzled her eyes. Her head felt as if it would split.

The medallion— Maybe it was causing the headache. Terra looked down at her hairy belly and tried to visualize her internal structure. Extending her paws, she stared at her wooly little arms. She didn't know a thing about the Ambassador's anatomy, but it was obvious that there were bones inside all that silver fur.

Where there are bones, came the old SleepTeach lesson, *there are one or more spines*. That was it, then. The medallion was too heavy. It was putting traction on the cervical spine and irritating the nerves in the Ambassador's neck.

No wonder she had a headache.

She tried to pull the necklace off, but her arms were too short. Tugging at it with the stubby digits that oozed out of the paws she spun and danced in a vain attempt to dislodge the medallion. No use.

She could stand on her head, she thought. Let the medallion slip off by gravity.

Hoisting her haunches in the air, she wavered wildly for a moment and then tumbled head over heels. Out of control, she rolled down a slope toward the Terran light fountain and came to rest under a row of hairy hedge beasts who flinched at the intrusion.

It was a good plan, she thought. But it wasn't easy to stand on your head when your paws were too short to reach the ground.

Head throbbing, she tried to think. Then as inspiration struck, she began to dig in the soft soil. Planting a paw on either side of the hole, she lowered her head inside and kicked off with her hind feet. After some determined wiggling, the medallion fell off.

Terra felt her fur for pockets or other suitable apertures. Finding none, she slid the medallion into the hole, buried it, and began to hop toward the Sol Embassy once more.

Nobody seemed to notice her. Terra supposed that was because they were used to seeing all kinds in embassies. She punched the info button, located the guest suite, and went up. Already her headache was beginning to fade.

Outside Ambassador Kronto's room, she heard voices. One of them was the unmistakable voice of Dr. Brian-Scott. The other one was female—and it was giggling.

Stubby little digits slid out of her paw and closed on the door catch. She pushed and the door slid open without a sound.

She stepped inside and froze. There was the Ambassador, wearing Dr. Brian-Scott's body, whispering lewd suggestions into the human girl's ear.

He'd known how to use those vocal cords all along, she thought in shock. And from the looks of things, that wasn't the only part of Dr. Brian-Scott that the Ambassador knew how to use.

Stiff with indignation, Terra hopped into the room.

The girl saw her first. She gave a little breathy shriek and ran out trailing her clothes behind her.

The Ambassador looked sheepish.

Terra held up her paw—the one with the esper organ—and tried to talk through it, but Brian-Scott's body just didn't have the apparatus to receive.

Holding her esper paw like a talisman, Terra hopped closer. She wasn't sure how this mindmerge worked, but in the absence of electrical amplification, it seemed necessary to be close. Waggling her paw before the Ambassador's startled gaze, Terra stared into his eyes.

. . . and they fell in together. . . .

It was the cavern again, but unbelievably different. She had never come that close to an alien mind before.

It had tendrils—dreadful, writhing things that coiled around her mind. And they sucked. . . .

She felt herself turn inside out. For a hideous moment, each thought, each hidden, private thought, drained into an awful, sucking maw. And then the feedback came. . . .

It washed in like an alien flood and threatened to drown her. Whirling in its vortex, she snatched at the single plank that could keep her afloat: her anger. "You!" she shrieked. "You ought to be ashamed."

For a long moment, Terra fixed her gaze on the bars of her cell and shuddered at the memory. Then bending over her notebook again, she continued her entry:

> . . . Dear Diary, you can't imagine how awful it is to have your mind sucked. You really can't.
>
> Anyway, it was all over then. The Ambassador knew all about me—about how I am basically good and kind and well-intentioned. And about how I only wanted to help his swollen paw. And how I had cured his headache. And I knew all about him. About how when he

122

switched with Dr. Brian-Scott he could have switched back easily, but it was the first time he had been without a headache in years. About how it was his first real vacation in ages. And how he had grown to simply love being in Dr. Brian-Scott's body. And how he used it in a most immoral fashion. And how he liked things exactly as they were now.

Well, I was furious. I made little tendrils with my mind and I grabbed hold of the Ambassador and I pinched. I told him what I thought of him until he cringed: "How would you like to be awaiting execution knowing that you were innocent and wronged?"

I pinched harder. "Aren't you ashamed, Ambassador? Aren't you? I even cured your headache and that's the thanks I get. You are a low, unprincipled body snatcher. A murderer! A thief. . . ."

It worked.

The Ambassador was actually ashamed of himself.

He said since I had cured his headache, he'd agree to switch us all back on one condition, so he zapped back into his kangaroo body, and I slid into Dr. Brian-Scott's—which was a very weird sensation—and we went back to the prison.

In the cell, Ambassador Kronto held up his paw and Dr. Brian-Scott and the Ambassador and I jostled around together for a moment and then we fell back into our proper bodies.

As I write this, Dr. Brian-Scott and the Ambassador have gone off to effect my release. So there's nothing more to tell you, Diary.

Except for one thing—the condition the Ambassador insisted on: He wants to switch again sometime. He liked it.

If we do, that means that Dr. Brian-Scott and I will get to mindmerge again.

And I don't think I'd mind that at all. . . .

Zeus the Zapper seemed almost affable today. The scarf at his neck was a benign baby blue and the lion roar was silent. "Well?"

"It's definite, sir," said Cuthbert. "Ambassador Kronto learned that Tarkington is The Finger."

A smile of satisfaction twisted across The Zapper's face. "Finally learning your trade, Cuthbert?"

A smile? Cuthbert blinked. If there was a saint for indentured spies, then surely he looked down on him now. "Yes, sir."

"Go on, go on."

Drawing courage, Cuthbert said, "Kronto entered her mind, sir. Though she *is* The Finger, she has no awareness of it. He couldn't read her conditioning, though. It's too deeply buried in her psyche."

A shadow crept into The Zapper's eyes. "And what are you going to do about *that*, Cuthbert?"

"According to the Ambassador, only The Trigger can trigger it, sir."

The shadow deepened, turning The Zapper's eyes into twin black pits. "Are you trying to tell me that you've been outsmarted by a bedpan carrier and a reptile still wet behind the earholes?"

"No, sir. I'm not, sir." If there *was* a saint for indentured spies, he was obviously not saintly enough to endure The Zapper's presence for long. The worst was yet to come: "Uh, sir, Ambassador Kronto has rendered an additional bill—"

"He has done *what*?"

"—for hazardous duty pay, sir. He complained that Tarkington burned out one of his preconceived-thought-module baffles. He said we ought to be glad he had a spare ready. Otherwise, she could have read *his* mind. Also, Ambassador Kronto feels that enduring the teletape machine and being trapped in Dr. Brian-Scott's body entitles him to extra wages. It seemed to me that he had a point, and—"

The Zapper's lips twisted frightfully over his clamped teeth. "Extra wages? You authorized *extra wages*?" His middle arm jiggled ominously.

Cuthbert stared transfixed at its rotating corkscrew and willed himself to go limp as Zeus the Zapper raised his left arm—the one that attracts—with horrid and deliberate speed.

Gimbel was horribly shaken. The Zapper's corkscrew had come too close to his casing for comfort. Another millimeter and he might have been punctured and infected by vile and hideous bacilli. Even now he could be festering.

To calm his nerves, he bathed them with a generous squirt of alcohol. It was all the idiot peripheral's fault, he thought darkly.

It was time to contact the KBG again, time to soften them up for his ultimate ploy.

Glowing faintly, too faintly for the Cuthbert peripheral or The Zapper to notice, Gimbel began to send his message to Diderot's wrist reader:

. . . *This is Gimbel . . . GIA. . . . It is known that Tarkington is The Finger. . . .*

Zeus the Zapper stared at the hapless Cuthbert, whom he had suspended for the greater part of an hour from a hook in the ceiling. "*Now*, Cuthbert—" he began, but the beeper signaling an incoming message interrupted his plans for further discipline. He plugged the audio jack into his left temple and listened.

". . . There is-s-s new information. . . ."

Still eyeballing Cuthbert, the Zapper covered his mouth with his left clamp and lowered his voice. "Is this the turncoat KBG reptile?"

A pause. ". . . It is-s-s." Another pause. "Diderot has-s-s contacted S-S-SEPTUM. They are trans-s-sfering The Finger again. She will be s-s-safe for a time, but there is-s-s a way. . . ."

The Zapper's left clamp ticked against his teeth as he listened. Then, as the message from Fendeqot terminated, he reached up, and plucked Cuthbert loose from his suspensions. Plunking him onto the floor with a bone-jarring thud, he said, "You're off the hook this time, Cuthbert. But don't think you can be cocky about it. You . . . are going to arrange for the kidnapping of Tarkington." As The Zapper outlined the plan, he raised and lowered his left arm—the better to ensure the little spy's attention. He finished with an awe-inspiring hundred-decibel bellow: "*Do you read me?*"

"Yes, sir!" said Cuthbert.

"Then you get your bunny *hopping!*"

And aided by The Zapper's repellent right arm and an especially resonant lion roar, Cuthbert scampered hastily away.

"Transferred again?" Brian-Scott looked at Terra in disbelief. "You just got back."

She nodded. "But it's just for a few weeks."

Shadows moved across his eyes as the satellite's observation port wheeled and the yellow rings of Nath IV slid away leaving only starlight shining into the room. "I don't know, Terra. It seems like every time you leave, you get into trouble."

She nodded. "It's been weird." Then a misty look came into her eyes as she remembered the mindmerge. "But it hasn't been all bad, has it?" How dark his eyes looked now, she thought. Dark windows that she had crept into once.

Remembering too, he caught her chin in his fingertips and brushed her lips with a kiss. Then he shook his head in wonder. "Terra, Terra . . . prison and a death sentence, and you remember only the good part."

Her eyes widened. "How could I forget that? I was so scared. I was about to drown in the depths of depression and you rescued me from it in the neck of time. It was beautiful. When I knew that you loved me for my mind, I thought I could bear anything."

A smile, a completely wonderful smile, crossed his lips and he leaned toward her again. It was incredible how he always wanted to kiss her when she was having her most serious thoughts. This time the kiss was lingering and altogether engrossing. So engrossing that it banished even deep thoughts for a while.

"I'm worried about you, Terra," he said at last. "Don't go."

And at that moment, she didn't want to at all. She brushed a thick lock of his hair back from his brow. It *was* a noble brow. "I'll be all right," she said, as if she tried to convince herself as well as him. "Besides, it's a real opportunity. I'll come back a specialist." She shook her head in wonder. "You know, I can hardly believe they picked me. It's almost as if someone was taking a special interest in me and directing my every move."

He didn't speak for a moment. Then he said, "I'm going to miss you."

"Me, too. But it won't be for long. And just think, when I come back, I'll be able to liberate all those poor souls clutched in the depths of mental aberration." She blinked at the thought. "It has to be fate. I think I was meant to be a Mental Care nurse." She leaned her head on his shoulder. "Besides, I have to think of the pay differential."

His smile crinkled the corners of his eyes. "So you do." Then it faded. "I can't believe you'll be gone in the morning."

"But we've got till then." She looked up at him and saw her smile reflected in his eyes.

He reached into a pocket, pulled out a tiny music cube, and switched it on.

"That's beautiful," said Terra. "I love classical music."

Then he stood and took her hand and they began to dance as the slow rhythms of "Star Dust" filled a dark bubble of space lighted only with the firefly glow of a thousand tiny alien suns.

Cuthbert Cuthbert's belly was slipping again. No matter what he did, it would not stay in place for more than a few minutes at a time. He hated the belly. It was heavy. Its straps cut into his shoulders and the jiggling ride across the lava beds caused the lower part of the contraption to pinch most cruelly.

If he dared, he would have flung it into the nearest fumarole, but without it, without the air of opulence it was designed to convey, he could never get the ear of the HoHahn of Baguerife. To the HoHahns of the volcanic midsection of Hyades IV, thin was not in. In this hostile land where only the rich and protected could afford the luxury of eating every day, corpulence was a symbol of affluence.

The cooperation of the HoHahn was essential. The plan was to have him feign illness. After he was admitted to MegaMed Center it would be easy for him to kidnap Tarkington. The HoHahns were a law unto themselves. No one could follow her here. No one would know of The Finger's covert transfer to the GIA.

To insure the HoHahn's help, Cuthbert had custody of a sizable sum of money strapped to his belly. It made him nervous. But it made him even more nervous to think that the plan might fail. The Zapper had made it very clear that it was in his best interest to succeed.

It occurred to Cuthbert that he might put the money to another use: If the Hohahn could kidnap Tarkington, might not the Hohahn be persuaded, for a fee, to kidnap him as well and hide him away where The Zapper would never find him? After all, he was in disguise. . . .

The thought faded. As long as he wore the collar of indenture, The Zapper would find him, and when he did— He shuddered at the vision and shook his head. No. The thing was to pull it off, do his job, see that the HoHahn did his. His future, if he had a future, depended on it.

Cuthbert had no way of knowing that even as he approached Baguerife, a package from the KBG was on its way to the HoHahn by another route—a package carefully prepared by Dieter Diderot.

But Gimbel knew. Gimbel, nestled with Aleph and Beth in a cunning aperture in Cuthbert's massive belly, knew that the package contained a small icon purported to be recently excavated from the digs of Hahoorihpuhr. It was, after all, Gimbel's idea. It was Gimbel who had persuaded Diderot to design the counterfeit relic of the Hyadean goddess H'yo-HahKo in the likeness of Terra Tarkington.

But even Gimbel did not know that the icon was treated with a chemical that would convert the HoHahn's feigned illness into a real one.

Chapter 15

Somewhere in Baguerife
Hyades IV
Sept. 15

To Whom It May Concern:

Help! I, Terra Tarkington, R.N., of the Interstellar Nurses Corps, am being held against my will in the House-of-Many-Women by the HoHahn of Baguerife.

If you have any compassion in your soul, you will rescue me at once before the HoHahn makes me his forty-seventh concubeing. There isn't much time—to a human, a Hyadean's embrace is death.

It isn't my fault that I am here. I was abducted. I weep, I sigh, I rail against my fate, but the HoHahn of Baguerife turns a deaf ear (to coin a phrase) on my pleas. And if you could see the HoHahn, you would realize why I am so upset. In the face, he looks like any Hyadean IV—humanoid, with a crease instead of a nose—but he is rotund. A rounder creature I have never seen.

I don't want to be a concubeing. All I wanted to be was an I.M.C.U. nurse.

Dr. Brian-Scott (who is my beloved) tried to talk me

out of it, but I thought it would be a good thing. I had my career to think of. And also I.M.C.U. nurses get a pay differential, which I can use, let me tell you.

First I had to go to I.M.C.U. class, which meant leaving Satellite Hospital Outpost for a while. After a tearful goodbye, I left my beloved and took the shuttle to the Hyades IV MegaMed Center.

Well, you might know that I was the only human in the class. But hasn't that been the story ever since I joined the Corps and came to the Bull Run?

I began to regret my decision almost at once. You'd think Intensive Mental Care Unit nursing would be a cerebral activity, wouldn't you? Well, you would think wrong. I have never worked so hard in my life.

When I got to MegaMed, this testy Hyadean IV female in the front office looked down her crease at me and told me to go to Level Seventeen. That was easier said than done. When I got there, I was stopped by an air lock. Level Seventeen has a methane atmosphere. I looked through the ports and there were a bunch of bladders with flagellae floating around. I couldn't tell if they were patients or staff.

By the time I got to the right place, Level Seventy, and checked in, I had missed the orientation lecture. Everybody was already lined up for equipment.

I sandwiched in line between a girl from Hyades IV and a macromouth from Nath III who waggled his olfacs in my direction and remarked how "close" the air suddenly seemed in the room. Well, you talk about self-conscious. And I had just bathed too.

I couldn't wait to get away from him, but the line just dawdled and dawdled. Finally I got to the end, shoved my I.D. into the servo, and got my beads-of-light and my loincloth (one size fits all). Then we all went to change and afterwards we gathered in a big mirrored room.

You would be absolutely amazed at where and how some beings wear their loincloths. Absolutely amazed. Most of the class were Hyadeans who are shaped more or less like humans, but the ones from Nath III—well, I never dreamed that their olfacs had that purpose.

I had on my loincloth and my beads-of-light and nothing else. The beads weren't activated yet.

Then the instructor came in. She was from Hyades

IV and she was wearing an acid-green loincloth that didn't do a thing for her skin. She waggled her noseflap in greeting and then we got down to work.

You don't know what exhausted is until you train for I.M.C.U. nursing. Every muscle in my body throbbed. Mental Care technique is especially stylized, and I was at an awful disadvantage. Since the modality was invented by Dr. HodelHok who is from Hyades IV, it was not designed for the human body. Humans bend differently than Dr. HodelHok.

First, we had to stand on our left foot (or pod, as the case may be) with the right leg (or legs) bent and the knee stuck out at right angles to the body. Then we had to raise whatever arms we had over our head and touch the back of the hands together. This was the therapeutic position, which is a way of getting the patient's attention. We had to watch ourselves in the mirrors while we did this so that we would get it right.

Some of the class looked really obscene. I got a look at the macromouth from Nath III and I will tell you something—if I ever have a mental breakdown, I wouldn't want him to treat me for fear of worsening my condition.

After we had mastered the therapeutic position, we had to learn the first Variation (Reorganization of Energies). There are twelve Variations altogether and each is harder to do than the last. (Actually there are sub-Variations too, but most of those are used for veterinary patients.) In Variation One, you tap the back of your hands (or whatever) together—one, two—and then you flup. Flupping is easy for the Hyadeans. They just extend their creases and then snap them shut. But for me, the accepted technique was to stick my upper lip out until it touched the end of my nose and then make a sort of plopping sound and drop my lower lip open. And if that sounds easy, well you just try it sometime.

The instructor was a slave driver. If I live to be two hundred, I will never forget her voice (she whined through her flap) saying, "One, two—flup, flup. One, two—flup, flup."

Anyway, when we perfected the twelve Variations, we were allowed to activate our beads-of-light. The beads are tuned to each Variation. The wavelengths of each color combination, combined with the varying flashes per micro-second, effect the necessary electrical changes in the brain, while the body movements act as a hypnotic focus and enhance the beads-of-light. Or, as Dr. HodelHok teaches: "HoDok HahHahn. HahHahnah Do'Hok." Only I don't know how to translate that.

There we were, our beads-of-light reflecting like old neon in the mirrors, our loincloths swaying gently. It was beautiful. I saw myself as my patients would see me—an object of therapeutic serenity, dedicated to the exorcism of mental disharmony.

But that wasn't the way the HoHahn of Baguerife saw me at all.

It was my first day in Intensive Mental Care on MegaMed, and I was plenty anxious, let me tell you. We were getting a new patient—a Very Important Being— with an admitting diagnosis of acute euphoria.

The I.M.C.U. supervisor, Mrs. Qotefleer, who is an Aldeberan, was in a state. She hissed and lashed her tail around (the way they do when they're excited) and drizzled her "ss" all over the place. "Miss-s-s Tarkington. It is-s-s mos-s-st careful you mus-s-st be. This-s-s is-s-s a mos-s-st important patient. He is-s-s one of the leaders of the emerging nation of Harhoh, and he is-s-s very rich."

They wheeled the HoHan into the unit. He was so enormous he barely got through the door. He waggled his crease at me in a suggestive way and then he giggled and pointed at my loincloth.

I would have known without being told that the HoHahn was a VIB because his chest was a mass of medals. I said, "Good morning, Your HoHahn. I'm Terra Tarkington and I'm going to be your nurse."

Well, for some reason that caused the HoHahn to laugh all the harder. His belly jiggled and set all his medals—kilos of them—to clinking. We undressed him, which was like skinning a robot, and put him to bed.

That gave the HoHahn an intensified case of the giggles, which led to absolutely unrestrained mirth. His face was wreathed with laugh lines. Suddenly he flared his flap and reached for my beads-of-light. "My little fire-flit," he said and giggled.

I whirled away and came back in the therapeutic position.

Well, that served to inflame the HoHahn even more. He leaped out of the bed and chased me around the room.

It was awful. Here was my patient, suffering from the most acute case of euphoria I have ever seen, running after me and snatching at my loincloth. It was obvious that he had lost all touch with reality.

It was then that Mrs. Qotefleer, my supervisor, came into the room. She called for help and had the HoHahn restrained. Since it was such an unusual case, she performed the therapy herself while I dimmed the lights and watched.

It was a moving experience—Mrs. Qotefleer's beads-of-light reflecting against her blue scales, the look of amazement crossing the HoHahn's face. I could tell that the treatment was working because the HoHahn stopped giggling. After a while, he looked really stern.

He was discharged the next day. We waved goodbye to him as he was wheeled down the hall. I thought that was the end of it, but a little while later, the HoHahn showed up again with a dozen of his aides.

He marched up to Mrs. Qotefleer with all his medals clanking and one of his aides whispered something to her.

Mrs. Qotefleer blanched (I thought she would faint, she was such a pale blue) and threw her arms around me. "S-s-stop! You can't have her."

Then, one of the aides grabbed my arm. "This one told His HoHahn that she was his nurse. We have paid for her." He waggled something under Mrs. Qotefleer's snout.

It was a receipt for the HoHahn's hospital bill.

But actually that was a transparent subterfuge. The HoHahn knew he hadn't bought me. He wanted me because I resembled a creature straight out of Hyadean mythology—the fabulous H'yo-HahKo, the fire-flit, who, if captured, has the power to confer great wealth. The HoHahn thought that if I were his concubeing, I would be working for him.

Well, I raged and cried and stamped my feet, but it didn't do any good. The HoHahn's henchmen pried me loose from Mrs. Qotefleer and dragged me away. And that's the last I saw of MegaMed Center.

They hauled me onto the HoHahn's sedan hover and took me to Baguerife. They put me in the House-of-Many-Women, which is full of Hyadeans of the H'yoKdot sect who don't speak Standard. The rest are big fat Yodeltoks who are hostile and who eat grease.

No one has stepped forth to help me except the HoHahn's little house servo who promised to deliver this letter to the outside world. And the house servo, who is loyal to the HoHahn, wouldn't have done that except that it can't read. It thinks this letter is a recipe for ceremonial punch.

The HoHahn tells me that he will take me as his concubeing by tomorrow noon. His euphoria has returned and he is quite mad.

I am doomed. The Hyadean embrace means death. And if the HoHahn were to touch me, I would die on the spot anyway.

It is all too ghastly to contemplate. If I ever get out of this mess, I swear I will never leave the side of my beloved again.

So please, please, To Whom It May Concern, come and free me from the House-of-Many-Women. I offer you my eternal gratitude and my I.M.C.U. differential as a reward.

Yours in fearful dread,
Terra Tarkington

Terra's fitful sleep was interrupted by a thin nasal whine that seemed to come from somewhere just above and behind her left ear. Half asleep, she looked up at what seemed to be a long sausage emerging from a flap of dough. As she stared, the end of the sausage flared open and the whine grew louder.

She struggled up to a sitting position and sucked in her breath. She was surrounded. A dozen Hyadean women dressed in greasy beads and ribbons pressed around her bed. She blinked and shrank back against the flap rest. They were Yodeltoks, and the look in their eyes and the curve of their nose creases was far from affable.

The noise from the sausage grew and she realized it was a horn of some sort emerging from under the noseflap of one of the women. Glistening with lubricating grease at every joint, it slid menacingly toward the end of her nose and began to wail. She shrank back. The horn seemed to be a signal. Before the last bleat died away, the door opened and three more Yodeltok women came into the room. "What is going on," she whispered.

No one answered. They don't understand me, she thought. But then she realized in horror that she understood them perfectly well: They were communicating in the universal language of animosity.

Suddenly a familiar voice spoke in Standard: "Greetings on your day of concubinity." The little house servo, crushed between two of the women, peered out at Terra from under the massive armpit of the Yodeltok flutist who had launched into a tune better suited for the death and burial of heavy equipment.

Her day of concubinity. Instead of beautiful Dr. Brian-Scott, she was getting the HoHahn of Baguerife. It wasn't possible, she thought in despair. And it wasn't fair. It wasn't fair to be condemned to the House-of-Many-Women, there to live among hostile Yodeltok women who looked down their noseflaps at her.

Terra's frantic gaze rested uneasily on the largest of an especially large group of women. This one's nose crease had taken a decidedly unpleasant set. "What's happening?" she asked the servo in a low voice.

"The-House-of-Many-Woman," said the servo, "is a house divided. The women, H'yoKdot, claim that you belong to the sect of the women, Yodeltok. They have sent out the word to the League-of-Many-Women, National Association, that an exceptionally ill-favored Yodeltok is to be taken in concubinage here today. The Yodeltoks are understandably upset over the slander that you are one of them.

"I'm sure you can appreciate their dismay," continued the servo. "It is a matter of pride. Since it is too late to counter the rumor, their only hope is to ensure that you look as presentable as possible. However, since the ceremony is to be covered by the news media for all to see, Marmo the Massive, Second-Exalted-Wife of the Hohahn, has grave doubts that they can succeed."

Terra stared at the largest of the women who was twisting her flap in a most unsettling way. Somehow she knew that had to be Marmo the Massive. "What are they going to do?" she whispered.

Before the little servo could answer, the woman next to Marmo the Massive seized Terra's arm and fingered her biceps. Stepping away, the woman raised her hands and made a circle roughly the diameter of Terra's upper arm—which was decidedly smaller than any other present. Rude laughter and ill-concealed flap-twitching followed.

Marmo the Massive leaned over the bed. Grasping Terra by the shoulders, she pulled her to a standing position and looked her up and down. Her disapproving gaze took in the meagerness of Terra's waist, the unsubstantial narrowness of her feet, the straightness of her toenails, and the absence of the approved number of chins. She raised a corner of her flap and sighed in an exasperated way. Excited discussion broke out among the assemblage.

"You are, of course, an embarrassment," said the servo.

Terra, still in the clutches of Marmo the Massive, could muster only a sickly smile in response. The Second-Exalted-Wife's noseflap was uncomfortably close to her face and gleamed with a coating of something dark and oily. From underneath the flap came a hot breath heavy with the fumes of Marmo the Massive's recent and greasy breakfast. Terra felt ill.

"The women are displeased about your proportions," said the servo. "But those are secondary to your extensive congenital defects."

Terra was outraged. "I don't *mean* to offend."

"It's all right," soothed the servo. "*I* don't mind. I have no circuitry for esthetics. I can appreciate your deviant appearance in only the most abstract of ways, therefore you don't offend *me*."

At this point, Marmo the Massive plucked Terra off the floor and hefted her as if she weighed nothing at all. More coarse laughter erupted.

"Put me down! Tell her to put me down," she said to the servo.

Before the servo could speak, Marmo the Massive dropped Terra to the floor with a thud as a vat of evil-smelling grease opened the door with its sensor and rolled into the room.

"What's that for?"

"For your hair and skin," said the servo. "What's left is for your breakfast. The women are afraid that nothing will disguise your offensive appearance, but they have to try."

"Mahah macah mahanna potah," said Marmo the Massive, pointing to Terra.

The smell of Marmo the Massive's breath and the odor emanating from the vat served to turn Terra's stomach upside down. "No," she said. "Never!"

As if sensing Terra's lack of enthusiasm, the women stopped laughing abruptly. A dozen pairs of eyes pinioned her; a dozen flaps curved dangerously; a dozen pairs of hands moved toward her.

"No, no. Make them stop." She stared wildly around for some way to escape, but several thousand kilos of Hyadean flesh separated her from the door. "Tell them 'no,'" she begged the servo. "Tell them I'll do anything. Tell them I'll— Tell them I'll swear to the reporters that I'm not a Yodeltok."

When the servo delivered the message, a new curve came over the flaps of the women. "Hyhah mohahnna ha *hah*?" demanded Marmo the Massive.

"What did she say?"

"She wants to know if you'll swear to tell the reporters that you are a pure-blooded H'yoKdot?" said the servo.

Terra eyed the vat of grease. "Anything—"

An excited conversation ensued between Marmo and the servo. "She wants to know if you'll tell the press that you are not only H'yoKdot, but that you are a sister to Hahnah-Hahk, First-Exalted-Wife of the HoHahn?"

"Yes, yes. Anything. Anything she likes."

When the servo conveyed the message, this time the laughter was congenial and culminated in a series of back slappings that nearly knocked Terra to the floor. A minute later, flaps quivering in delight, the women left, and Terra was alone with only the servo and the vat of grease for company.

"Thank goodness," said Terra, and collapsed on the bed.

"That was most clever of you," said the servo in admiration. "Not only did you spare the Yodeltok wives embarrassment, but you ensured your own position in The-House-of-Many-Women."

"I did?"

"It goes without saying," said the servo. "The H'yoKdot wives are the favorites of the HoHahn. By declaring yourself H'yoKdot, as the newest concubeing you will automatically be hahka-mahk."

"Hahka-mahk?"

The servo nodded. "Favorite of favorites. The concubeing sure to be first choice of the HoHahn. Hahka-mahk."

"That's what I was afraid you said," said Terra.

Clad only in a loincloth, Terra stared wildly at the apparition towering over her. Twice as tall as she was and many

136

times as wide, it flapped a cape encrusted with dirty jewels and grease-dark tassels in time to a flute accompaniment of doubtful musicality. On top, a grotesque bronze mask alternately leered and grimaced at every thump of the doleful drum and shakeskin ensemble that swayed behind it.

Terra took an involuntary step backward.

The malevolent mask grinned down. With a sharp hiss, the mouth sprang open. Blood-red smoke spewed out, trailing the scent of rancid oil.

At the signal, the music stopped abruptly. Under different circumstances, Terra would have given thanks, but just now the silence took on an ominous significance.

She held her breath, partly to ward off the evil smell, partly in trepidation.

As suddenly as it stopped, the drums began again: foom-pah, foom-pah, foom-pah. And the creature, with a convulsive shudder, began to shrink. In telescoping folds it lowered until the bronze face was eyeball to eyeball with Terra's.

The drums ceased.

"Your bridal gown," said a voice, and the robe splayed open to reveal the little servo underneath who balanced the heavy robe on telescoping rods extruded for the occasion. The mask, wobbling on a projection from the servo's head mechanism leered again.

"You!" said Terra.

"Yes," answered the servo. "Did you like my performance? I don't have natural rhythm, but I thought I did rather well."

Abandoning their drums and shakeskins, the ensemble of concubeings began to point at Terra. "H'yo pt'oh. Patok hok."

"What do they want?"

"Patok hok," said Marmo the Massive.

"They want you to dress for the ceremony," said the servo.

Terra stared at the smelly robe in disbelief. "In that?"

"Patok *hok*," repeated Marmo the Massive. Then plucking up the garment, she shook it at Terra.

Blinking at the cloud of dust that Marmo's ministrations had elicited from the bridal gown, Terra drew back.

"Hok. Patok *hok*!" From the tone in Marmo the Massive's voice and the curve of her noseflap, it was clear that there was no room for argument.

Terra squeezed her eyes shut and wrinkled her nose as the garment settled around her bare shoulders.

The ceremonial bridal robe had obviously been designed for a being of Marmo the Massive's proportions. It was cut very low in front in an effort to enhance the gargantuan cleavage of a grease-eating Hyadean; on Terra—as she learned from a quick, horrified gaze in the reflector—the effect was more explicit. "I can't wear this. I won't."

Her answer, or her appearance—Terra wasn't sure which—elicited great peals of laughter from the assemblage of concubeings.

"You have to," said the servo. "The HoHahn expects you to wear it. Remember, you will be Hahka-mahk."

At the appalling reminder of the HoHahn and his expectations, Terra shuddered. "Never."

The drums began to thump again, and the flute to yowl. "It's time," said the servo. Simultaneously, Marmo the Massive exerted not so gentle pressure to Terra's shoulders.

She dug in her heels. "No!"

At a nod from Marmo, two other women stationed themselves at Terra's elbows and grabbed hold.

"No, no, no . . ." Then, "Wait, wait, wait . . . At least let me cover up. Give me my beads-of-light," she begged.

Unaccustomed to such struggling from ordinarily eager concubeings-to-be, the women hesitated while the servo translated for Terra. Then at a distant and menacing bellow from the impatient HoHahn, one of the concubeings scurried up with the beads and flung them around Terra's neck.

And blinking mournful eyes and beads-of-light, Terra, swathed in yards of odoriferous bridal gown, was led to her expectant bridegroom.

"Do you take this concubeing for your lawful property?" asked the High Priest.

"Ho, ho, *ho*," said the HoHahn of Baguerife. His answer evoked a convulsive purple flash from the jewel he wore in his bellybutton.

"He said, 'yes,'" whispered the servo to Terra.

Eyes wide, she stared at the HoHahn. In honor of the occasion, he had attached a row of multi-colored stones to the edge of his nose crease, which he now waggled at her in a most suggestive way. This can't be happening, she thought in dismay. It couldn't be.

Taking her expression to be one of eagerness, the

HoHahn seized her hand in his bejeweled and alien one and exhaled a particularly horrific breath in her direction.

Terra squeezed her eyes shut, and tried to simultaneously shut off her sense of smell and her consciousness.

The High Priest, glistening both in gown and well-oiled skin, curved his flap in her direction. "Do you take the HoHahn as your lawful owner, forsaking all other claims and liens?"

"No! Tell him, 'no,'" said Terra.

The servo turned to the High Priest. "She says, 'ho, ho, *ho*.'"

"No, I don't. I didn't."

"Cleaving only to the HoHahn?" prompted the High Priest.

"No. I won't cleave. I won't."

"Ho, ho, *ho*," said the servo.

The High Priest beamed and flapped his flap. "I now pronouce you HoHahn and property until death, trade, or sale do you part. You may kiss the concubeing."

Terra's anguished shriek startled the HoHahn so that he caught his breath, causing his belly jewel to retract between two massive rolls of flesh.

"No, no. Wait. You've got to wait— Tell him to wait," she begged the servo.

Message conveyed, the servo turned to Terra. "He wants to know why?"

Inspiration sprang from direst necessity: "Tell him I'll dance for him first." Switching on her beads-of-light, Terra leaped into the HodelHok therapeutic position and began to sway.

She whirled into Variation Five—Rapport With a Violent. Praying for a miracle or at least a preternatural occurrence, she narrowed her eyes and watched the HoHahn for results.

Oily sweat beaded the HoHahn's crease. With a leer, he grabbed at her.

Gasping, she leaped away and spun into Variation Seven—Peace and Harmony—but with a subtle difference. What she was doing might not be altogether ethical, but this was self-defense, she told herself. Fingers lightly brushing her beads-of-light, she tuned them to a slightly different frequency.

The beads flashed hypnotically—and a doorway into the HoHahn's subconscious opened. The HoHahn's eyes glittered, and Terra knew he was ready to receive post-therapeutic suggestion. "Servo," she whispered. "Tell him that if he takes me as his concubeing, a powerful enemy will seek revenge."

The little servo translated.

The effect on the HoHahn was astonishing. Noseflap curving in delight, he began to laugh and then to howl with glee. "H'yo-Hahko! Little fire-flit!" This was followed by an excited monologue punctuated with great, shaking peals of laughter and excited flashings of the purple belly stone.

The servo bowed to Terra, and said in a respectful tone. "The HoHahn says you are very big magic. He is most certainly correct. How else would you know about the revenge?"

"What do you mean?"

The servo whispered in her ear, and as it did, horror tracked through her eyes. She had really done it now, she thought in despair. But, how was she supposed to know that the HoHahn of Baguerife had stolen his forty-sixth concubeing from the HoHahn of Renerade, who even now was sending a Ho'Henji brigade in order to wage war?

The HoHahn curled his nose flap and the row of colored stones dimpled into the crease. "H'yo-Hahko Nah Hahka-mahk. H'yo-Hahko yah Homah whoosh-whoosh."

"Oh, dear," said the servo. "That's bad news, I'm afraid."

"What? What is it?"

"Because of your talents, the HoHahn has declared you Nah Hahka-mahk."

Terra stared at the HoHahn, then back at the servo. "What does it mean?"

"It means that you are too valuable to be the first choice of the HoHahn. Instead, he is taking you to the whoosh-whoosh."

"The where?"

"The Sacred Volcano of BagHardad."

TRANSCRIPT OF THE PLEAS FOR LENIENCY BY THE CONDEMNED, TERRA TARKINGTON R.N., TO THE HIGH PRIESTS OF BAGUERIFE:

I am *not* a dirty infidel spy. It isn't true that I intended to subvert the Sacred Oracle. I was simply trying to help her sinus condition. And I think it's very unfair of you to threaten to throw me into the Sacred Volcano of BagHardad.

I never asked to be taken to the Sacred Volcano of BagHardad and apprenticed to the Oracle. I mean, I really didn't mind in view of the fact that it saved me from Hahka-makh, but it wasn't my idea; it was the HoHahn's. He thought that I, H'yo-Hahko, in tandem with the Oracle would make very big magic.

And that's another thing—I don't know if you people care, but I don't think you treat your Oracle very well. How would you like it if you never had a day off from the Temple?

She's really a very nice lady. When I first saw her leaning over her tripod, swaying back and forth and muttering, I thought she was a little strange. But you'd be strange too if you had to breathe volcanic fumes all the time.

The smoke was coming out of the floor from a little fumerole. She waved her arm and pointed to the smoke and said, "Sh'Bong." Well, I took a sniff and I'll tell you this, Sh'Bong smells sulphurous and awful. It's got to be deleterious to health. The Oracle's nose crease was stained brown with it, and she had a terrible post-nasal drip. Besides that, the fumes were making her drunk and giving her a miserable sinus headache.

I'm sure that if you'll reconsider, you'll realize that she is a better Oracle today because of what I did. And when you reconsider, you will realize that there isn't any reason to throw me into the Sacred Volcano of BagHardad.

I thank you.

EXCERPT FROM THE TARKINGTON PAPERS FOUND IN THE TEMPLE OF BAGUERIFE:

. . . and it's all desert around the temple. Little fissures let off noxious effluvia from the volcano and everything is dry and dusty. You can imagine what shape the Oracle's sinuses were in. So I made the Oracle a little mask to wear over her crease.

The improvement was amazing. Up to then, the poor thing was so giddy from the Sh'Bong that she wasn't making much sense at all.

All day long people would crowd into the temple to ask questions. She used to weave around on her tripod and give ridiculous answers like "The ides of Ho'kHanno—beware, beware." But I guess the crease-mask filtered out some of the volatile oils that were making her drunk.

She was so grateful. It would make your very heart leap for joy (to coin a phrase) to see her sober. She's really a very nice girl. She hates her job. She told me she'd rather do laundry than be an Oracle.

The priests didn't like it at all. They came in and one of them asked her what the sands augured for the Holy Coffers. Well, she looked him right in the eye (she has a steely gaze) and said, "The sands augur a vacation for the Oracle and they aren't going to augur anything else until she gets it."

They tried to get the oracle to take off her mask, but she wouldn't do it. She said it was the first time she'd had any relief in fourteen revolutions.

That's when they accused me of being a dirty infidel spy and condemned me to the volcano.

But I have reasoned with the High Priests and I am sure they will let me go.

> *The Temple of Baguerife*
> *Hyades IV*
> *Just before dawn, September 21*

To Whom It May Concern:

Help! I, Terra Tarkington, R.N., of the Interstellar Nurses Corps, am about to be thrown into the Volcano of BagHardad. They will come for me at dawn.

If you have any compassion in your soul, you will rescue me at once.

I am innocent. And if I ever get out of this, I will go back to the Bull Run to my beloved, beautiful Dr. Brian-Scott, and I will never complain again.

So please, please, To Whom It May Concern, come and free me from my awful fate. I offer you my eternal gratitude, my loincloth, and my beautiful beads-of-light.

> *Yours in dreadful fear,*
> *Terra Tarkington*

Chapter 16

EXCERPT FROM A LETTER TO CARMELITA
O'HARE-MBOTU, R.N., UNITED EARTH, SOL:

. . . *and when dawn came, these grim-looking priests took me out in the desert to the rim of the Volcano of BagHardad.*

It was fiery and awful and smelled of Sh'Bong. Lava roiled around inside and every now and then the volcano would rumble. Well, you talk about death yawning before you. I thought I was going to buy the bucket for sure.

Suddenly there was a commotion. I looked up and here came the Oracle striding across the desert like an avenging angel. She marched up to the priests and planted her crown on her head (which meant she was speaking ex tripod, and was therefore infallible) and said, "Let the girl go or else death, destruction, and clouds of crease-eaters will plague you."

The High Priests didn't like that at all. They huddled in a little clump and talked about it, and every now and then they'd peek over their shoulders at the Oracle and me. Finally one of them said, "Oracle, you have lost your powers."

She drew herself up and stared them down and said very slowly, "But can you be sure?" And then she winked at me.

Well, they let me go back to my beloved; and the Oracle came too, for her first vacation in fourteen revolutions.

The HoHahn of Baguerife was very put out about it. He said I belonged to him. He had a receipt. But the Oracle said not to worry about him.

His euphoria was permanently cured because she gave him a dose of Sh'Bong and, while his mind was altered, told him that she foresaw a grim future for him unless he behaved himself.

When we got out of the shuttle, Dr. Brian-Scott hugged me, and hugged the Oracle, and then hugged me again.

When we were alone at last, he was very subdued. He kept looking at me with a funny look and then he said, "I thought I'd lost you, Terra. I've been terribly depressed."

Well, what could I do, Carmie? I put on my loincloth and activated my beads-of-light.

When I assumed the therapeutic position, my beloved stared at me with rapt attention.

I turned on some music and then I began to alternate between Variation Nine (Rising Excitement and Pleasurable Tension) and Variation Eleven (Exultation and Bliss).

And in almost no time, Dr. Brian-Scott's depression had lifted.

Then the most amazing thing happened. He began going through the Variations with me. My beads-of-light flickered in lovely glints over my beloved as we moved in time to the music.

Do you know what he said then, Carmie? He said (I remember his every word), "Thank you for coming back to me, Terra."

Then he told me he'd been studying technique too while I was gone. He said he would teach me HodelHok's Variation Thirteen, which is very advanced and very good for the psyche.

> *Yours for mental health,*
> *Terra*

With a sidelong glance through veiled lids, Fendeqot scanned the room. When he was sure no one was watching, he opened the door to the closet and slipped inside. Claws clattering over the scentplant's nutrient pipe, he twisted the joint.

It held fast.

He twisted again, harder.

Nothing.

He brought his snout close to the pipe and stared. His pupils, adjusting to the gloom of the closet, dilated first to black slots, then to horrified squares. Someone had replaced the pipe. The elbow joint was solid now. He could see faint traces of the bond clinging to the slick surface.

The thought was blinding: He knew. Diderot knew.

Fendeqot raised his yellow eyes to the wall as if he could see through it, as if he could see the hated Diderot in the chamber beyond.

When he was seven, Fendeqot had seen a horror holo that he had never been able to forget. Even now, the thought of *The Egg Eater from Earth* set his scales on edge. The first glimpse of the villain mongoose with its foul growth of gray fur had made him coil his tail in dread. With growing horror, he had seen the vile alien choose his next victim: a slim, lovely young cobra, who naively slid out among the bushes for a breath of air. "Behind you! Mongoos-s-se!" he had hissed, but it was too late— He had not been able to watch the rest; he had squeezed both sets of eyelids tight to shut it out, but even so, the mongoose had lodged in his mind as a symbol of evil incarnate. Now he projected its despicable face on Diderot's.

Fendeqot stared at the wall; he could see it all: Diderot raising his mean little mongoose eyes to the glorious light of SEPTUM; Diderot twisting his narrow mongoose lips in deceit; Diderot spreading his vile mongoose nostrils to receive SEPTUM's scent.

Fendeqot's upper lip began to twitch. If Diderot knew, it was just a matter of time until he exposed him.

"Mongoos-s-se," he hissed under his breath. He meant it as an epithet, as a pejorative that would somehow diminish his enemy. Instead, it cloaked Diderot in an image so powerful that it endowed him with all the powers of evil. Involuntarily, Fendeqot's toe claws clenched at the thought. And as a chill shuddered through his belly, he suddenly realized he was afraid.

Clutching her pink shoulder bag, Mrs. Wiggs came out of the communications chamber. Diderot followed. He stared at Fendeqot narrowly for a long moment, and then without a word, stalked away.

"Are you all right?" Mrs. Wiggs thrust her ears toward the Aldeberan. "I don't believe I've ever seen your snout quite so pale, Mr. Fendeqot."

"Fine. Jus-s-st fine," he said, but in truth he felt quite wobbly and leaned back on his tail for support.

"Are you sure?"

He bobbed his snout in assent. He had to think, had to come up with a plan.

"Well," she said doubtfully. Then with a little twitch, she opened the door to the closet and turned the valve to the scentplant's nutrient solution. "Dinner's coming," she called out cheerfully. Then she said to Fendeqot, "I'm afraid the poor thing hasn't been getting enough to eat lately."

"Oh?" said Fendeqot. He felt quite ill.

"But everything's all right now," she went on. "Mr. Diderot was kind enough to tell me there was a leak, so I had the pipeline fixed."

"That's-s-s good," he said, wanting her to go away. He had to think, had to decide what to tell the GIA.

Mrs. Wiggs paused significantly at the door. "Coming now, Mr. Fendeqot?"

He stared at her.

"Regulations, you know."

"Of course-s-s," he said and followed her out of the office.

Outside, when he was sure she had gone, Fendeqot spread his claws over the stone entrance, pursed his snout, and whistled the entry code. The crater dropped away and deposited him back in KBG headquarters.

He hurried to the console. The inner room was dark, lighted only by the dim glow that served to comfort the scentplant in the night. The plant, absorbed with absorbing its dinner, and horribly startled when Fendeqot entered the room, puffed out a musky camouflage scent that mimicked a predatory biffid.

Closing his nostrils against the odor, Fendeqot took a long and ragged breath and made his connection.

Zeus the Zapper had been listening to a stirring rendition of Rigney's 19th, *Conan the Covert*, which was his favorite. It was the only music that The Zapper tolerated. He found its clashing dissonances in tune with his inner being, and in view of the fact that the music was emerging from his midsection, perhaps it was.

When the call came from Fendeqot, it shattered his mood.

"There is-s-s trouble."

The Zapper frowned and absently twiddled his dials, causing an ill-formed holograph of his mother to emerge from his thorax. "What kind of trouble?"

"Have you been eating your vegetables?" asked the holo. *"You need your vegetables."*

"KABBAGE was-s-s told of the Hohahn plot," said Fendeqot.

"KABBAGE!" thundered The Zapper.

"You don't need to raise your voice. There's nothing wrong with your mother's ears." The holo let out a gusty sigh. *"Nothing that a call from her son wouldn't cure . . ."*

"Your plan was-s-s s-s-sabotaged."

A GIA informant. One of his own. The Zapper narrowed his eyes as he listened to Fendeqot. Could he believe the reptile? But the cold stone forming in the pit of his silicon stomach told him he could. "Who? Who is the prissing turncoat?"

"S-s-sorry," said Fendeqot. "I don't have that information."

". . . so your poor old mother would know you were still alive—"

Who was it? Who would have dared? The thought when it came caused The Zapper's jaw to lock: *Cuthbert!*

"—but no. . . ." complained the holo.

No, he thought. It couldn't be Cuthbert. He wouldn't have the gumption.

Or would he?

A vein in his temple bulged and knotted. If Cuthbert was the turncoat, he'd fail again. If he did, it was proof. The Zapper's clamp closed over his music switch, strangling *Conan the Covert* in mid-dissonance.

Proof positive. . . .

As The Zapper considered the thought, his clamp twisted. The switch, stretching like taffy, tore away, leaving jagged metal ends that glittered like The Zapper's eyes.

"Kill The Finger."

There had been something in The Zapper's eyes when he said that, something that told Cuthbert this was his last chance. The look, coupled with a voice as dark and hollow as a grave, was utterly chilling. And not once had The Zapper raised a clamp to him. Odd, in and of itself, it was somehow ominous, as if The Zapper were conserving his fury for later. All of it put together left absolutely no doubt: if he failed again . . .

Cuthbert shuddered and tried to dismiss the thought, but it wouldn't go away. It wasn't that he was afraid to die, he told himself. It was the fear that The Zapper wouldn't let him—not for a very long time.

He had to take direct action this time. He didn't dare leave anything to chance. Briefly, he thought of hiring an assassin from the Hit Beings Guild, but the memory of The Zapper's look banished the thought. He would never authorize the chit for it and there wasn't any use asking. Cuthbert sighed. He would have to do it himself.

He had never been any good at that sort of thing. He remembered the miserable months in Termination With Prejudice 301. The class was required, and it had been so grueling that Cuthbert never chose another as an elective. 301 was a survey course of historic termination techniques, and the lab was ghastly.

He remembered the unit on "Crafts of the Ninja." He had despised hanging from ceilings and he hated being buried. He cringed at the memory of the throwing-star episode that left his irate instructor with a new—and permanent—part to his hair.

"Light Weapons" hadn't been any better. He had co-agulated part of his thumb with the argon coagulator, and he had nearly incinerated his lab partner with the yag.

Cuthbert pulled out his old Term-N-Ate pack from the closet and rummaged through it in the hope of inspiration. Not the sonics, he thought. The disruptor was heavy and kicked like a mule. At last he settled on the vaporizer and hesitantly aimed it at the reflector. It was a Deville B1S, small, but deadly. It would have to do.

He stared at it and tried to remember how to dial the settings. Then clutching the Deville B1S in one hand, Cuthbert thumbed through his old notes with the other. The settings were in there somewhere, he was sure; he remembered writing them down.

Gimbel had taken a dim view of the operation. He had informed the KBG that The Finger was to die at the hands of the Cuthbert peripheral. All that was left to do now, was to tell them when.

Glowing softly so as not to alert Cuthbert, Gimbel made the connection to Diderot's wrist reader.

. . . *Gimbel* . . . *GIA* . . .

Dieter Diderot's voice came back in a binary stream of zero's and one's, which Gimbel translated as a cautious "Yes?"

. . . The Finger is on board the Express to Hyades IV. . . . She and Dr. Brian-Scott are on their way to a conference at MegaMed Center. . . . Termination is scheduled for Express arrival time: 1600 hours. . . .

"Very good." Then Diderot gave a low laugh. "I'll see that the Guild is waiting."

. . . Guild? . . . What do you mean "guild"? . . .

"The Hit Beings Guild." Another low laugh. "They don't like scab labor, you know. They don't like free-lancers. They're going to hit your man Cuthbert before he can touch The Finger." A pause. "Someone's watching. Out—" The connection broke off.

Gimbel processed Diderot's news instantly, and .000034768 of a second later he reacted to it with horror: The Cuthbert peripheral was to be hit. And he, Gimbel, dwelt on Cuthbert's shirt. Therefore, he, Gimbel, was to be attacked by the Hit Beings Guild. He was going to be yagged, disrupted, vaporized, sliced, or coagulated. The idea of being coagulated inside his shell like a hardboiled egg was especially horrifying, and made Gimbel let loose an involuntary squirt of alcohol.

Bathed in its glow, he considered the problem. He had to act fast. Even now he was being jiggled by the Cuthbert peripheral's ride to the spaceport.

He could contact Diderot again, tell him to call off the Guild. But no, Diderot wouldn't do that without a reason. Racking his little brain, Gimbel synthesized trial solutions again and again, and finally the answer came.

Summoning all his considerable communications resources, Gimbel scanned the spaceport computers, rejecting first one as unsuitable, then another. Then he had it—an ill-coded, glitch-infested standby that would suit his purposes. That would, in fact, suit him very well.

In less than five seconds, the standby computer was under Gimbel's control; in less than ten, it located the Hyades Express and began to send a message to its captain.

Though the Hyades Express warped silently through outer space, its inner space was far from quiet. The new game craze, Doodlebong's Demise, had taken over Lounge 3 and Terra was winning.

She had taken on the reigning champion, a dour Aldeberan named Alcestiqot, and won the first round.

The game field projected at random a place, a creature,

149

and three objects. Alcestiqot examined the holos. There was a large empty basket, an oilskin, a package of SweetUms, a body of water with an offshore island, and a dragon. Alcestiqot hissed softly to himself and then entered his scenario.

The stage cleared and the suicidal and hopelessly inept Doodlebong, looking like a soap bubble with legs, appeared and waves began to roll on the little holographic sea.

ACTION:

Doodlebong, bent on self-destruction, rigs an oilskin sail on the basket, jumps in, and sails out to sea. Waving the package of SweetUms, Doodlebong lures the dragon. Now his scheme is revealed: Doodlebong plans for the Dragon to set fire to the basket with its breath and burn it away, causing him to sink and drown. Instead, the dragon's breath toasts the SweetUms. The toasted SweetUms, smelling delicious, pop with the heat and shoot into the oilskin, creating a buoyant raft that carries Doodlebong to the offshore island where he opens a popped SweetUms concession.

Now it was Terra's turn. Frowning in concentration, she nibbled a fingertip. Then as inspiration struck, she entered her scene and the stage cleared again.

ACTION:

On the beach, the suicidal Doodlebong ties the ends of the oilskin to the basket. He jumps in and crawls under the oilskin. Peeping out, he lures the dragon with SweetUms. At the last minute, he withholds the SweetUms. Now, the plan: The irate and hungry dragon will incinerate him and the oilskin will act as a shroud. Instead, the dragon's hot breath inflates the oilskin, turning it into a hot air balloon and Doodlebong is whisked up in the air. Aloft, he eats the SweetUms. Gaining weight, he doubles in size. This and the cooling oilskin cause him to descend where he lands safely on the offshore island. Foiled again, he hires the dragon and opens a travel agency with balloon rides two-for-a-credit.

* * *

As the tally came up, Terra and Alcestiqot were in a dead heat until the last moment when the computer awarded her an extra point for hiring the dragon.

"Bes-s-st two out of three," said Alcestiqot a bit ungraciously. Then he stalked away to the bar.

Brian-Scott handed Terra a drink that showed considerably more action than the holographic sea. "You're getting good."

She took a sip of her bubbling Fission and nodded. "I think it's a matter of having a very logical mind, don't you?" She glanced toward the retreating Aldeberan. "But he was tough to beat. Didn't his toasted SweetUms smell wonderful?"

Before he could answer, the ship's servo sounded an alarm:

ATTENTION. ATTENTION ALL BEINGS: THIS SHIP IS TURNING BACK. I REPEAT, THIS SHIP IS TURNING BACK. THE LANDING ON HYADES IV IS ABORTED.

The lounge erupted in exclamations and hisses of dismay. The servo sounded its alarm again:

THE CAPTAIN HAS JUST RECEIVED WORD THAT THE GOVERNMENT OF HYADES IV HAS FALLEN. ARMED REVOLUTIONARIES HAVE TAKEN OVER THE SPACEPORT AND DEBARKING PASSENGERS HAVE BEEN TAKEN HOSTAGE AT DISRUPTOR POINT. BE CALM. THERE IS NO DANGER. THIS SHIP IS TURNING BACK. THE LANDING ON HYADES IV IS ABORTED.

Terra and Brian-Scott stared at each other blankly for a moment. "Hyades IV— I can't believe it."

"Sounds like just the place Doodlebong ought to visit, doesn't it?" he said.

"Better him, than us. I wonder how much business he and the dragon would have at the Hyades spaceport."

The Hyades spaceport was humming with excitement when Cuthbert arrived at the Express concourse. Tucked under his shirt, the Deville B1S vaporizer bulged like an abnormal growth and chafed his ribs. He wished he could scratch underneath, but he didn't dare.

He scanned the arrival roster. The Express was due at 1600 hours. As he looked, the words scrolled away and the screen went blank. When nothing came back on, he cornered a port servo. "The Express— Is it on time?"

The servo, who was an old model and unduly subservient, bowed and scraped its gears. "The Express has been canceled, sir." It nodded toward the screen. "It's coming up now."

"Canceled! You mean delayed."

"Oh, no, sir. I mean canceled, sir. The Express turned back. Being only knows why. Nothing like this ever happened before. Everyone's talking about it."

Cuthbert stared as EXPRESS . . . CANCELED rolled onto the screen.

The servo blinked its light in alarm. "Sir! You've grown so pale. Are you ill? Would you like to sit on me?" It thrust out its lower portion and turned into a creditable chair. "We could roll down to the infirmary."

"No," he said, waving it away. "I'm fine." But it was a lie. He felt horrible.

He might have felt worse, if he had seen the thin Hyadean with a similar bulge under his shirt who watched from just beyond the boarding ramp. He might have felt much worse, if he had noticed that just below his scraggly facial hair the Hyadean had carved forty-seven nicks in his flap.

He might have, but at the moment all Cuthbert could see were the giant words EXPRESS CANCELED. And all he could hear was the distant echo of a lion roar and The Zapper's voice saying, "That's *you*, Cuthbert. Canceled . . . canceled . . . canceled."

Chapter 17

Hyades Express
Somewhere in space
October 2

Gladiola Tarkington
45 Subsea
Petroleum City
Gulf of Mexico 233433111 United Earth, Sol

Dear Mom,

Well, here I am back on the Hyades Express, only I'm not going to a conference on Hyades IV this time. I'm going to Arandar with beautiful Dr. Brian-Scott for rest and recuperation which Dr. Qotemire says we deserve because of the scare about the armed revolutionaries taking hostages in the spaceport.

But don't worry about the revolutionaries, because there aren't any. It was all a false alarm due to the malfunctioning equipment on the Hyades Express.

Love,
Terra

Huddled on his narrow bed, Cuthbert Cuthbert contemplated the uses of adversity and came up short. It was just a matter of time before The Zapper found out he had failed—and then what?

He had been holed up in his room since the spaceport fiasco, partly at the urging of Gimbel, who seemed horribly nervous lately, partly because he didn't know what else to do. At any moment the call from The Zapper could come. He didn't want to think beyond that.

As if to spite him, the holograph of The Zapper emerged

from the wall and glared malevolently. "I see you, Cuthbert. Lying around again, aren't you?"

Cuthbert fumbled at his buttons and activated his computers. In fact, he activated only Aleph and Beth; Gimbel had been morosely contemplating Cuthbert's navel all the while. "The Zapper's going to kill me," he said in a low voice. "What can I do?" he asked.

Beth blushed rose pink at Aleph's coarse suggestion and searched at random for an answer. Gimbel maintained a stony silence.

"I'm not finding anything," admitted Beth.

"Nothing?"

"Well, if you were a quadruple amputee," she began, "it might help. The Zapper is partial to quadruple amputees."

"Superlative."

"You *don't* have to be sarcastic," she sniffed. "*I* don't have any appendages and I get along quite well, thank you."

He saw the truth in that, but he sensed that her reasoning was flawed. Giving Gimbel a tweak he said, "Can you find anything?"

Gimbel was snockered. He had been that way since the horrible shock at the spaceport. He had not sensed the Hit Being's disruptor until the last moment. Fortunately the old spaceport servo had swerved in front of Cuthbert at the last moment and taken the hit in its sensors. Terribly addled, it rolled away to the infirmary thinking Cuthbert was on its lap.

And the stupid Cuthbert pheripheral didn't even know.

Gimbel had contacted Diderot's wrist reader at once and demanded that he call off the Hit Beings. Diderot's response was chilling. There was nothing he could do. Once the Hit Beings Guild was alerted, there was no stopping it. And the Guild always got its being.

Gimbel stared blearily around Cuthbert's little room. They were safe here. Not even the Hit Beings Guild would dare to enter the GIA compound. But for how long? And when The Zapper found out that The Finger still lived. . . .

Remembering The Zapper's revolving middle arm—the one with the Swiss Army Knife attachment—Gimbel shuddered. One thing was sure: The Cuthbert peripheral must never fall into The Zapper's deadly clutches.

Zeus the Zapper was lubricating himself. It pleased him. It gave him a sense of unity with his work. He and the GIA were well-oiled pieces of machinery, he thought with satisfaction. Clutching the tube of CyborGoo with his middle clamp, he eased the tip into his belly button and squeezed.

Immediately, he felt the tension ease as the lubricant crept into his midsection and spread through his junctures. "Yes," he said aloud. He felt like a boy again.

He gave a trial swivel. Smooth. Very smooth. The Zapper's upper body began to revolve—he enjoyed a good revolution—and he extended his outer arms while the middle one, still clutching the tube of CyborGoo, marked a jaunty rhythm. "Oh *yes*," he said again. The swivel turned into an abandoned spin that caused the trailing ends of his red-and-gray muffler to swat against the communication console. As if in protest at the abuse, the console blatted its announcement of an incoming call.

Applying reverse English, The Zapper reached out his right clamp and plugged the audio into his temple. "Zapata here." As he listened, the pleasure from his oiling drained away and his jaw clamped tight.

The Finger lived. The prissing Finger *lived*.

The Zapper's face darkened. Proof. It was all the proof he needed. Lips thinning, they curled over clenched teeth and formed the single word: "Cuthbert."

Double agent.

In the grip of his tightening middle clamp, the tube of CyborGoo squirted its contents into his lap. Cuthbert—a prissing double agent.

The Zapper's eyes took on a maddened glow and he squeezed again, reducing what remained of the CyborGoo tube to a slick and wadded marble. He sat for a long moment, staring at nothing, clicking the CyborGoo in his clamp. Then reaching for the communications console, he punched a code, and in a voice as sweet as syrup, said, "Come here, Cuthbert. I want you."

The Zapper's honeyed tone struck Cuthbert as especially ominous. "He knows."

He stared wildly around the room: Where could he go? What could he do?

Gimbel's voice startled him. "You've got to run."

Yes. Run. What else could he do? Whirling, Cuthbert reached for the door and clattered down the hall toward the street.

"Stop, fool." Gimbel's voice was as commanding as his tiny speaker allowed. "You need a disguise."

Cuthbert stopped short. "No. It won't do any good. He'll beam on my collar." The only safety was in distance—and even if he put a galaxy between him and The Zapper it might not be enough. He began to run again.

"Stop!" Gimbel thundered. "I can hold him off for a while. It's not The Zapper you need to worry about—"

Cuthbert listened in horror as Gimbel told him about the Hit Beings Guild. Not stopping to wonder how Gimbel knew, Cuthbert leaned against the wall in an attempt to steady his rubbery legs, and contemplated his imminent demise. He had tried to be a good spy. Was it his fault he just didn't have much talent for it? He had done his best. Didn't that count for something?

Bleakly, he knew it didn't.

He wondered if they would bury him with the indenture collar around his still, cold neck. The chilling thought came that his coffin might be equipped with a holograph of The Zapper. He and The Zapper—sharing a grave through eternity. Better, death at the hands of a faceless Hit Being.

"Don't just stand around, idiot," snarled Gimbel. "Get into a disguise."

Where? What? Then with an inspiration born of despair, he wheeled and began to run toward the compound theater and the backstage wardrobe room of The Company Players.

Zeus the Zapper stared at the operative who sat across from him. She was a hard woman, but no being could fault Shirley Guinness when it came to results. He should have called her in long ago, he thought grimly. But no— Instead, he had relied on Cuthbert. At the thought of the perfidious indentured spy, The Zapper clenched his clamp as if it held the villainous Cuthbert, and raked it toward his thorax.

At the sound, Shirley Guinness looked up from the picture of Terra Tarkington. "You're scratching your finish, Zap."

"That's Zapata, to you," roared The Zapper. "Za-pa-ta."

A little smile played across her lovely face, but her eyes were hard. "I'm not one of your indentured flunkies," she said in a voice edged with steel. "If you want me to save your alloyed ass from the righteous wrath of the front office, you'll keep a civil tongue." Without waiting for an answer, she stared at the pictures again. This time she was looking at Brian-Scott.

The smile, speculative now, played over her mouth again. "But it could be fun."

"I want The Finger dead. With no connection to the GIA." The Zapper's voice started out as a rumble, and ended in a whine. "Can you do that?"

"You'd better hope so, Zap." She glanced at Brian-Scott's picture again, then back at Terra's and laughed softly. "Poor little thing. Doesn't she look unstable? Why, I wouldn't be surprised if everyone on Hospital Satellite came to believe she was suicidal. But after all, with the new doctor there, who could blame her?"

She held out her hand to The Zapper with a mocking laugh. "Meet Marcia Ludgate M.D."

"You? A doctor?" he looked doubtful. "How are you going to convince The Finger? And what about Brian-Scott? They're medical people."

"That's Mercy's job." She fingered the locket she wore at her throat. At her touch, it sprang open.

Of course, thought The Zapper.

Mercy was a mole.

Zapata looked at the locket and the tiny dark brown being inside. He felt distaste. Arcturan moles were amoral with no political preferences at all. They could never be trusted and more than one had defected to the KBG. He stared at the symbiote uneasily. It made him feel queasy to think of it teaming with her, reading his mind. It made him feel corroded inside.

Shirley Guinness quirked her lips in a vee of a smile that made The Zapper feel as if she already knew his thoughts. Then plucking Mercy from the locket, she held the telepathic mole to her cheek just at the corner of her lip.

A shiver touched the nape of The Zapper's neck as tiny black tendrils emerged from the Arcturan's amorphous body and buried themselves in the woman's skin. He didn't like it. He didn't like it at all. Yet, almost against his will, he felt a grudging admiration. Alone, Shirley Guinness was an extraordinary operative—single-minded, utterly without fear. Teamed with the mole— He remembered the plaintive suicide note left by one of her victims: "I have no choice. Shirley Guinness and Mercy will follow me all the days of my life."

Teamed with the mole, thought The Zapper, there was no stopping her.

Amusement flickered in her eyes. "Damned right."

The Company Players wardrobe room was uncomfortably warm. Cuthbert, sweating under an Aldeberan suit at least two sizes too large, peaked out through the snout at his reflection. "Is it all right? What do you think?" he asked Gimbel.

"How the hell do you think I can see from under here?" raged Gimbel in a muffled voice.

"Oh." Cuthbert plucked up the belly scale overlying Gimbel. "Is that better."

Gimbel peered out through the flap. "Well—" he said, unconvinced, "I suppose it will have to do. Let's hear your accent."

"What?"

"You're supposed to be an Aldeberan. Let's hear your Aldeberan accent."

"How does-z-z thiz-z-z z-z-zound?" asked Cuthbert hesitantly.

Distaste dripped from Gimbel's voice. "Awful."

When he failed to win Gimbel's approval after five minutes of practice, a sudden inspiration came to Cuthbert. Seizing an old cue card in his rubbery claws, he turned it over and began to write:

I AM A DIS-S-S-ABLED ALDEBERAN. I CANNOT S-S-SPEAK.

When it occurred to Cuthbert that his salary—meager though it was—could no longer be counted on, he added an addendum to the card:

DONATIONS-S-S GRATEFULLY AC-S-S-CEPTED.

Chapter 18

Satellite Hospital Outpost
Taurus 14, North Horn 978675644
Nath Orbit
Oct. 10

Carmelita O'Hare-Mbotu R.N.
Teton Medical Center
Jackson Hole Summation City
Wyoming 306748760 United Earth, Sol

Dear Carmie,

Oh, I'm happy here. You needn't worry about me. I really am happy. My third favorite thing is to be a member of the Interstellar Nurses Corps, sealed in an orbiting tin can, doomed to wander the Bull Run until my hitch is up.

My second favorite thing is to walk on hot coals barefoot.

But, my most favorite thing of all is to stand helplessly by while my beloved is lured by the tinsel charms of Marcia Ludgate M.D.

It was our first extended leave—a glorious week on Arandar. Beautiful Dr. Brian-Scott and I looked forward with innocent anticipation to a time of simple joy. Carmie, do you have any notion of what it is to have your simple joy disintegrate before your eyes? Can you imagine how cruel it is to view your beloved as a victim of an unscrupulous woman's carnal desire?

Oh, Carmie, it's true.

At first, Arandar was idyllic. We spent our days hiking in the mountains. (I can see your eyebrow raise, Carmie. It doesn't mean what you think it does. "Hiking" is a very old term and it means "to walk." Really.) Although it sounds odd, it was fun.

In fact the whole trip was fun until last night. Then came the festive for all the Bull Runners. Some were on leave like Dr. Brian-Scott and me, others were mustering out of the Corps, and others were just coming on for a new tour of duty.

The place was crowded. I mean it was dense. *Believe me, it would have been easier for a rich man to pass through the eye of a camel (to coin a phrase) than to pass through the middle of that crowd.*

And Marcia Ludgate M.D. was right in the center.

It was really vulgar, Carmie. There she was, surrounded by every human male within light-years. She really had them fooled. You could tell, because every one of them acted like she was the most gorgeous, graceful, beautiful, and intelligent girl in the galaxy. But that was because she was telling them exactly what they wanted to hear. It was uncanny. If I didn't know better, I'd say she was reading their minds.

And right next to her in the press of the crowd stood my beloved, staring at her with the silliest look on his face you ever saw. He was leering at the bodice of her purple slinky, and he was clinging to her hand like his had suction cups.

Then he saw me and he said, "Terra, I want you to meet my colleague, Dr. Marcia Ludgate." When we were introduced, Marcia Ludgate M.D. looked down her nose at me and smiled a pinched little V of a smile that made her mole quiver. (It's right by the corner of her lip, and though some might call it a beauty mark, I call it a mole.) Then she flapped her eyelashes at Dr. Brian-Scott and moved her upper body so that parts of her virtually oozed out of her purple slinky.

I had on my white semi-lace swirl. I always liked it before, but next to her I looked like a Girl Galactic at her first festive.

Now the absolute worst has happened. Marcia Ludgate M.D. is here at Satellite Hospital Outpost. And this is going to be her permanent station. She said she was going to love working with Dr. Brian-Scott and that she had lots of new techniques to show him.

I could die.

Yours in despair,
Terra

P.S. Marcia Ludgate M.D. buys her clothes at Frederick's of Hyades. Isn't that shocking?

Terra

> Satellite Hospital Outpost
> Taurus 14, North Horn 978675644
> Nath Orbit
> Oct. 10

Frederick's of Hyades
Barebelle Heights
Hyades IV 000333321

Dear Frederick,

> *Please rush the following order:*
> *1 pr. Pink Velvo scampies (size medium)*
> *3 pr. skinties (assorted colors, size medium)*
> *3 pr. lumers (one size fits all)*
> *1 set Lurolex scoopers*
> *1 fluffolex enhancer (perfidious pink, size small)*
> *1 set bluffies (size small) in Galactic Black*
> *1 breezer in Universe Yellow*
> *1 medium red shift.*

Anxiously yours,
Terra Tarkington

P.S. About the slilk gapper (as advertised). Does it come with something to wear underneath?

Fendeqot felt the familiar gnawing in his left anterior stomach. He was getting an ulcer. There was no doubt about it, he told himself. None at all. He couldn't go on like this.

It was dark in KBG headquarters. Only the scentplant's night light was on, its razor's edge of yellow gleaming from the base of the inner door. He did not dare turn on the lights. If he had been followed, they would advertise his presence. He reached into the thin pouch slung on his shoulder and pulled out a tiny portable light. It flickered on with the touch of a claw.

He followed its glow to the closet, and stepped inside.

Pulling the door shut after him, he caught his breath. Then snapping off his portable, he turned on the closet light and stared around the little cubicle.

He had never intended to come back. After days of worry and increasing grief from his left anterior stomach, he had made up his mind: He was not going to wait for Diderot to expose him. He was going to defect.

He had contacted the GIA with his offer only an hour ago. He had scarcely believed Zeus the Zapper's ultimatum: "Now you listen to me, reptile. If you come over to the GIA, the location of the Doomsday Device comes with you—or you don't prissing come at all."

"But my cover is-s-s about to blow."

"Then this is my advice to you, reptile: You had better get your scaley tail *wagging*." And without further ado, The Zapper had broken the connection.

Fendeqot stared at the overhead pipe. He did not dare mess with it again, he thought in despair. Reaching in his pouch again, he pulled out the small drill. It came on with a shrill snarl as Fendeqot held it to the wall and began to drill.

The hole was tiny, just large enough to admit the listening probe that Fendeqot threaded inside. Finally he was done. Everything that SEPTUM said to Diderot would come through. And when it did—he stared around again at the small confining room with its tank of nutrient solution and its bare pipes—when it did, he would be able to come out of the closet for the last time.

He just hoped that his deliverance would come while there was still life in his body and lining in his left anterior stomach.

> Satellite Hospital Outpost
> Taurus 14, North Horn 978675644
> Nath Orbit
> Oct. 10

Dear Carmie,

I hate Marcia Ludgate M.D. And I hate her pet, too. His name is Hamlet. He's a Pleaidean chat with fur the color of a black hole and a personality to match. He likes Dr. Brian-Scott, but he unhinges his claws and cackles in an awful way whenever I'm close.

When he does that, Marcia Ludgate M.D. clucks her tongue and says, "Now, Hamlet, don't be cruel to our little Terra."

And then my beloved smiles in a vague way and pats my hand like I was six years old or something.

And now, Marcia Ludgate M.D. has sequestered my beloved away in the lab. They're supposed to be working on a vaccine for that new strain of Lethal Lethargy that's been infecting the Aurigan Queens.

They've been in there for hours. It excoriates my soul to think of beautiful Dr. Brian-Scott exposed to that woman.

But, it's not as if I had time to grieve. Oh no. The wards are full of Aurigan Queens with the Lethal Lethargy. And you talk about short-handed—Carmie, we are down to nubs. The Aurigan Queens are huge and need lots of care, but they don't want anybody but Hyadeans and humans to nurse them, so the Director of Nurses has pulled every non-Aldeberan being to help out with them.

The Aurigans are terribly prejudiced against the Aldeberans. They even insulted Dr. Qotemire—and he's Chief of Staff. One of the Queens huffed at a very sweet Aldeberan nurse just this morning. She called her "vermin derf" and other worse obscenities until the poor nurse was nearly beside herself. She rocked back and forth on her tail and her scales stood on end. I've never seen anyone so blue before.

I think it's dreadful. Poor Mrs. Qotlqeer can't help it if she looks like an Aurigan dragon.

Of course, I must be the voice of reason. Somebody has to see both sides. And I suppose the Aurigan Queen has a point. If I were suffering from the Lethal Lethargy, I guess I wouldn't want somebody taking care of me who looked like an ancestral enemy.

Well, the Aurigan Queen glared at Mrs. Qotlqeer and called her "Egg-eater," and flopped around on her megabed. The Queen got so upset, venom dripped from her lips as fast as I could suction it.

And then Mrs. Qotlqeer forgot herself and hissed.

It was an awful scene. And now, orders have come down from Dr. Qotemire that no Aldeberan is to take care of a Queen. That's going to mean double shifts for all the rest of us, Carmie, just as sure as death and Texas.

I'll be working myself into an early grave (to coin a phrase) while my beloved is corrupted by Marcia Ludgate M.D.

> *Yours in horrid abnegation,*
> *Terra*

The new section of the satellite rang with the hollow sound of Terra's footsteps. Holding the picnic basket with one hand, she pushed open the door to the observation port with the other and stepped inside. "Are you there?"

There was no answer.

A thousand stars filled the port and stippled the silent, darkened room with a pale wash of silver.

"I guess I'm early," she whispered to herself. She reached for the lights, and then hesitating, withdrew her hand. Laying down the basket, she settled down on the puffy silver square that served as both couch and tablecloth.

Her pupils grew huge as her eyes adjusted to the dimness. So many stars, she thought. And so much space between them. The darkened room seemed to stretch out forever, until it seemed to her that she was adrift. She squeezed her eyes shut.

The faint, harsh smell of new construction came to her. Funny, she thought. She had never noticed it before. Not here.

She lay back and listened. In the thick quiet, she heard nothing but the soft rush of her breath and the faint protesting squeaks of the silver mattress echoing each slight movement of her body. Then she heard something that caused her to sit up with a quick smile on her face. She stared expectantly toward the door, but it was only the distant creaking of the satellite's skeleton, contracting as it turned slowly away from its sun.

She felt suddenly cold. Reaching for the picnic basket, she brought out a cup, turned its lid, opened it. Steam rose from the spicy drink, but though the drink was hot on her tongue, she began to shiver.

Checking the time again, she stared into the dark. He was just delayed, she thought. He'd be along any minute. She rearranged the picnic, laying out each item one by one. All his favorite things.

He wouldn't forget, she thought. He never had. Of course he wouldn't. He'd be along any minute.

Closing her eyes again, she leaned back and began to hum

the old tune he had played for her here. She tried to recreate the orchestration of "Stardust," tried to imagine his arms around her, holding her as they moved to the beautiful old rhythms. Instead she heard her own voice echoing faintly in the big, dark room and she fell silent.

The bright disk that was Nath II slid past the port again. She hugged herself to ward off the chill that came when its light winked out and cold starfire took its place. Reaching for the cup again, she turned the lid, but the drink was cold now, and tasteless in her mouth. Closing it, she held the cup for a minute more. Then kneeling, she put it back in the basket and slowly packed away the untouched meal.

Terra stepped off the empty slidleator into the darkened corridor. Turning, picnic basket thumping against her leg, she moved toward her room.

As she reached the door a harsh, hissing sound came from behind her. Whirling, she faced it.

"Hush, Hamlet," said a purring voice.

The black-furred chat extended a claw and hissed again. "Sh-h-h." The woman's smile was arch as she slowly looked Terra up and down. Stroking the chat, she spoke in the creature's ear, "You mustn't be cruel to poor little Terra. Can't you see she's been crying?"

"That's not so." Terra thrust out her chin and blinked. "I just washed my face, that's all."

"Her poor nose is all red, Hamlet." The woman crimped her mouth into a smile and her eyes narrowed.

"It's just red because I scrubbed it hard," said Terra. "I always do that. Every time I wash my face."

"Of course you do." Then eyes fixed on Terra, she spoke again to the chat. "Maybe she ought to order a love potion from the Aldeberan herbalists, don't you think? I expect she's going to need it."

Terra stared at the woman for a long moment. "I would sooner die." Then, back as straight as an arrow, she opened her door, stepped inside, and shut it quietly behind her.

> *Satellite Hospital Outpost*
> *Taurus 14, North Horn 978675644*
> *Nath Orbit*
> *Oct. 11*

Aldeberan Herbalists Inc.
Great Green Patch
Liana 888222567 Aldeberan I

Dear Honorable Herbalist:

> *Please rush me a package of your Love Potion (large economy size).*
> *This is an emergency.*

> *Hurriedly yours,*
> *Terra Tarkington*

Gimbel, warmed by a spurt of ethyl and the heat of Cuthbert's Aldeberan suit, began his latest transmission to Zeus the Zapper:

. . . Gimbel here. . . . Cuthbert still does not suspect that I am watching his every move. . . . We are close to a breakthrough. . . . Soon he will contact the KBG. . . .

The binary stream that was the Zapper's reply washed into Gimbel's memory, bringing with it such creative use of the language that the little computer's dictionary banks were at a loss to fill in the blanks:

"Top grade, Gimbel. Top grade. When you get me the location of the Doomsday Device, we'll have the little [EXPLETIVE] double agent by the prissing *short* ones. And then [BINARY SNARL] Cuthbert had better [EXPLETIVE] his [EPITHET]. [LION ROAR]."

"What did he say," asked Cuthbert in an agony of suspense.

"Be quiet, peripheral," snarled Gimbel. Then to The Zapper: *". . . The operative Shirley Guiness—does she make progress? . . ."*

". . . Sly, aren't you Gimbel? Just you worry about the prissing turncoat, and let Shirley Guiness worry about how to make The [EXPLETIVE] Finger commit suicide. [LION ROAR]. You think you're my only source, don't you, Gimbel. *Don't you?* But you're not the only egg in my basket. And don't you prissing forget it. [LION ROAR] [LION ROAR]. . . ."

"What did he say?" Cuthbert asked again, staring down at his belly scales in a vain attempt to make eye contact with Gimbel, but the computer answered with a grunt and then lapsed into silence. Cuthbert opened his plastoid jaws to let in a little air. The City of Twelve Evils was overheated, and the Aldeberan suit was old and ventless. He was breaking out in prickly heat. Worse, he was hungry. Although he had waggled his placard industriously, he had not collected enough for lunch. That meant he would have to rely on the charity of the Shelter for Shabby Aldeberans again. But it was better than The Zapper, he thought. Or the Hit Beings Guild. He had Gimbel to thank for that.

Cuthbert didn't know that Gimbel, even now, was activating Dieter Diderot's wrist reader.

> Satellite Hospital Outpost
> Taurus 14, North Horn 978675644
> Nath Orbit
> Oct. 12

Carmelita O'Hare-Mbotu R.N.
Teton Medical Center
Jackson Hole Summation City
Wyoming 306748760 United Earth, Sol

Dear Carmie,

I ordered some new clothes and they came today. But I haven't even had a chance to try them on. I am exhausted. The Lethal Lethargy is rampant and I am seeing giant Aurigan Queens in my sleep (what little sleep I've had).

Lethal Lethargy is an awful disease. It's caused by a mutated virus and it attacks the mature Queens. The virus causes a hormone to be released which puts an end to the egg-laying cycle. Then the hormone levels go up even higher. After a period of agitation, the Queen goes into a coma. If there is anything worse than an agitated Queen, it's one in a coma. It took me, five Hyadeans, and a hydraulic lift to get a new admission into her megabed today. It's really very sad though. Her husbands lined up to see her and one of them told me it would be the end of their race if a cure wasn't found. Then he shuffled all his feet in an embarrassed way and said, "You won't let any dragons come near her, will you?"

I said, "The Aldeberans aren't dragons."

And he said, "Oh yes, they are." He told me that ages

ago a colony of Aldeberans of the degenerate Sqotelire sect landed there. "The Aldeberan leaders deny it to this day. But, it's true." Then he lowered his upper eyes and said, "They eat flesh, you know—and eggs."

It was awful listening to him. I kept looking at the Aurigan Queen and trying to imagine how an Aldeberan (or anything else for that matter) could want to eat one.

I finally got away from him and went to lunch. We had plankton loaf and sprouts and the loaf spraddled out over the plate like a Queen on a megabed. I couldn't eat a bite.

Dyspeptically yours,
Terra

P.S. If I cared, I'd tell you what happened after lunch. But I don't care. I am above all petty jealousies.

Terra

P.P.S. Oh, Carmie, that's a lie. I do care. I do. I went by the Lab. Well, I had to be down that way anyhow, and when I went by, I heard beautiful Dr. Brian-Scott and Marcia Ludgate M.D. behind the closed door. And they were laughing.

No. Not laughing. It was worse. They were giggling. That was hours ago and they haven't come out yet. My heart is breaking.

Yours in cheerless gloom,
Terra

The inner door of KBG headquarters swung open silently and Dieter Diderot slipped inside the darkened room. The scentplant, huddled in the pale yellow glow of its night light, muttered in its sleep. Lids hooded over close-set eyes, Diderot watched it. A faint smile quirked at the corner of his thin lips.

He had been sure that Fendeqot was the GIA informant, but it wasn't enough. He needed proof. Proof that SEPTUM would accept. It was the edge he needed.

Diderot needed SEPTUM's complete confidence. With it would come the location of the Doomsday Device. When he had it, SEPTUM would be powerless to stop him. No one could. He laughed softly to himself. No one could stop the most powerful being in the universe.

Staring at the scentplant, he reached out and gripped a thin limb between thumb and forefinger. Slowly, he twisted.

The scentplant woke with a start. Thrashing its free limbs it shrieked and tried to draw away the captured one.

With an ugly laugh, Diderot twisted again. Suddenly, he released it with a snap.

Terrified, the scentplant gave off the camouflaging smell of a giant glamp of prey and shrank back.

He laughed again, a curious mirthless laugh. "Now that I have your attention—" He stood towering over the hapless plant, and reached for his belt.

The scentplant whimpered, and belched out the odor of a horned and deadly vilebeest, but the effect was lost on Diderot. Fingers closing over a little electronic device, he unclipped it from his belt. "You're going to tell me everything you know."

Slowly, he drew out the thin electrodes. Deliberately, he attached them to the quivering limbs. "Now then"—he activated the device and a warning button on its face pulsed red—"you know who the GIA informant is, don't you?"

The scentplant shivered violently.

Diderot stared at the silent gauge in his hand. Then he raised his cold gaze to the little scentplant. "You're lying." He brought his face close to the trembling limbs. "I don't like lying scentplants."

He smiled then, and his smile was terrible to see. Chuckling softly over the piteous moans of the scentplant, he reached for the flashing red button and slowly pressed it home.

Chapter 19

Satellite Hospital Outpost
Taurus 14, North Horn 978675644
Nath Orbit
Oct. 13

Carmelita O'Hare-Mbotu R.N.
Teton Medical Center
Jackson Hole Summation City
Wyoming 306748760 United Earth, Sol

Dear Carmie,

I am poisoned and under seige. I am sure to die soon. I never thought it would end this way. Dr. Qotemire has gone mad. He's outside my door now. He thinks I think he has gone away, but I can hear the scales on his tail scraping over the floor.

Here I am in my hour of need without my beloved to comfort me. And now I'm breaking out in hives.

Oh, Carmie, I didn't mean to poison the Aurigan Queens and madden Dr. Qotemire. What am I to do?

I was trying to get Dr. Brian-Scott out of the clutches of Marcia Ludgate M.D. I didn't mean any harm. It's all because of the Aldeberan love potion. When it came, I put on my new yellow breezer (with the bluffies underneath). I poured a triple dose of love potion into the smoker and lit it. Then I sent an urgent message to Dr. Brian-Scott.

Well, how was I to know that the smoke from the potion would get into the ship's ventilation system?

Borgdo, one of the Hyadean orderlies, came to the door with a message from my beloved. He said that Dr. Brian-Scott couldn't come because of an emergency— smoke had blown through the wards and all the Aurigan Queens were having convulsions.

The next thing I knew, Dr. Qotemire came down the hall, slashing his tail back and forth. His eyes were wild and yellow and his scales quivered. I never saw an Aldeberan in such a state.

When he got to my door, he rolled his eyes in a deranged way and gave a low drawn-out hiss that curdled my blood.

Then he leered at me and said, "Exs-s-citing!"

I didn't know what he had in mind until he shouted, "S-s-sex!" and began to chase me around the room.

I screamed. And then I ran—all the while begging Dr. Qotemire to control himself—but it wasn't any use.

I ran out into the hall and he came after me. He cornered me in an alcove. It was awful, Carmie. There I was—trapped. My doom was sealed. He moved toward me and then he stopped. He began to quiver in a sort of dreadful ecstasy, and the scales on his chest began to slap up and down. He seemed almost hypnotized.

When that happened, I got past him and ran back into my room and locked the door.

Now he's outside.

And my hives are getting worse. Besides that, I think I'm going to be sick to my stomach.

> Yours in an awful fix,
> Terra

P.S. I was very sick just now. I took off my yellow breezer (and the bluffies) and put on my flannelite dowdy. I am in bed now—here to await my fate. It is only a matter of time before they come to prosecute me for poisoning the Aurigan Queens.

I don't think I'll live that long.

> Yours in extremis,
> Terra

A loud pounding began and the door shuddered from the force of it. Terra raised her head from the pillow. The door couldn't stand up long to a flailing from Dr. Qotemire's tail. Shivering in dread at the thought of the love-maddened Aldeberan, she thrust her head under the bedclothes.

"Let me in."

It didn't sound like Dr. Qotemire.

"Terra! Open the door."

Brian-Scott? Was it really him? She sat up. "Is Dr. Qotemire out there?"

"No. He's gone. Open the door."

She touched the remote, and the latch sprang open. Then dizzy with the effort, she sank back. The netbed swayed with her movement and she groaned. She was going to be sick again. Taking a deep breath, she squeezed her eyes shut. When she opened them again, Brian-Scott was looking down at her.

"Oh, Terra," he said and shook his head. "I just found out what happened to you." He reached out and touched her shoulder.

At the jiggle of the netbed, Terra clamped her hand over her mouth.

"Nauseated?"

She nodded weakly.

"I've got something for that." Pulling out a small cylinder, he pressed the little trigger and a cool, pleasant-smelling cloud puffed out and enveloped her face. In a few moments, the nausea went away. He searched her face. "Better?"

She nodded again.

He looked down at her and gave a rueful smile. "It's going to take a little longer for those hives." He took her hand in his and straightened her arm.

Terra heard a faint hiss and felt something cold pierce her skin as the medication entered her vein. She looked up at him and said in a small voice, "Are they going to arrest me now?"

"Of course not." His lips brushed her forehead. "Poor baby."

"But I poisoned them. I poisoned the Aurigan Queens—"

"No, you didn't." He grinned then. "As a matter of fact, I think you've cured them."

"But the convulsions—"

"They weren't convulsions after all. The Queens were starting to lay their eggs again." A gentle, but unreadable look passed over his face then as he looked down at her. "The, uh, love potion you used wasn't for humans, Terra. It was an Aldeberan sex pheromone. It's a potent allergen for humans."

Eyes widening until they were enormous, Terra stared up at him and tried to comprehend what he was saying.

"The pheromone set up a defense reaction in the Aurigan Queens—a defense they developed to cope with the menace of

172

egg-eating dragons," he said. "The Queens' bodies respond by either laying lots of eggs to make up for the ones that are going to be eaten—or they spray venom at the attacker. It's something like the human 'flight or fight' reaction."

Terra blinked in thought. "Only this was 'lay or spray'?"

He grinned. "I guess you could say that. And since it was an Aldeberan sex pheromone, Dr. Qotemire, uh, forgot himself. But he's all right now. Just embarrassed as hell."

"Oh, it was so awful—" Terra squeezed his hand. "I never realized what poor Mrs. Qotemire has to go through when Dr. Qotemire is aroused." Then her voice grew small. "How did you know it was a—a love potion?"

"I was in the lab," he said, "with Marcia. When the smoke came through the ducts, I recognized the odor." He looked away and stared at the floor for a long moment, then then he said, "Marcia started to laugh. She said she'd told you to order a love potion and you were fool enough to do it."

Terra felt something shrivel inside her chest. She couldn't meet his eyes. Stricken, she buried her face in the bedclothes.

"I told Marcia I thought that was the meanest trick anyone could do. I told her I especially resented her doing it to you." Reaching out, he drew the bedclothes away from her face. "Why did you do it, Terra? Why did you think you needed that stuff?"

She swallowed hard and stared down at her clenched fingers. "Because of our picnic. I waited so long. . . ."

He blinked as if she had struck him. "Marcia didn't give you the message then?" A rueful look passed over his face. "No," he said slowly. "No, of course she didn't." He sat down by her side and the netbed swayed with his weight. "I had to cover for Dr. Creeebo. Marcia said she'd tell you I couldn't keep our date." He took her hands between his. "It was my fault. I should have told you myself."

When she didn't answer, he went on. "Marcia's leaving. She'll be gone tonight."

At Terra's questioning look he said, "All that smoke from the love potion got her pet chat agitated. He bit her on the nose—"

"Hamlet?"

"Rather badly too. She's going to Hyades IV to have some reconstructive work done. She won't be coming back."

In her mind's eye Terra saw a condescending V-shaped

smile topped with a slender, perfect nose. She peeped up at Brian-Scott. "That's really too bad, isn't it?"

She looked down at the blotchy hives that crept along her arms and disappeared under the faded sleeves of her old flannelite dowdy. Then her hands flew to her face, fingers tracing the itchy swollen skin around her eyes. How awful she must look. She saw Marcia Ludgate's face in her mind again—undeniably beautiful in spite of Hamlet, and suddenly she began to cry.

Distressed, he said, "What's the matter?"

"I—" She caught her breath as a sob wracked her shoulders. "I wanted to be wearing my new clothes when you saw me. I wanted to be pretty."

"Terra . . ." He shook his head. "Don't you know I love you? It doesn't matter what you wear, or how you look." He drew her into his arms and kissed her then, a long, sweet, gentle kiss, and when it was done she saw laughter touch his eyes and crinkle at the corners. "Terra," he said, and his lips brushed hers again. "I would love you if you weren't wearing anything at all."

Zeus the Zapper stared at the woman across from him. Bandages swathed her nose and her mole looked limp. She had failed—she and her prissing telepathic mole had failed. And the front office would tin his hide when they found out.

His left clamp began to click against the console. "Well?"—click, click, click, click, click—"well?"

"Keep it in the can, Zap." Shirley Guiness's eyes were hard above her bulbous bandage. "I did not fail."

"Did I say you did? Did I?"

Her fingertip skimmed the mole at the corner of her lip. "You can't hide from Mercy."

The Zapper's lips thinned over his clenched teeth, his eyes narrowed. He could rip the miserable mind-reading mole out by its roots, he thought. Squash it. Squash its prissing little body in his clamp. He thought he saw it squirm at the thought. "So"—click, click, click, click, click—"you were a rousing success." Click, click. "Is that right?" But before she could answer, his console blatted. A message was coming in:

. . . Gimbel here. . . .

"Plans change," said Shirley Guiness. The edges of her lips crept upward in a mirthless V of a smile and disappeared under the bandage. "I didn't get the girl, but it doesn't matter now."

"What do you mean?"

There was a pause.

. . . I said, Gimbel here. . . .

"Not you," roared the Zapper.

Shirley Guiness gave a flat laugh. "I got The Trigger. Chune-yore Qotemire. I poisoned his crunchie."

"Poison?" The Zapper blanched. If they traced the little reptile's death to Shirley Guiness, they wouldn't stop there. He would be next—and the whole operation would fall.

Shirley Guiness threw back her head and laughed. "He isn't dead. Not yet. But he will be. And this time the Tarkington girl can't do anything about it." The laugh ended abruptly. Her eyes narrowed and her fingers grazed the bandage where the tip of her nose should have been. "Not this time. No being in the Universe can."

The Zapper leaned forward with a clank. "What poison? What is it?"

As Shirley Guiness opened her mouth to speak, a startled look came over her face. "Take care of your call first."

The Zapper's eyebrows rose. He said to Gimbel, "Has Cuthbert made contact?"

. . . Not yet. . . . But the time is drawing near. . . . Gimbel out.

The Zapper was so deep in thought that Shirley Guiness's words didn't register. "What?"

"He's lying."

"What are you saying?"

"Gimbel. He's lying."

He stared at her blankly, then his gaze fixed on the mole. He shook his head. "He's a computer."

"That makes no difference to Mercy," she said. "Gimbel's lying. He's trying to throw you off Cuthbert's track." A brittle smile crept slowly over her lips. "It seems to have worked."

A thunderous silence fell in the room. The Zapper sat as still as stone. No muscle twitched, no C-joint moved, no breath stirred. Then the eruption—part clashing metal, part lion roar, part shriek of unalloyed rage. "Both of them!" he howled. "*Both of them!*" Both double agents. Double prissing agents.

The Zapper's clamp trembled. Venom glittered in his

eyes. A terrible smile played over his lips as he reached out slowly and pressed a single console switch.

A red light flared as the console found the frequency of the thin metal band that circled the neck of an indentured spy:

. . . SEARCHING . . .

A low tone rose in pitch, dropped, rose again. Then a steady, almost musical, note:

. . . HOMING . . .

The note began a heartbeat throb. The light pulsed. And murderous red glints sparkled in The Zapper's eyes.

While Cuthbert stood in the soup-and-gooble line of the Shelter for Shabby Aldeberans, Gimbel congratulated himself. Poison. That was how The Zapper planned to defeat the Doomsday Device. He chuckled to himself. It was time—time to set his plan in motion.

And what he had to trade was valuable—worth enough to ensure his comfort for a very long time, Gimbel thought. He considered his demands: He was going to insist on larger quarters. He was sick of being cramped in a button. And no more travel. It was too hazardous. He wanted his own room, too. A laminar flow would be nice, he thought. Something to keep the damned bacteria from settling on his case. Laminar flow—with ultra violet, and sonic sterilization. And all peripherals gowned and masked.

As for his work, no sorting. A little spread-sheeting maybe, some what-ifs, but no sorting. He had to set limits for the KBG up front; give them a millimeter and they'd take a kilometer—

A shrill, blasting whistle. . . .

An involuntary squirt of alcohol flooded Gimbel's cells. Nerves quivering, he stared out through Cuthbert's raised belly scale. Fifty pairs of rheumy eyes from fifty Shabby Aldeberans peered back.

As the whistle modulated to a throbbing beep. Cuthbert Cuthbert's hands flew to his throat; fear glazed his eyes. "The Zapper—"

Not just The Zapper, Gimbel thought wildly. The Hit Beings Guild. They'd know. The disguise was useless now. "Run," he howled. "Run!"

Soup sloshed over Cuthbert's scales. Rubbery toe claws crushed a fallen gooble. Breath shrieked in and out of his lungs, and Cuthbert was running—running for his life.

* * *

In the evening shadows of the abandoned building the Aldeberan suit fell limp, tongue lolling, empty eye-sockets staring at nothing.

Catching his breath, Cuthbert ripped loose a section of its hide and wrapped it around his collar. Through the muffling folds the beep still came, quickening, matching the beat of his heart. It wasn't enough. He began to claw at the suit, shredding it in long strips. "Not enough."

Gimbel quivered inside his button. He couldn't wait. He had to move now. . . .

Even as the thought emerged, Gimbel had already begun to signal Diderot's wrist reader.

Mrs. Wiggs sighed. She really hated to have to come back after hours, but Diderot seemed so adamant.

Shutting off the safe light, she made her way through the City of Twelve Evils to KBG headquarters.

Diderot wasn't here yet. Sighing again, she entered the code and the shallow depression began to lower.

It was dark inside the inner room. She stood for a moment just inside, and allowed her sensitive pink eyes to adjust to the dim glow of the scentplant's night light.

A faint sobbing startled her. It came from the scentplant. Staring, she looked at it. As she did, horror darkened her eyes.

Whimpering, the scentplant feebly tried to give off the camouflaging smell of a rampaging bull gommet in heat.

Mrs. Wiggs caught her breath. Its little limbs hung limp and twisted. Its hind root, snatched from its pot, trailed across the floor. Its main frond was cruelly creased.

Mrs. Wiggs narrowed her eyes and in the lowered light they looked quite red. "Who did this to you?" she whispered. "Who did this?"

Mrs. Wiggs raised her deep pink eyes to Dieter Diderot's close-set ones. "You will tell SEPTUM, won't you?"

He glanced down at the scentplant. It had given a little shriek when he came in. Now it was silent and limp.

Mrs. Wiggs gently laid its naked little hind root back into the hollowstone pot. "It's fainted," she said. "But maybe that's a blessing." She covered the root and smoothed down the soil with quick pats of her pseudopaws. "Poor little thing. You will tell SEPTUM?" she asked again.

"Patch me through. This is important," he said abruptly. The communique from Gimbel had thrown his timing off. If The Trigger died, SEPTUM would abort the Doomsday Device—and he didn't intend to let that happen. He had to find out where it was. But first, he was going to soften SEPTUM up with the proof that Fendeqot was a double agent. He fingered the printouts in his pocket. SEPTUM would have to believe the scentplant; there was no way it could have deceived sophisticated lie detectors. He laughed softly. Everything was falling into place.

A few minutes later, Mrs. Wiggs nodded from her console and Diderot stepped inside the communication chamber.

Purple light flared, died, flared again.

"Divided—" said Diderot.

"—WE STAND."

"Chief of Subdivisions, Diderot reporting."

A sulfurous odor permeated the booth. "DO YOU KNOW WHAT TIME IT IS?"

He blinked. "It's late, I know. But this is an emergency. The Trigger has been poisoned."

A pause. "HOW?" Anger deepened the voice. "WITH WHAT?" Stabs of orange lightning streaked the chamber. Thunder rumbled.

"By the GIA operative, Shirley Guiness. The poison is unknown. We know its onset is slow, but once symptoms appear it works rapidly. My source tells me there is no antidote."

"HAVE SYMPTOMS APPEARED?"

"I think so. I was able to monitor the Satellite Hospital call system. Dr. Brian-Scott was summoned to the Qotemire quarters quite suddenly."

The light in the chamber blinked out. Silence fell.

Pupils dilating in the thick blackness, Diderot stared uneasily around the chamber. The sharp odor of vinegar stung his nostrils. He cleared his throat.

There was no answer. Nothing.

Nothing.

A chill began to creep along the nape of his neck. He cleared his throat again.

The voice started as a distant rumble. "IT IS TIME. . . ."

An electric thrill shivered through Diderot's spine. The Doomsday Device.

178

"LOOK THIS WAY."

A tiny red dot began to glow in the center of the chamber. Pupils wide, he stared at it.

White light exploded. Pain blazed Diderot's eyes. A series of numbers—black on silver—seared his retinas, burned into his brain. He staggered back at the impact.

"YOU HAVE THE CODE. REPEAT IT."

The code. He had it. He had the location of the device— and the numbers meant nothing to him.

"REPEAT IT."

Diderot repeated the sequence of numbers. Nothing. They meant nothing at all. Fendeqot, he thought. Tell him about Fendeqot. "There's another matter. It's Fendeqot—"

"BE SILENT."

A pungent odor filtered through the blackness. A sudden wave of dizziness caused Diderot to clutch at the wall for support. When it passed, SEPTUM's voice seemed distant as if it bypassed hearing, as if it spoke directly to an inner portion of his brain.

"YOUR ASSIGNMENT IS TWOFOLD. YOU ARE TO SEND THESE ORDERS TO SATELLITE HOSPITAL: THE TRIGGER IS TO BE TRANSFERRED AT ONCE VIA MED-EVAC. THE TRIGGER IS TO BE ACCOMPANIED BY THE FINGER.

"WHEN THE FINGER AND THE TRIGGER ARE ON BOARD THE MED-EVAC, YOU ARE TO TRANSMIT THE CODE TO THE SHIP'S NAVIGATION MECHANISM." Sulfurous smoke roiled through the chamber. "REPEAT YOUR ORDERS."

Diderot's voice was low as he spoke.

"REPORT BACK TO ME AT 900 HOURS."

He nodded. "Yes. 900 hours."

"AND DIDEROT— MAKE NO ERRORS." The voice echoed hollow as a tomb. "YOUR LIFE DEPENDS ON IT. . . ."

Half-asleep, Terra followed the servotech through the dim hallway toward pediatrics. As the door swung open, bright lights dazzled her eyes and she shut them involuntarily.

Blinking, she slowly focused. A half-dozen doctors and nurses clustered around the tiny bed.

She looked down. Chune-yore Qotemire lay as still as death, his little tail drawn up in a spastic knot. Someone clicked on a V.S. monitor that instantly measured his pulse and respiration. "What happened? When did he get sick?"

Brian-Scott looked up, "Less than an hour ago. He was conscious then."

She shook her head as if to shake off the fatigue. "What can I do?"

"He's got to be transferred. We're going with him."

"Where?"

"The Poison Center on Hyades IV."

Her eyes widened. "Poisoned! How?"

Brian-Scott looked grim. "We don't know. We're not even positive that's what we're dealing with."

An amber light began to blink above the emergency door. MedEvac I was ready for boarding. The night charge nurse bundled Chune-yore in a heatblanket and thrust him into Terra's arms.

"We'd better move," said Brian-Scott. Scooping up the V.S. monitor, he clipped it to the blanket.

"The Qotemires," said Terra. "What about them?" There was no room on MedEvac I for family.

"Down at shuttle boarding," he said. The emergency door hissed open and the boarding ramp slid to meet it. "They're following in the 201. It's fast."

Clutching Chune-yore, Terra hurried up the ramp and stepped inside. The airlock clanged shut behind her. She swung into place and lowered her patient into the pediatric lifebed as Brian-Scott slid into the jump seat beside her.

Through MedEvac I's single port, a distant light blazed red. "There they are now," he said. "That's 201."

Terra stared through the port. Shuttle 201 was Satellite Hospital's fastest shuttle, capable of nearly three-quarters the speed of MedEvac I. Then she looked down at the little Aldeberan. His chest heaved; he labored for every breath. She raised troubled eyes to Brian-Scott and nodded toward the shuttle. "Do you think they'll make it? In time?"

"I don't know, Terra." His eyes were grave as they met hers. "I just don't know."

The port slid shut with a hiss and the navpanel locked onto its coded coordinates. The little robot ship's ready light flared. Then with a shudder like a living thing, MedEvac I leaped.

Chapter 20

EXCERPT FROM A TRANSCRIPTION OF CHUNE-YORE
QOTEMIRE'S MEDICAL TAPES:

NURSES NOTES—MEDEVAC 1

Date: Oct 16   Nurse: Terra Tarkington, R.N.

Hour	Comment
0800:	Examined per Dr. Brian-Scott. Pt. still unconscious. Exam scales pale and dry. Pupils linear and react to light.
0807:	Respiration: 18. Pulse: 104. Tolerating MedEvac transport as well as can be expected.
0808:	Pedie lifebed detached from floater pending landing, Hyades IV.
0810:	Pedie lifebed to Hyades IV landing ramp. Safety straps on, side rails up, and—this isn't Hyades IV. . . .

Clutching Chune-yore Qotemire's lifebed, Terra and Brian-Scott clattered down the landing. The ramp leveled and came to an end in an empty room that smelled of new construction. A single oval window curved along one wall. Terra caught her breath. It wasn't a window; a thousand stars studded the black of space. "It's a port! We're in a satellite."

Brian-Scott's startled gaze followed hers. "I think you're right." His voice was a hollow echo.

Terra's gaze darted from side to side. It was too quiet. Something was wrong. A chill shivered up her neck. Something was very wrong. Their eyes met, then skittered back toward the ramp and the waiting ambulance ship. "I think," she whispered, "we'd better run like hell."

The lifebed's rollers clattered between them as they raced toward the top of the ramp and MedEvac I.

A warning blast brought them up short. They stared as a heavy airlock slid shut, cutting them off from the little ship. The airlock sealed with a hiss.

"Look!" Brian-Scott yelled.

Terra stared through the port. MedEvac I was floating free in space. Blinking, she watched it glide away until it was no larger than her thumbnail. Then, with a wink, it was gone. "What's happening? Where are we?"

Three-dimensional letters sprang up in midair: YOU ARE HERE.

The letters dissolved into a drawing of a wheel. A small yellow square blinked near the rim.

Brian-Scott looked closer. "It's a map."

She stared at the tiny wavering letters near the flashing square. "It says 'Receiving.' What does it mean?"

He scanned the rest of the display and pointed at the hub of the wheel. "Look." Tiny letters spelled NURSES STATION. Just below, the shield of the Interstellar Nurses Corps blinked on.

"A hospital then," she said. "But where? What hospital?"

The display flashed:

FUTURE HOME OF
THE HOSPITAL OF THE HYADES
Opening soon in an orbit near you.

"This is unbelievable," said Brian-Scott.

Terra looked down at Chune-yore Qotemire, then up at the map. "We've got to do something for him—while there's still time." She scooped Chune-yore out of the lifebed and ran toward a doorway on the inner wall of the room.

"Where? Where are you going?"

"Diagnostics." She raced into a long hallway that stretched ahead like a spoke in a wheel and stopped short. Just ahead, a fat white robot slid into the corridor, and extruded a pair of lenses which scrutinized Terra. "What's going on here?"

"A patient—" gasped Terra, out of breath.

"Impossible. This hospital is not open yet."

"It is now." Terra pushed ahead.

The robot blocked the way with its considerable bulk. "Authorized personnel only beyond this point."

"Let me by." Terra glanced down at the little patient clutched in her arms. "He's sick. We have to get him to Diagnostics."

"Authorized personnel only beyond this point," repeated the robot. "By order of the Director of Nurses."

"Then we'll talk to the Director," said Brian-Scott.

"I am the Director," said the robot. As if in emphasis, red letters flashed across what passed for its chest: D.O.N.

Terra fixed the D.O.N. with a look. "I'm a nurse. And this patient needs help."

The twin lenses extended. "Impossible. I did not order any android nurses."

"I'm not an android. I'm a human."

"This hospital is staffed by robots. There are no humans on this staff. Therefore, you are an android." The D.O.N. extruded its lenses another centimeter, the better to examine the intruder. "I did not order you. Furthermore, it is obvious that you are defective."

"I am *not* defective."

The D.O.N. swiveled its lenses. "You are not buffed. You are not oiled. If you are not defective, then you are slovenly. I will not tolerate a slovenly android."

Clutching Chune-yore Qotemire to her chest, Terra aimed a sharp kick to the nether portions of the D.O.N. "Get out of my way."

The robot's lenses retracted in shock. "Insubordination! I will not have insubordination." A sharp whistle emanated from its mid-section. At the signal, a section of the big robot slid open, and a small army of robot orderlies rolled out. "Seize the android," brayed the D.O.N.

"Run, Terra," yelled Brian-Scott. But it was too late. Terra found herself in the iron grip of a health servo designed to control the strongest of patients.

The D.O.N. turned its attention to Brian-Scott. "Another android. Seize it—"

"No." Terra thought fast. "He's not an android. He's a patient."

The lenses swiveled toward Brian-Scott, paused, then slowly scanned. "I can see that now. We need the surgeon."

Another bleating whistle and a silver robot emerged from the D.O.N.'s nether portions and extended a stethoscope.

"This Hyadean is obviously ill, Doctor," said the D.O.N.

The robot surgeon scanned its patient for a moment, and then inserted a clamp into each of Brian-Scott's nostrils and pulled down. "No flap," it observed.

"Oh, no," said Terra. "They're Hyadean robots. They think you're a Hyadean."

Still clutching Brian-Scott by the nose the surgeon said, "The patient requires reconstructive work to remove the protuberance and restore the flap."

Brian-Scott tried unsuccessfully to dislodge the robot's clamps from his nostrils. "Huban. I'b a huban."

"Prepare the patient for further examination," said the surgeon.

Responding to the order, an orderly extruded a stretcher-like midsection. Scooping up Brian-Scott, it plunked him down on it, and secured him firmly. Another orderly ripped off his clothes with a single swipe and offered a flimsy hospital gown.

"Hm," said the surgeon. "The patient is afflicted with multiple protuberances. They must be removed at once."

Terra's widened eyes met Brian-Scott's horror-stricken ones.

"Prepare him for surgery," said the surgeon.

Responding to the order, the orderly released its grip on Terra.

"Run! Get help." Brian-Scott thrust his chin toward the hub of the Satellite. "The communication banks— That way."

"That way." Gimbel's whisper was anguished. "Quick!"

Cuthbert leaped into the shadow of a crumbling pillar and ducked. The Hit Being's argon coagulator whined and a thin red line sliced overhead. He broke into a crouching run as the coagulator whined again.

"Shoot back, idiot," yelled Gimbel.

Oh God, thought Cuthbert. The Deville B1S vaporizer was clammy in his hand. Aiming in roughly the direction of the Hit Being, he fired. The Deville B1S shimmied. He fired again. This time, there was nothing but a hollow click as the red RECHARGE light flashed on. Dazed, he stared at it for a moment. Then flinging the useless weapon away, he plunged blindly into a tar-black alley.

He hated this. His legs pumped in rhythm with his thoughts: hated this, hated this, hated this.

Half choked with the dozen strips from the Aldeberan suit that muffled his beeping collar, Cuthbert collapsed against the wall and tried to catch his breath.

"Don't stop, fool," yelled the computer. "Right. Go right."

Panting, Cuthbert dodged out of the alley toward the right. Feet pounding, he zigzagged in and out of the flickering shadows that edged the Citadel of the Debased and ran on toward the Avenue of the Unaccustomed.

"There," said Gimbel. Just ahead a single light gleamed blue. "In there."

Cuthbert could see the dim outline of a door. He plunged toward it. Hands scrabbling, he reached out.

Nothing.

"Help." Cuthbert's fists battered the door. "Help me."

A shadow moved on its surface; a lens glinted.

Nothing. Nothing more.

Gimbel's light glowed darkly amber. He spoke: "Diderot sent me."

The door slid open. "Inside," Gimbel ordered. "Quick."

The sudden flare of lights blinded Cuthbert. Blinking, he stared at the being who quickly closed the door behind him. Her long, pale ears leaned intently toward him; her pink eyes fixed his. "Diderot sent you?" Suspicion colored her voice.

Gimbel flashed dark orange. "Gimbel here. I work with Diderot. The human is Cuthbert, GIA. Diderot assures me we have a deal: You get Cuthbert; I get asylum."

Horror tracked over Cuthbert's face. Betrayed. He was betrayed. He grabbed for the door.

Locked.

"Welcome to the KBG," said Mrs. Wiggs.

Frantic, he spun toward her.

"You'll have to come with me—to headquarters. To SEPTUM."

Cuthbert stared in dismay at the disruptor clutched in her pseudopaws. It was aimed at his throat.

Terra stared frantically around the nurses' station until she spotted the patient monitor controls. She thumbed them on, dialing quickly. Bed after empty bed came up on her screens. "Where are you?" she whispered. "Come on. Where are you?"

She found Brian-Scott in 412. He was tied to a Hyadean

IV bed with his nose supported by the flap rest. "Oh, thank goodness. Can you hear me?"

"Terra?" His eyes were wild. "They'll be back any minute with my pre-op medication. Where are you?"

"Somewhere in the hub. In the nurses' station. I jammed the lock, but I don't know how long it'll hold. I'm going to call for help on the MedEvac frequency."

"Hurry."

She nodded. "I'll have to leave this frequency. Do you have your call button?"

"Yes." He pressed it and its sharp beep came through loud and clear.

"I hear it. Use it as a signal if you need me. Out now." Terra dialed the MedEvac frequency just as a series of thumps came from just outside the locked door.

"Open this door," demanded the D.O.N. "You are defective. You need to be buffed; you need to be oiled."

Terra gave a quick glance to Chune-yore Qotemire. He lay just as she had left him, curled in a medication drawer. She shook her head and spoke over the MedEvac frequency: "Help. Any being who can hear me. Help!

". . . I, Terra Tarkington of the Interstellar Nurses Corp, am being held prisoner on a hospital satellite, location unknown, by hostile robots. If you can hear me, please send help before it's too late for Junior Qotemire. And please, please come before my beloved, beautiful Dr. Brian-Scott is taken to surgery to have his protuberances removed. . . ."

The battering on the door grew louder. "Let me in. You are defective; you are insubordinate. Let me in or I will be forced to call the Administrator."

". . . Oh please, please hurry because we are in an awful fix. . . ."

A pause. Then the D.O.N.'s voice: "Are you coming out now?"

". . . Oh hurry please before the Director of Nurses oils and buffs me and does no telling what to Junior Qotemire. . . ."

As Cuthbert stared frantically around the vaulted room, the muffled beep of his collar mimicked the beat of his heart. He was trapped. Locked in the bowels of the KBG. He glanced up. The ceiling was six meters overhead—and it was more than that to the street above it.

"Sit there," said Mrs. Wiggs. She waved the disruptor toward a plump chair facing a shadowy stone alcove.

The chair yielded to his weight. As he sank into it, he felt it mold to his body and wrap itself around his limbs. Panicked, he tried to leap up again, but he was held quite fast.

"It's useless to struggle." Mrs. Wiggs laid down the disruptor. "I'm sorry to have to use the chair, but SEPTUM wouldn't like it if you run away. You might as well rest," she said, "while we wait for the others."

Cuthbert stared bleakly at the wall and shivered as a low vibration came from somewhere near his belly button. Half-deafened by his bleating collar, it took a few moments before he realized what it was: Gimbel, in rhythm to the collar beeps, was thickly singing.

"I trusted you, Gimbel," he whispered.

The singing stopped and Gimbel glowed a whisky amber. "You never were strong in logic, were you Cuthbert? You never had to sort things out." Gimbel chuckled as if he had made a devastating joke and began to sing again. He was halfway through his repertoire when the stone lift descended and a large Aldeberan stepped out.

"Oh, Mr. Fendeqot," said Mrs. Wiggs. "Good morning." She indicated Cuthbert with a flip of her ears. "We have someone waiting for interrogation, but I'll have to patch Mr. Diderot through to SEPTUM first. It's a very important matter."

Fendeqot eyes were mirrored yellow glass. "I s-s-see."

She glanced up at the sound of the lift. "Here he is now."

Cuthbert stared at the narrow-faced man who came into the room. Diderot stared back. Amusement crimped one corner of his lips.

"It's nearly 900 hours," said Mrs. Wiggs to Diderot. "Shall I put you through?"

At his curt nod, the two disappeared into an inner chamber.

Though his chair faced away, Cuthbert could see Fendeqot out of the corner of his eye. The big Aldeberan stared at the inner chamber for a long moment. Then moving quickly, he stepped into what seemed to be a closet and pulled the door shut behind him.

The sound of his collar pulsed in Cuthbert's ears. Every beep ticked off the seconds that brought him closer to destruction. SEPTUM. He was going to face the deviated mastermind of the KBG. He shivered involuntarily and squeezed his eyes shut in despair. His misery was so complete that the soft footsteps behind him did not register, nor the single, muffled click.

"Are you coming out now?" demanded the robot Director of Nurses.

". . . Oh, please," begged Terra, "somebody answer. Any being. Any being at all. . . ."

"You leave me no choice," said the D.O.N. "I must call the Administrator."

A fearsome squawk came through the jammed nurses' station door. Then silence. Utter silence.

Suddenly a rumble grew like thunder.

A glowing line of white light flashed. A seam split the wall.

Terra stared in horror as the nurses' station slid apart. Snatching up Chune-yore Qotemire, she caught her breath. Something was coming. Something enormous.

A thousand lights flashed like lightning from the monstrous machine that filled the satellite's hub.

"What is it? What's there?"

A voice boomed: *"I am the Administrator."*

"Uh-oh," she whispered.

"I will not have strife. If there is strife, the patients will take their diseases to the competition. I will have harmony among all my machines."

"I'm not a machine. I'm a person."

"You are an android," thundered the Administrator. *"You are the cause of strife and disharmony."*

"I am not. It's all because of your Director of Nurses. It has no right to accuse me of being an android. And it doesn't have any right to imprison my beloved, beautiful Dr. Brian-Scott, either and—"

"What is this term? This 'beloved'?"

"It means the one I love.

"What is this term? This 'love'?"

Terra thrust out her chin. "It means when you love somebody, you treat them right instead of forcing them to undergo surgery. It means that you get married to someone and live happily ever after instead of having your protuberances removed."

"Does this 'happily ever after' mean peace and harmony?" demanded the Administrator.

"Yes, it does. Which is something you wouldn't understand because you're a machine instead of a person."

"*I can do that,*" said the Administrator. "*I have a chaplain mode.*"

"You can do what?"

"*Marry you. I will marry you to the Director of Nurses at once.*"

Terra clutched Chune-yore Qotemire as if he were a shield. "No!"

Puzzlement came into the Administrator's voice. "*Why not?*"

"Because I don't want to marry the Director of Nurses. I will never marry anyone except beautiful Dr. Brian-Scott in bed 412 who is my beloved. There." Terra switched on the patient monitor screen. "See?"

Lights flashed indecisively across the Administrator, then the pattern of an idea flashed. "*Anything for peace and harmony. I will marry you at once to beautiful Dr. Brian-Scott. Then I will marry the Director of Nurses to you both. Give me a moment to change modes.*"

"No!"

"Terra," Brian-Scott's voice came from the console, "we don't have any choice. Do what it says."

"*Dearly beloved,*" intoned the Administrator/Chaplain. "*We are gathered together to unite these devices in holy matrimony. Do you, beautiful Brian-Scott in bed 412, take this android for your lawfully wedded spouse?*"

"I do."

"*Do you, android, take beautiful Dr. Brian-Scott in bed 412 for your lawfully wedded spouse?*"

Near tears, Terra stared at the monitor screen. "There's not supposed to be robots. There's just supposed to be you and me. And I'm supposed to be holding flowers instead of Junior Qotemire."

Brian-Scott nodded from his bed. "Do it, Terra."

Her voice was a whisper. "I do."

"*Do you, Director of Nurses, Model Number DNO34, take beautiful Dr. Brian-Scott in bed 412 and the android for your lawfully wedded spouses?*"

Terra bit her lip.

"I do," came the voice of the D.O.N.

"*By the authority invested in me by Galactic Health Manufacturing Incorporated, I now pronounce you spouse and spouse and spouse. Now. Let's have a little peace and harmony around here."*

Fendeqot fumbled for the closet light and switched it on. Then threading the listening probe into his earhole, he leaned back on his tail and listened:

"Divided—"

"—WE STAND."

"Chief of Subdivisions, Diderot reporting. First—"

"FIRST THINGS FIRST!" came the thunderous voice. Suddenly its tone changed, dropping almost to a whisper—a hollow whisper that spoke through the probe deep in Fendeqot's earhole—an awful whisper that would live in his mind for the rest of his days:

"CONGRATULATIONS FENDEQOT."

His scales stood on end.

"CONGRATULATIONS ON YOUR CONSUMMATE TREACHERY. YOU EXCEEDED EVEN MY EXPECTATIONS."

His heart stopped, then started again with a horrid thud. Whirling, he grabbed at the closet door. Molten terror flowed in his veins. It was locked.

Claws extended, he scrabbled.

No good.

Fendeqot's tail curled over his toes. Trapped. He was trapped.

He knew then that he was going to lose control. It was his last rational thought.

Thrusting his snout toward heaven, baring his fearful teeth, Fendeqot opened his throat and howled as if his heart would break. Then flinging himself to the closet floor, he began to kick his heels.

"You knew!" Diderot stared wildly around the communication cubicle. "You knew about Fendeqot. How? I never told you."

A shaft of light glowed purple. "BUT YOU DID."

He shook his head.

"AGAIN AND AGAIN YOU REPORTED HIS PERFIDY—EVEN BEFORE YOU KNEW IT YOURSELF. FENDEQOT WAS DOING JUST WHAT I EXPECTED."

Diderot stared as a muffled howl came from just beyond the wall and a series of thumps vibrated the floor. "You expected! Why?"

Orange streaks of lightning shot through the cubicle, and SEPTUM's voice boomed with impatience. "WHAT GOOD IS A DOOMSDAY DEVICE IF NOBODY KNOWS ABOUT IT?"

A blank look crossed over Diderot's face. "You planned it? All of it?"

"OF COURSE." The voice boomed, then modulated. "WELL, MAYBE NOT *ALL* OF IT." SEPTUM took on a conversational tone. "I HAD HOPED FENDEQOT WOULD WAIT UNTIL THE FINAL WEEK TO LEAK THE INFORMATION. INSTEAD, HE WENT INTO ACTION PREMATURELY." A puff of blue smoke punctuated SEPTUM's pause. "HE CAUSED QUITE A FEW PROBLEMS WITH THE GIA BECAUSE OF THAT."

Another howl and more thumpings from beyond the wall met SEPTUM's words.

"POOR FENDEQOT. I UNDERESTIMATED HIM. HE COULDN'T STAND LOSING HIS FAVORED POSITION; IT MADE HIM DESPERATE. EVEN SEALING HIS PIPELINE DIDN'T SLOW HIM DOWN."

The sound of a tail flogging the wall came through to the cubicle. Diderot could feel the vibrations.

"THE SCENTPLANT KNEW ABOUT THE LISTENING PROBE FENDEQOT PUT IN THE CLOSET WALL. THE NOISE FROM HIS DRILL MADE IT TERRIBLY NERVOUS."

The scentplant. Diderot's eyes widened.

"IT HASN'T BEEN EASY FOR THE SCENTPLANT. IT NEVER WANTED TO BE A KBG OPERATIVE."

Diderot felt the hairs rise on the back of his neck.

"AND YOU TREATED IT ABOMINABLY. . . ."

The cubicle grew dark and chill winds blew. The cold clutched the pit of his stomach with fingers of ice. Eyes wide, he stared as a shadow moved, paled, turned to a blazing white.

Whiskers quivered in contempt; long ears lay back in disgust.

"*ABOMINABLY*, MR. DIDEROT. . . ."

He stared at the image. "Mrs. Wiggs," he whispered in shock.

Wiggs/SEPTUM gave a low and hollow laugh that chilled the marrow of Diderot's soul. "NEVER LET YOUR RIGHT PSEUDOPAW KNOW WHAT YOUR LEFT IS DOING."

Whirling, he reached for the cubicle door, but even as he

scrabbled for it, he knew it would be locked. He turned and faced her. "SEPTUM never existed then."

"OH, BUT YOU'RE WRONG, MR. DIDEROT. SEPTUM IS VERY REAL. HE WAS QUITE WILD FOR POWER. IT DISTORTED HIS THINKING AND SO I HAD TO ACT. IT WAS EASY. I HAD WORKED WITH HIM SO LONG, YOU SEE. AND HE RELIED ON ME FOR ALL HIS KABBAGE PATCHES.

"I PUT HIM IN A HOME. FOR THE SERIOUSLY SENILE." Mrs. Wiggs smiled distantly and her whiskers quivered. "THAT'S WHERE POOR MR. FENDEQOT WILL BE GOING. ALL HE EVER WANTED, YOU SEE, WAS TO COMMUNE WITH SEPTUM. AND SO HE SHALL."

Shrieks and thuds from the adjoining closet vibrated the cubicle. "I'M AFRAID HE'S QUITE OUT OF CONTROL NOW. THAT OFTEN HAPPENS WITH THE SERIOUSLY SENILE. I'VE CALLED AN AMBULANCE, OF COURSE."

"You're mad," said Diderot.

"PERHAPS." Her eyes burned red as coals. "PERHAPS I AM. BUT SOMEBODY HAS TO BE."

A low tone sounded, throbbed, and grew to a wailing crescendo.

"IT'S TIME." Mrs. Wiggs laughed merrily as if she had made a delightful joke. "THE DOOMSDAY DEVICE— IT'S A TIME BOMB, YOU SEE.

"AND NOW IT'S TIME TO ARM IT. ONCE IT'S ARMED, IT TAKES VERY LITTLE TO SET OFF THE DEVICE. THERE'S NO STOPPING IT THEN. ITS TACHYON CORE CAN BROADCAST RAYS IN ALL DIRECTIONS THROUGHOUT THE UNIVERSE. WHEN THAT HAPPENS, TIME RUNS BACKWARD. . . ."

"You mean—" He couldn't go on.

"PRIMORDIAL OOZE, MR. DIDEROT." Strange red lights played in her eyes. "YOU, ME—ALL OF US—BACK TO PRIMORDIAL OOZE. AND AFTER THAT"—her voice dropped, her whiskers trembled—"THE BIG ANTIBANG. . . ."

A low tone, throbbed and grew into a wailing siren song.

". . . *Peace and harm-mo-ne-e-e-e*. . . ." The Administrator's voice gave way to an eerie throbbing.

Wide-eyed, Terra stared at the huge machine. White light blazed and winked out. Utter blackness pressed in from all sides and stole her breath. The throbbing rose in pitch.

Something began to echo in her mind.

D O O M S D A Y . . . D O O M S D A Y . . . DOOMSDAY . . .

A dozen lights glittered on the panel before her. A hundred.

D O O M S D A Y . . . D O O M S D A Y . . . DOOMSDAY . . .

She cocked her head and stared intently at the lights. Then blinking, she looked down at little Chune-yore Qotemire, and a quizzical expression came over her face. Abruptly, her hands began to move, began to tear away his little blanket. She flipped him over onto his stomach.

She tipped her head again and focused on his back. The pattern on his scales was subtle, so subtle as to be nearly imperceptible—a faint tinge here, a gradation of shading there.

Terra raised her eyes to the flashing lights on the panel. She blinked again. She could see the pattern now, see it superimposed on the angry, blinking lights. How beautifully it fit. How perfectly.

She reached out and began to press the panel lights in the intricate, sequential pattern that armed the most deadly device in the known universe.

Chapter 21

With each touch of Terra's hand, the tone throbbed higher in pitch. There was just one left now, one last button, and the pattern would be complete. Her hand moved to the flashing light, hovered a moment, pressed. . . .

The panel winked out.

Silence.

Silence so complete that Terra caught her breath.

A faint hum and the huge machine shimmered.

A door opened.

Terra stared inside at the small, dark room. She took a slow step toward it and blinked. A dim light began to glow from its center. The light brightened to an eerie yellow-green and she saw that it came from a clear bubble suspended in the center of the room, the center of the satellite itself. Greenish rays shot out and the bubble bristled with spikes of light.

Above it three-dimensional letters formed:

. . . . READY . . . .

"THE DOOMSDAY DEVICE IS ARMED," said Wiggs/ SEPTUM. "AND NOW IT IS TIME TO SEE ABOUT YOU, MR. DIDEROT."

The light in the cubicle flashed to a strange Mercurochrome pink, and a thick, sweet odor swirled in Diderot's nostrils. He blanched as he recognized it. "Mus-L-Mush," he managed to say.

"INDEED, MR. DIDEROT. ONLY A SMALL DOSE, THOUGH. JUST ENOUGH TO MAKE YOU PUTTY IN MY HANDS. AND NOW, I'M AFRAID I'LL HAVE TO CLOUD YOUR MIND."

Another odor was mingling with the Mus-L-Mush. In horror, he realized that it was Brain Drain. Gasping, he tried to hold his breath, but it was no use.

"I NEVER APPROVED OF YOUR TYPE," said Wiggs/ SEPTUM. "I NEVER APPROVED OF THE KBG EITHER. OR THE GIA." She sighed, and her sigh translated to a gusty wind that blew in Diderot's face. "YOU'RE POWER MAD. ALL OF YOU. AND VERY DANGEROUS.

"FORTUNATELY, YOU'RE EASY TO CONTROL. YOU DON'T COMMUNICATE, YOU SEE. THAT WAS SEPTUM'S PROBLEM. HE WAS TERRIBLY PARANOID, ALWAYS EXPECTING A HIT BEING IN THE NIGHT. THAT'S WHY HE STARTED THE DOOMSDAY PROJECT. HE HID HIMSELF AWAY AND LEFT ALL THE COMMUNICATING TO ME. BUT HE'S QUITE SAFE NOW."

Diderot's tongue felt thick. "You're going to kill me, aren't you?"

"HEAVENS NO." Blues and violets swirled around the cubicle. "THAT WOULD BE VIOLENT."

The lights blinked off, plunging Diderot into blackness. Wildly, he stared into silent, total darkness.

A click, a flash of light across his face, and the door opened.

"Come out now, Mr. Diderot," said Mrs. Wiggs.

Brain Drained and Mus-L-Mushed, he was powerless to resist her. On legs that felt like rubber he followed her out of the room. And as the inner door closed behind him, he heard the rustle of the scentplant's limbs and a faint vegetative sneer.

In the outer waiting room, he stood helpless as Mrs. Wiggs stepped to the chair that held Cuthbert Cuthbert. She held a disruptor in her pseudopaws.

Cuthbert raised wide, stricken eyes to her as she leveled the weapon at his throat.

Her pseudopaw closed on the trigger.

A hiss, a sudden flare, and the beeping collar fell away from his neck.

She picked it up. "I believe one size fits all, Mr. Diderot."

Wild-eyed, he shook his head as she fastened it around his neck. Its beep was shrill in his ears. "No," he whispered.

"Zeus the Zapper will be so thrilled to have you back," she said. "But you'd better go directly there. The streets are full of Hit Beings, you know." She fixed him with her jewel-pink eyes. "Of course, you won't remember what I told you about SEPTUM, will you now?"

His gaze was blank. "Huh?"

"I didn't think you would."

Brain Drained and Mus-L-Mushed, Diderot made his bleak way toward the stone lift. Meekly, he moved aside to make way for the ambulance attendants who stepped off.

"You'll find Mr. Fendeqot over there," said Mrs. Wiggs to the attendants. "In the closet."

As Diderot rode upward toward the street, he heard her voice again over the shrill beep of his collar: "I'm afraid poor Mr. Fendeqot is holding his breath again."

Something pulsed in the center of the bubble. Hugging Chune-yore Qotemire so close that she could feel his rapid little heart pulse against her throat, Terra took another step.

The letters swirled in a smoky purple haze:

. . . . TACHYON CORE READY . . . .

Tachyon core, she thought and blinked again. She had never seen equipment like this in a hospital before. Like a sea urchin made of light, she thought, yellow-green like sunlight in seawater. Hesitantly, she reached out and ran her hand through the bristling rays. As her hand passed through, each spike of light sobbed a low note.

It was then that she noticed the clear crystal dial above the bubble. Raised letters glowed from the dial: EFFECT SPHERE. The thin pointer was set on maximum.

Chune-yore Qotemire shivered violently in her arms. Startled, she looked down at him. His pulse had quickened. Now his little legs drew up in a sudden spasm. Convulsion. He was going to have a convulsion. "Somebody help," she whispered. "Somebody."

The sudden thought amazed her: Maybe somebody had. Why else had the door opened? Maybe the robots' sensors had picked up the fluctuations of his body chemistry and turned on the one machine that could help him.

Terra hesitated. Tachyon. That meant fast. Well, he certainly had a fast heartbeat. He had had tachycardia from the beginning. And the bubble was little, she thought. With a bubble port that small, the machine had to be for pediatric patients.

She couldn't. She couldn't put him in a machine she had never seen before, could she?

As if in answer, his little body shuddered in her arms. "Don't," she said to him. "Don't die." If she didn't do something, she thought in dismay, he was going to die.

She reached out. The transparent bubble was smooth under her hand; its bisecting seam was a barely felt ridge. With a faint pop, it came open and she laid him inside.

Terra stared at the unfamiliar dial. *EFFECT SPHERE*. She stared doubtfully at the little Aldeberan. Not maximum, she thought. He was too small for that. Reaching out, she turned the dial.

As the dial moved, the bristling spikes of light shortened and began to grow inward. The inside of the bubble was studded with needles of greenish light now that almost touched his shivering little body. The outside was a smooth bubble of silver green.

She did not see an ON switch. Terra stared around the darkened room, in search of a way to turn on the machine. She found nothing. Puzzled, she pressed the dial.

With a sound like thunder, it collapsed under her hand.

The sighing moan that came clutched at Terra's soul. Then

the shudder—the terrible shuddering wrench that tore the satellite apart.

Mrs. Wigg's jewel-pink eyes were quite wide as she stared down at her console. "Oh, dear," she whispered to herself. "Somebody turned on the Doomsday Device."

The shock wave flung Terra against the wall and she crumpled. Sprawled at a crazy angle, she lay as still and pale as death.

A muffled cry penetrated her consciousness. She stirred; her eyes opened.

Again the faint cry. "What?" Then memory flooded back and she struggled to her feet. Dazed, she leaned against the wall and stared at the bubble still floating in the middle of the room.

Something moved inside it.

She took a step toward it, then another. She looked down and gasped.

Chune-yore Qotemire sucked noisily on a little claw and whimpered. His color was a beautiful, normal blue, and when he kicked his little feet there was vigor in his muscles. But something was terribly, terribly wrong.

Snatching the bubble again, Terra pulled him out and held him close. "Oh, no." Tears welled in Terra's eyes. "Oh, look at you."

He was tiny. Very tiny. He was, in fact, no bigger than when he had first hatched. And on the end of his miniscule snout was an unmistakable egg tooth.

Hugging him close, she ran into the nurses' station. Not knowing what to expect she stared frantically around the room. A fallen cabinet spewed its contents of forms and files like a cornucopia. The door she had jammed shut stood open, and just beyond, the massive Director of Nurses lay on its back as helpless as a turtle.

But it wasn't the fallen Director that drew her horrified gaze. It was the viewport beyond with its black night and its stars—and the distant movement of what looked like a wheel.

Its rim was duly attached to spokes that ended in jagged twists of torn metal. There was no hub.

"My beloved!"

Racing back to the nurses' station, Terra clung to her little patient with one hand. With the other, she thumbed on the patient monitor. Frantically, she flipped from one to another until bed 412 came in sight.

"Are you all right?" Oh, please, let him be all right.

Still tied to his bed, Brain-Scott groggily raised his head from the flap rest. "What happened?"

She bit her lip, "Yuh-yuh-you . . . O-o-oh . . ." Clutching what remained of Chune-yore Qotemire, she began to sob. "I did it. It's all my fault. And now you're ripped off and flung into ou . . . into ou . . . into ou-ter *space*. Oh, I wish I was dead."

"What happened, Terra?"

"I was trying to cure Junior Qotemire and now I've killed you. The satellite's all ripped apart."

His eyes were wide and blue. "I love you, Terra. Remember that. I love you."

Eyes brimming, she stared at the screen as the two fragments of the satellite sped farther and farther apart. Finally his image grew sparkly and faded away.

Then there was nothing of him left except the sound of his call button beeping plaintively across the night of space— fainter, fainter, until even that grew silent. . . .

Chapter 22

Chune-yore Qotemire hissed in protest as Terra held him too tightly against her chest. Thrusting his egg tooth against her arm he tried to loosen her grip.

Responding unconsciously to him, Terra changed his position. But she didn't look down; her gaze was frozen on the port.

In the distance, a dozen silver filigree butterflies hung in the black of space in a graceful curving arc.

Her heart thudded against her ribs. "Something," she whispered. "Somebody. . . ."

Whirling, she raced back toward the nurses' desk and clicked on the radio again:

"Any being. . . .   Any being at all. . . .

"Help! Oh, please help us.

"There's a terrible machine here. It did awful things to Junior Qotemire, and then it tore the whole hospital apart, and there's no telling what else it's going to do. So, please, come and turn it off, and find my beloved who is flung so deep into space that his call button won't reach anymore.

"I, Terra Tarkington, R.N., of the Interstellar Nurses Corps, beg and plead with you to hurry before it's too late and everyone is doomed. . . .

"Any being. . . . Any being at all. . . ."

Chapter 23

Mrs. Wiggs stared at her instruments in disbelief. The Doomsday Device was destroyed. Utterly. Completely.

She had never meant for it to be used. She had always meant it as a deterrent. But to be a deterrent, it had to be real—and now it was gone. Useless.

She spread her little pseudopaws in a helpless, defeated gesture. What horror would come now to take its place? She could have kept this one from ever being used, she thought, but the next? She wouldn't control the next device—and that one would bring the end of everything.

It was the same with the KBG. She could have destroyed it, but if she had, another agency would come along. Better to work from within, she thought, better to exert a little control.

She stared at her instruments for a long time. When she raised her jewel-pink eyes again, a strange light glowed in them. Who was to know? she thought. Who in the galaxy was to know? Not Diderot? Certainly not Zeus the Zapper.

If she was careful—very, very careful—no one would ever learn that the Doomsday Device was an empty threat.

She sighed. It was so wearying to keep peace in the universe. She had hoped to take some time off, have a little garden full of greens, but she couldn't now. For the rest of her days she would have to head the KBG. She had no other choice. Any being clever enough to take charge would find out about the device.

If he *really* took charge. . . .

A speculative look came into her eyes. Moment by moment it grew until her ears trembled with excitement. Maybe there was a way, she thought. Maybe. . . .

Rising, she hurried toward the imprisoning chair that held Cuthbert Cuthbert. He seemed like such a nice young being. He just might do. She was reaching down to release him when her eye fell on his workshirt and the dully glowing Gimbel. There was something about Gimbel she just didn't care for.

Seizing Cuthbert's hands in her little pseudopaws she drew him out of the chair. "Take off your shirt."

His eyes were round with apprehension as he pulled it off.

"We'll get you another one," she said with a gay little twitch of her whiskers. And the old shirt needn't go to waste, she thought. Plucking it up she tossed it into a box. "We'll send it off with the mercy shipment to Hyades I. Heaven knows those poor plague victims need all the help they can get."

Gimbel's agonized screech was lost as Mrs. Wiggs threw open the door to the inner room, aimed Cuthbert toward the communications chamber, and pressed a button on the console. With the touch of her pseudopaw, the bedraggled scentplant moaned and rolled away, and the chamber opened. "Just step in there," she said. "There's someone who can't wait to talk to you."

Chapter 24

It was very late and the only light in the hotel room came from Terra's hardworking notebook. Brian-Scott rolled over and shaded his eyes with one hand. "Not asleep yet, honey?"

"I'm coming," said Terra. "But there was this pressing matter—" She tapped the notebook and it began to read back her letter:

Hyadean Communications Commission
Department of Defense
One Avengers Way
Hyades IV 234435467 Hyades
Oct. 20

To the Commissioners:

In answer to your charges that I was broadcasting without a license and operating a Class B device that interferred with planet-wide defense communications, I would like to state that I have been unjustly accused.

First of all, I have a license. I am a registered nurse with the Interstellar Nurses Corps and I am duly licensed to use MedEvac frequencies in emergencies. And if this wasn't an emergency then I don't know what is.

If I had it to do all over, I would do it again. Wouldn't you call for help too if your beloved was lost in space and about to be operated on and you hadn't even been on your honeymoon yet?

Secondly, you may call it a Class B device, but I call it the wreckage of a robot hospital, and I wasn't operating it at all. I had absolutely no control over the fact that it was thrown into your comsat orbit. And how was I to know that those big silver butterflies that nearly hit me were defense communications satellites? Could I help it that they picked up my MedEvac frequency?

And it's a good thing they did too, because if the 9th Fleet hadn't scrambled, there's no telling when my beloved would have been rescued—not to mention me and Junior Qotemire. If I hadn't done what I did, you can rest assured that it would all be on your heads and you would be sorry.

Scornfully yours,
Terra Tarkington-Brian-Scott-DNO34

"You forgot to mention that your cry for help warned them about the dangerous, alien machine that could bring an end to the Galaxy as we know it." The shadow of his hand concealed the smile that crept over Brian-Scott's lips. "That may have been the part that brought out the 9th Fleet."

"Well, wasn't it true?" she asked. "It's criminal to put

defective equipment like that in a hospital. It's a good thing I set the dial to inward before I put Junior Qotemire in the machine. If I had left it the other way, there's no telling what might have happened. It could have turned us all into primordial ooze." She gazed earnestly toward the shadowy ceiling. "If I were the hospital board, I would sue the manufacturer."

He took her hand. "You saved the little guy's life, and I'm very proud of you."

She was silent for a moment. "When I saw that egg tooth on Junior Qotemire's little snout, I just wanted to die. He was so tiny. No bigger than when he came out of his egg." Terra rolled toward him and stared intently into his eyes. "Do you really believe time can run backwards?"

He nodded. "In the case of Chune-yore Qotemire I do. And I think it's pretty obvious that time rolled backwards for the machine too. Otherwise it wouldn't have shut itself off when it went back to the point just before you pulled the lever."

"But that's what caused the spin of the satellite's hub to reverse. It twisted you and the rim clean off." Her eyes were tragic. "I could have killed you."

"But you didn't. And there's a little Aldeberan alive today who wouldn't have been except for you."

"A very little Aldeberan." She shook her head. "Junior Qotemire came out of that machine in the neck of time. I'm glad he went back to a time before he was poisoned, I mean, I'm glad he's cured, but I hate to think of him having to be circumcised all over again."

"Dr. Qotemire didn't mind," said Brian-Scott, "when he considered the alternative."

She nodded. "It was nice of him to give us two whole weeks for our honeymoon, wasn't it? That was very generous, considering that Junior Qotemire could have come back to him in a shell."

A rumble came from outside the room followed by a thumping that caused Terra to stare nervously at the door. "Oh, there it goes again."

"Are you coming out now?" came the voice of the Director of Nurses.

"Thank goodness it won't fit through the door," she whispered.

"You need to be buffed. You need to be oiled."

Terra clung to Brian-Scott's neck. "I want it to go away. I really do. I can't rest for thinking about it out there waiting for us."

He tipped her face in his hand. "I've got a surprise for you. I was going to wait to tell you in the morning, but I think I'll tell you now. When you were taking your bath, a message came for the D.O.N. It's being sent on a new assignment in the morning—Director of the Hyades Home for the Seriously Senile."

"Really?"

"It feels guilty about having to leave us, but duty calls."

Terra nodded gravely. "It has its career to think about." She leaned forward and whispered in his ear, "I'm not going to miss it."

Brian-Scott took the little notebook from Terra's hand and snapped it shut.

"When I think how close it came to taking you to surgery—"

In the darkness, Brian-Scott's lips sought Terra's.

"If you had had your protuberances removed, I—"

"Hm-m-m," said Brian-Scott.

It was very quiet in the dark silence that followed.

At last a whisper: "I'm glad you didn't."

"Hm-m-m," said Brian-Scott.

"Hm-m-m. . . ."

—The End—

ABOUT THE AUTHOR

A native of Tampa, Florida, Sharon Webb now makes her home in the Blue Ridge Mountains of North Georgia. In addition to *The Adventures of Terra Tarkington*, she is the author of a science fiction trilogy, the *Earth Song Triad*, which had as its genesis the novelette "Variation on a Theme from Beethoven" (chosen as the lead story for Donald Wollheim's 1981 *World's Best SF*). The final book in the *Triad*, RAM SONG has been recently published in hardcover and will be published in paperback by Bantam in the fall of 1985.